E. & M.A
WHO KILLED DIC

EDWIN ISAAC RADFORD (1891-1973) and MONA AUGUSTA RADFORD (1894-1990) were married in 1939. Edwin worked as a journalist, holding many editorial roles on Fleet Street in London, while Mona was a popular leading lady in musical-comedy and revues until her retirement from the stage.

The couple turned to crime fiction when they were both in their early fifties. Edwin described their collaborative formula as: "She kills them off, and I find out how she done it." Their primary series detective was Harry Manson who they introduced in 1944.

The Radfords spent their final years living in Worthing on the English South Coast. Dean Street Press have republished three of their classic mysteries: *Murder Jigsaw, Murder Isn't Cricket* and *Who Killed Dick Whittington?*

E. & M.A. Radford Mysteries
Available from Dean Street Press

E. & M.A. RADFORD

WHO KILLED DICK WHITTINGTON?

With an introduction by Nigel Moss

DEAN STREET PRESS

INTRODUCTION

DOCTOR HARRY MANSON is a neglected figure, unjustly so, amongst Golden Age crime fiction detectives. The fictional creation of husband and wife authors Edwin and Mona Radford, who wrote as E. & M.A. Radford, Manson was their leading series detective featuring in 35 of 38 mystery novels published between 1944 and 1972. A Chief Detective-Inspector of Scotland Yard and Head of its Crime Research Laboratory, Manson was also a leading authority on medical jurisprudence. Arguably the Radfords' best work is to be found in their early Doctor Manson series novels which have remained out of print since first publication. Commendably, Dean Street Press has now made available three novels from that early period – *Murder Jigsaw* (1944), *Murder Isn't Cricket* (1946), and *Who Killed Dick Whittington?* (1947) – titles selected for their strong plots, clever detection and evocative settings. They are examples of Manson at his finest, portraying the appealing combination of powerful intellect and reasoning and creative scientific methods of investigation, while never losing awareness and sensitivity concerning the human predicaments encountered.

The Radfords sought to create in Doctor Manson a leading scientific police detective, and an investigator in the same mould as R. Austin Freeman's Dr John Thorndyke. Edwin Radford was a keen admirer of the popular Dr Thorndyke novels and short stories. T.J. Binyon in *Murder Will Out* (1989), a study of the detective in fiction, maintains that the Radfords were protesting against the idea that in Golden Age crime fiction science is always the preserve of the amateur detective, and they wanted to be different. In the preface to the first Manson novel *Inspector Manson's Success* (1944), they announced: "We have had the audacity – for which we make no apology – to present here the Almost Incredible: a detective story in which the scientific deduction by a police officer uncovers the crime and the criminal entirely without the aid, ladies and gentlemen, of any outside assistance!" The emphasis is on Manson as both policeman and scientist.

The first two Manson novels, *Inspector Manson's Success* and *Murder Jigsaw* (both 1944), contain introductory prefaces which acquaint the reader with Doctor Manson in some detail. He is a man of many talents and qualifications: aged in his early 50s and a Cambridge MA (both attributes shared by Edwin Radford at the time), Manson is a Doctor of Science, a Doctor of Laws and author of several standard works on medical jurisprudence (of which he is a Professor) and criminal pathology. He is slightly over 6 feet in height, although he does not look it owing to the stoop of his shoulders, habitual in a scholar and scientist. His physiology displays interesting features and characteristics: a long face, with a broad and abnormally high forehead; grey eyes wide set, though lying deep in their sockets, which "have a habit of just passing over a person on introduction; but when that person chances to turn in the direction of the Inspector, he is disconcerted to find that the eyes have returned to his face and are seemingly engaged on long and careful scrutiny. There is left the impression that one's face is being photographed on the Inspector's mind." Manson's hands are often the first thing a stranger will notice. "The long delicate fingers are exceedingly restless – twisting and turning on anything which lies handy to them. While he stands, chatting, they are liable to stray to a waistcoat pocket and emerge with a tiny magnifying glass, or a micrometer rule, to occupy their energy."

During his long career at Scotland Yard, Manson rises from Chief Detective-Inspector to the rank of Commander; always retaining his dual role of a senior police investigating officer as well as Head of the Forensic Research Laboratory. Manson is ably assisted by his Yard colleagues – Sergeant Merry, a science graduate and Deputy Lab Head; and by two CID officers, Superintendent Jones ('the Fat Man of the Yard') and Inspector Kenway. Jones is weighty and ponderous, given to grunts and short staccato sentences, and with a habit of lapsing into American 'tec slang in moments of stress; but a stolid, determined detective and reliable fact searcher. He often serves as a humorous foil to Manson and the Assistant Commissioner. By contrast, Kenway is volatile and imaginative. Together, Jones and Kenway make a powerful combination and an effective resource for the Doctor. In later books, Inspector Holroyd features as Manson's regular assistant. Holroyd is the lead detective in the non-series title *The Six Men* (1958), a novelisation of the earlier British detective film of the same name, directed by Michael Laws and released in 1951, and based on an original story idea by the Radfords. Their only other non-series detective, Superintendent Carmichael, appeared in just two novels: *Look in at Murder* (1956, with Manson) and *Married to Murder* (1959). None of the Radford books was ever published in the USA.

The first eight novels, all Manson series, were published by Andrew Melrose between 1944 to 1950. The early titles were slim volumes produced in accordance with authorised War Economy Standards. Many featured a distinctive motif on the front cover of the dust wrapper – a small white circle showing Manson's head superimposed against that of Sherlock Holmes (in black silhouette), with the title 'a Manson Mystery'. In these early novels, the Radfords made much of their practice of providing readers with all the facts and clues to give them a fair opportunity of solving the riddle of deduction. They interspersed the investigations with 'Challenges to the Reader', tropes closely associated with leading Golden Age crime authors John Dickson Carr and Ellery Queen. In *Murder Isn't Cricket* they claimed: "We have never, at any time, 'pulled anything out of the bag' at the last minute – a fact upon which three distinguished reviewers of books have most kindly commented and have commended." Favourable critical reviews of their early titles were received from Ralph Straus (*Sunday Times*) and George W. Bishop (*Daily Telegraph*), as well as novelist Elizabeth Bowen. The Radfords were held in sufficiently high regard by Sutherland Scott, writing in his *Blood in their Ink* (1953), a study of the modern mystery novel, to be afforded special mention alongside such distinguished Golden Age authors as Miles Burton, Richard Hull, Milward Kennedy and Vernon Loder.

After 1950 there was a gap of five years before the Radfords' next book. Mona's mother died in 1953; she had been living with them at the time. Starting in 1956, with a new publisher John Long (like Melrose, another Hutchinson company), the Radfords released two Manson titles in successive years. In 1958 they moved to the publisher Robert Hale, a prominent supplier to the public libraries. They began with two non-series titles *The Six Men* (1958) and *Married to Murder* (1959), before returning to Manson with *Death of a Frightened Editor* (1959). Thereafter, Manson was to feature in all but one of their remaining 25 crime novels, all published by Hale. Curiously, a revised and abridged version of the third Manson series novel *Crime Pays No Dividends* (1945) was later released under the new title *Death of a Peculiar Rabbit* (1969).

During the late 1950s and early 1960s the Radfords continued to write well-conceived and cleverly plotted murder mysteries that remain worth seeking out today. Notable examples are the atmospheric *Death on the Broads* (1957) set on the Norfolk Broads, and *Death of a Frightened Editor* (1959) involving the poisoning of an odious London newspaper gossip columnist aboard the London-to-Brighton Pullman Express (a familiar train journey for Edwin Radford, who had worked in Fleet Street while living in Brighton). *Death and the Professor* (1961), the only non-Manson series book released after 1959, is an unusual exception. It features Marcus Stubbs, Professor of Logic and the Dilettantes' Club, a small private dining circle in Soho which meets regularly to discuss informally unsolved cases. Conveniently, but improbably, the Assistant Commissioner of Scotland Yard is among its members. The book comprises a series of stories, often involving locked room murders or other 'impossible' crimes, solved by the logic and reasoning of Professor Stubbs following discussions around the dining table. There are similarities with Roger Sheringham's Crimes Circle in Anthony Berkeley's *The Poisoned Chocolates Case* (1937). The idea of a private dining club as a forum for mystery solving was later revived by the American author Isaac Asimov in *Tales of the Black Widowers* (1974).

Edwin Isaac Radford (1891-1973) and Mona Augusta Radford (1894-1990) were married in Aldershot in 1939. Born in West Bromwich, Edwin had spent his working life entirely in journalism, latterly in London's Fleet Street where he held various editorial roles, culminating as Arts Editor-in-Chief and Columnist for the *Daily Mirror* in 1937. Mona was the daughter of Irish poet and actor James Clarence Mangan and his actress wife Lily Johnson. Under the name 'Mona Magnet' she had performed on stage since childhood, touring with her mother, and later was for many years a popular leading lady in musical-comedy and revues until her retirement from the stage. She also authored numerous short plays and sketches for the stage, in addition to writing verse, particularly for children.

An article in *Books & Bookmen* magazine in 1959 recounts how Edwin and Mona, already in their early 50s, became detective fiction writers by accident. During one of Edwin's periodic attacks of lumbago, Mona trudged through snow and slush from their village home to a library for Dr Thorndyke detective stories by R. Austin Freeman, of which he was an avid reader. Unfortunately, Edwin had already read the three books with which she returned! Incensed at his grumbles, Mona retaliated with "Well for heaven's sake, why don't you write one instead of always reading them?" – and placed a writing pad and pencil on his bed. Within a month, Edwin had written six lengthy short stories, and with Mona's help in revising the MS, submitted them to a leading publisher. The recommendation came back that each of the stories had the potential to make an excellent full-length novel. The first short story was duly turned into a novel, which was promptly accepted for publication. Subsequently, their practice was to work together on writing novels – first in longhand, then typed and read through by each of them, and revised as necessary. The completed books were read through again by both, side by side, and final revisions made. The plot was usually developed by Mona and added to by Edwin during the writing. According to Edwin, the formula was: "She kills them off, and I find out how she done it."

As husband-and-wife novelists, the Radfords were in the company of other Golden Age crime writing couples – G.D.H. (Douglas) and Margaret Cole in the UK, and Gwen Bristow and husband Bruce Manning as well as Richard and Frances Lockridge in the USA. Their crime novels proved popular on the Continent and were published in translation in many European languages. However, the US market eluded them. Aside from crime fiction, the Radfords collaborated on authoring a wide range of other works, most notably *Crowther's Encyclopaedia of Phrases and Origins*, *Encyclopaedia of Superstitions* (a standard work on folklore), and a *Dictionary of Allusions*. Edwin was a Fellow of the Royal Society of Arts, and a member of both the Authors' Club and the Savage Club.

The Radfords proved to be an enduring writing team, working into their 80s. Both were also enthusiastic amateur artists in oils and water colours. They travelled extensively, and invariably spent the winter months writing in the warmer climes of Southern Europe. An article by Edwin in John Creasey's *Mystery Bedside Book* (1960) recounts his involvement in the late 1920s with an English society periodical for the winter set on the French Riviera, where he had socialised with such famous writers as Baroness Orczy, William Le Queux and E. Phillips Oppenheim. He recollects Oppenheim dictating up to three novels at once! The Radfords spent their final years living in Worthing on the English South Coast.

Who Killed Dick Whittington?

Who Killed Dick Whittington? (1947) is the sixth book in the Doctor Manson series. The early choice of a murder mystery in an atmospheric theatrical setting was perhaps predictable, given Mona Radford's acting background and writing for the stage, coupled with Edwin's role as an Arts journalist on Fleet Street. Indeed, they dedicated the novel to 'the Ladies and Gentlemen of the Footlights – for so many years our very Good Companions'. The first edition of 1947, published by Andrew Melrose, has a striking dust wrapper showing Dick Whittington lying asleep (or already murdered?) on a darkened stage, bathed in a light blue spotlight, with the Cat staring ahead at the audience.

Engagingly, the novel is prefaced with a theatre playbill for the Pavilion Theatre, Burlington-on-Sea, announcing the popular Christmas season pantomime *Dick Whittington* by the Henri de Benyat theatre company and listing the leading cast members. The Principal Boy playing Dick Whittington was a highly unpopular choice; and she had quarrelled publicly with several fellow artistes earlier in the run. Her demise occurs, in dramatic fashion, during an evening performance of the pantomime. In the well-known scene, Dick and the Cat are resting on a grassy bank by the milestone on Highgate Hill, where Dick sleeps and dreams of Bow Bells ringing "Turn Again, Whittington, Lord Mayor of London." But that evening the bells were not heard, for in the full glare of the stage lights and within sight of the large audience, Dick had been murdered by a fatal injection of prussic acid. Suspicion falls on the Cat, but this is quickly ruled out. Other cast members within easy reach of Dick when she was killed each had impenetrable alibis which made it impossible for them to have been the murderer.

Scotland Yard are called in by the local police. As Chief Detective-Inspector Manson is already preoccupied with investigating a complex series of commercial fraud cases involving arson, his CID colleagues Superintendent Jones and Inspector Kenway are assigned to the murder. But the respective investigations soon merge as links between the two are established, demonstrating some skilful plotting by the Radfords. Manson assumes overall charge and works out the solutions to both the murder mystery and related fraudulent fire-raising cases, deploying the powerful combination of forensic investigation, thoughtful analysis and logic. Several key findings result from scientific techniques used by the Doctor. The different strands of investigation tie in and the pieces of the overall picture gradually fall into place, with clever detection leading to a satisfying resolution. The denouement is handled in retrospect: on the opening night of a new theatre production by the Henri de Benyat company at the Pavilion Theatre, Burlington-on-Sea, the cast gather backstage to read the press report of Doctor Manson's evidence at the murder trial of the accused. Manson's measured and persuasive logic, delivered with great clarity of exposition, seems almost audible! The story-line is strengthened by the powerful and tragic human issues which underpin the motivation for the murder; these are woven into the plot with sensitivity and understanding, and make compelling reading. The Radfords follow their established practice of encouraging readers to follow the trail with Manson and providing them with all the vital clues and evidence which emerge from his investigations to reach their own conclusions. The novel is interspersed with 'Interludes', which serve as challenges to the reader.

The theatre is a popular milieu in which to set crime stories. It has a garish glamour, attracting flamboyant though often vulnerable and volatile artistic characters who work together in a confined atmosphere and are prone to personal and professional jealousies. There is also plenty of scope for satire. Stage production trappings, scenery, props and equipment, warrens of backstage dressing rooms and storerooms, and the crucial timings of actors entering and leaving the stage during a performance, offer prolific opportunities for the fertile minds of crime writers when it comes to devising plots and setting clues. The theatrical milieu has featured in some prominent Golden Age detective novels, including among others the following. Agatha Christie adapted several of her short stories into acclaimed stage plays, including *Witness for the Prosecution* and *The Mousetrap* (*Three Blind Mice*). Ngaio Marsh, creator of the Inspector Roderick Alleyn mysteries, was a celebrated theatre director as well as accomplished crime novelist, and wrote some excellent theatre-based murder mysteries: *Enter a Murderer* (1935) and *Overture to Death* (1939) both have performers murdered in full view before the audience. Marsh's *Vintage Murder* (1937) and *Opening Night* (1951) focus on murderous activities within small theatre companies; as do Douglas G. Browne's *The Looking Glass Murders* (1935), John Bude's *Death of a Cad* (1940) and Clifford Witting's *Measure for Murder* (1945). The latter is highly praised by the critics Barzun and Taylor, who regard it as Witting's best. *Hamlet Revenge* (1937) by Michael Innes, involves a country house performance of Shakespeare's play *Hamlet* during which an actor is murdered on stage by being stabbed through a curtain at the very moment Shakespeare's directions call for the same action. The theatrical superstitions around Shakespeare's Scottish play *Macbeth* are used to effect by Ngaio Marsh in her final novel *Light Thickens* (1982). Edmund Crispin (pseudonym of film composer Bruce Montgomery) featured a clever locked room murder amidst conflicts within a group of actors in Oxford in *The Case of the Gilded Fly* (1944), and later tackled the world of opera with a backstage murder in *Swan Song* (1947).

Nigel Moss

To

THE LADIES AND GENTLEMEN OF
THE FOOTLIGHTS

For so many years our very
Good Companions

PAVILION THEATRE

BURLINGTON-ON-SEA

Lessees . . . . . *The Burlington Corpn.*

Commencing BOXING DAY

Until further notice

Mr. Henri de Benyat presents the popular Pantomime

ONCE NIGHTLY AT 7

MATINEES on WEDNESDAYS and SATURDAYS at 2

DICK WHITTINGTON

AND HIS CAT

Book and Lyrics by William Lauriston

Spectacular Scenes : Gorgeous Costumes

With an All-Star cast, including :

Dick Whittington	NORMA DE GREY
Alice Fitzwarren	PEGGY PRUE
Idle Jack	FRANCIS BENSON
Alderman Fitzwarren . .	EVAN JAMES
Martha, the Cook . .	FREDDIE FOSSETT
Captain Heave-O } His Mate	{ THE GLEE BROTHERS
Fairy of the Bells . . .	HEATHER LOW
King Rat	FREDERICK BARNSON
The Cat	ENORA
Speciality Dancers . .	PEG ROFFE AND PARTNER

THE TEN LITTLE TWINKLE BELLES ;

MARCIA GARSON'S YOUNG LADIES ; AND

THE EIGHT GLEE SINGERS

Produced by ARTHUR FERN, under the
Direction of HENRI DE BENYAT

Manager for the Company . .	HARRY CASTLE
Stage Manager	WILLIAM TRIMBLE
Conductor	REGINALD HOWARD

CHAPTER I
INTRODUCING THE COMPANY

The Pavilion Theatre at Burlington-on-Sea was ablaze with twinkling lights which flickered with pleasing warmth from the revolving ball at the top of the theatre to the flickering colours which ran round the illuminated sign in front, telling of the programme that was being performed within.

Beneath the lights the dark streets were thronged with advancing columns of people jostling one another in a jolly and friendly way as they converged from various directions on the square of pavement before the vestibule of the theatre: old people, younger people and merry children, chattering with one another in joyful anticipation of the pleasures to come. For this was the annual pantomime season at the Pavilion; and the fairy story being played for old children as well as young ones was the popular favourite *Dick Whittington*.

And a very good production it was, too. The wide and revolving stage of the Pavilion lent itself particularly well to massive scenery; the modern stage lighting with which the Pavilion was wired gave every artifice of illusion. There was no stage superior to it in the West End of London, and very few comparable. Nor was there a back-stage to equal it.

Old actors who came out once a year—in pantomime engagements—entering a dressing-room at the Burlington Pavilion and being confronted with a bathroom leading off, equipped with shower, had been known hurriedly to retrace their steps to the street, dash round the corner for a couple of quick ones, and then, fortified, return to see if the bathroom was indeed a new elaboration of the 'Pink Elephant' hallucinations to which they were more accustomed. Add to the bathrooms the lift from stage to dressing-rooms, the real dressing tables, instead of a bare and dirty shelf running the length of the rooms, which is the average theatre dressing-room table, the mirrors, the brightly glazed walls, the easy chairs, the drying and ironing rooms, and the Green Room at the side of the stage, where the ladies and gentlemen waited their cues, or slipped out of the way of the revolving stage when it was in action, and you will realize why actors looked upon an engagement at Burlington as a week of holiday and ease at a good salary.

They gave of their best, too, for the artist in them responded to the ease, comfort, in fact, luxury, of their surroundings. Each year the pantomime of Mr. Henri de Benyat had been an improvement on the previous one. But *Dick Whittington* was, in Henri's own words, 'the daddy of the lot'.

Apart from the fact that *Dick Whittington* is always popular with children—even those up to ninety—Mr. de Benyat had produced it in its full glory, generously providing the Moroccan scene with camels (and the necessary attendants) the appearance of which delighted the audience, but put the fear of death into the hearts of the veiled Moroccan glamour girls whose part it was to lay posed about the stage and have the camels wend a graceful way between them, to the thunderous applause of the children. The applause on one occasion at least drowned the comment of one of the Moroccan maidens in an embarrassing moment. "Cor, lumme, Dais, it don't 'arf pong"—which was just as well, since the Lambeth accent did not come well from the damsel in Eastern robes.

The pantomime had run for a fortnight in Burlington, and this was its last week before finding new fields to conquer. Its success as an entertainment for the townspeople, and a financial triumph for the corporation of Burlington and the impresario, had not, alas, been shared by the company who, from its earliest hours had been beset by bickerings and quarrellings behind the scenes, and whispered asides in innuendo on the stage itself. It had, everybody agreed, been a most uncomfortable engagement.

This, as any stage associate could tell you, was decidedly unusual with a Henri de Benyat company. There are producers and impresarios whose misfortune it is never to be able to surround themselves with 'happy' companies. And for no definable reason. They are affable, they pay good salaries, they produce well and elegantly. Yet the players are invariably at sixes and sevens.

But this was not so with Mr. de Benyat. "It's always a happy crowd in a Henri show", was a by-word in the theatrical profession; and the genial, smiling producer had, accordingly, always a large repertoire of players upon whom to draw. The majority of the present crowd had been with Henri for some years. The rule is that re-engagement for pantomime in the following year is arranged before the current show is concluded. Unfortunately for the company this year, however, the Principal Boy of the last three years had taken on the role of leading lady to a principal comedian, and had vacated the Boards, she said, for ever. And Mr. de Benyat had engaged in her place Miss Norma de Grey. It was round Miss de Grey that the winter of discontent had circled. From the moment that she had swirled through the door of the Soho rehearsal room on a London November day, the company had taken a dislike to her, her voice, her bearing and her accent.

As the run of the piece proceeded the dislike and the discontent had grown in intensity, stoked by recriminations on both sides, by Miss de Grey as Principal Boy objecting to 'business', or interjections or gags which gave other members of the company more applause than she herself received; and by her insistence in interpolating songs to the exclusion of a song by somebody else—a necessary accompaniment since the scenes of the pantomime had to run to a time-table.

On the morning that our story opens a number of the principals on their pre-luncheon visit to the theatre for the purpose of collecting their mail, gathered in discourse in the Green Room, and there exchanged their conclusions on the date now drawing to its close. Their verdict was unanimous, and blunt.

It was given succinctly by the Demon King to the Captain. "My dear old boy, the lady's a complete cow," he said.

Why that noble animal, the cow, should have been thus anathematized so slanderously nobody seemed to know, or troubled to ascertain; but it seemed to be accepted by common agreement rather than as a considered opinion by the King. Nobody, as a rule, took much notice of what Freddie said. He was a little peculiar, temperamental some designated it, and though he knew almost everybody in the profession, he had very little good to say of any of them other than himself. Unsuccessful and warped actors are not infrequently taken that way. There was, on this occasion, however, no adverse comment, and Freddie, after a look round, continued.

"Yes, my dears, she's lousy, with a capital 'L.' Can't understand what Henri was doing to engage her. Legs, I suppose, though she can't use the blasted things."

He waxed warm with anger.

"Good Lord, the camel walks better than she does. Looks as if she's a lady with two professions. She must be damned good at the other one to get on in this."

A little restlessness betrayed itself among the company at this openness of expression, and Idle Jack intervened.

"Oh, don't take too much notice of Freddie," he urged. "He's always belly-aching about somebody. Miss de Grey was a bit hasty with Peggy about choosing the numbers, but we got over that. Peggy can sing anything." (Peggy Prue, the Principal Girl, was in private life Idle Jack's wife.)

"That's right," agreed Miss Prue. "We didn't let her worry us. There's too many real things in life to worry over, but it's funny how one in a company can create a nasty atmosphere. Still, we're happy enough. It's a good pantomime."

"Well, I think she's horrid," the Fairy announced; and the tone of Miss Low's voice suggested that there was more magic in the fairy's wand than would appear on the surface, since its dulcet nuances each night had wished the Boy good fortune. "I've only one song to sing," she continued, "and she had a verse cut out of that, because she said it was too long for her to lie on the Highgate Hill while I was singing it. The Principal Boy last year didn't complain. Mean, I call it. No voice herself, of course. Jealous, I suppose."

"Gor blimey, what a nark!" burst out the Captain. "A 'ambone, that's what she is. Throwin' her weight abaht. Why, my missus could run rings round her even now, though she do weigh sixteen stone. Ask Henri. He'll tell you. One of the finest Principal Boys as ever worked Merthyr Tydfil."

"Nanty polari—the mozzie's just comin' cross the green-gage." The Cat gave a whispered warning. "Good morning, Miss Grey. Nice day," he said, as the subject of the conversation walked past them. "There, see what I mean?" he added. "The perisher didn't even answer. Thinks she's the blooming queen of blooming Sheba. I'd like to dot her one, ripe and juicy. Allus on to me: 'Don't rub against my legs in the hill scene; you'll ladder me tights.' 'Don't scratch me legs.' Blimey, if you scratched her lousy legs sawdust'd come out."

He waxed more loquacious. "Wot a 'boy'. Complained about me to Henri, she did. Me, wot's worked circus and panto for Henri fifteen year. Miss de Grey. Wot a moniker for a louse." He spat in disgust. "Look at the way she talks to Bill here."

The stage-manager, thus dragged into the conversation, spread his hands deprecatingly. "As a matter of fact, old man, I usually keep my opinions to myself," he said. "It's safer in my position. But I must say Miss de Grey certainly causes difficulties. You usually get that kind of thing with newcomers. They don't understand the team spirit like the old troupers do. They get kind of selfish, I'm afraid. The guv'nor steers clear of Miss de Grey, so I have to use the kid gloves and sort things out for myself. There's always one line you can get away with with this type—just tell 'em they're wonderful."

"I should sum up the position this way." The understudy put in her oar. "The management engaged a special walking understudy just in case, which shows the lady's temperament. And Bill here keeps telling her how good I am, and so she keeps playing. Get me? I sit round, waiting to make my name in dead men's shoes, and I'd cut her throat for the chance. Four years I've understudied Dick Whittington now, with never a sound of Bow Bells for me. If it goes on much longer, I'll be so old when my chance comes they'll have to wheel me up Highgate Hill in a bath-chair."

It was left to a lady of the chorus to have the woman's last word. "I think you're all horrid," she announced. "I think Miss de Grey is wonderful. She wears such lovely diamond rings."

A ripple of laughter restored the company's good humour. One by one they wandered away for lunch, a drink and a rest before beginning the exertions of the evening.

Chapter II
THE STAGE IS SET

"OVERTURE and beginners, please—"

The voice of the diminutive call-boy rang out the ages'-old stage warning, the tocsin call to the boards that four hundred years ago brought running to the stage the actor Shakespeare, yet fresh from his old profession of holding horses' heads outside the theatre.

"Overture and beginners, Number One." The boy tapped on the star dressing-room of Miss Norma de Grey; he tapped on number two door, and on the door of number three room; and so on, to the corridor upon which the chorus rooms converged.

"Overture and beginners, PLEASE." He finished with a plaintive emphasis of his own on the last word, an appeal to avoid, if it were at all possible, another tour of the rooms.

Doors opened, and a bevy of laughing and chattering ballet and chorus girls came fluttering into the passage, and scurried away towards the Green Room. Others came staidly and industriously knitting jumpers; and still others, arms round companions' waists, whispering confidences of the day's happenings, or the happenings that were to follow when the curtain fell and the town's young gallants gathered outside the stage door. Still others there were hurriedly putting the finishing touches to their dressing and make-up. They were those who slipped into the theatre at the last moment. "Lor, girls, you'll never be ready in time," the dresser had warned them. One and all were making their way for the first scene, for which the stage was set—the market scene of *Dick Whittington*, traditional opening to the pantomime.

Behind the dropped curtain the scene stood waiting. Mr. Henri de Benyat prided himself on the picturesqueness of his stage settings. He felt that a spectacle that pleased the eye was half-way to the success of the performance, and it was the invariable rule that when the curtain went up on a Benyat production there was a general burst of applause from an appreciative audience for the work of Mr. de Benyat's brain and the work of the scene-makers and painters.

His Cheapside scene for this pantomime was no exception. The shops at the back looked too real to be painted canvas; the sets of plywood canvas and battens with a frontage and nothing behind looked as natural, for shops stocked with wares, as a real shop would have appeared had it been suddenly dumped in the same place on the stage. A fountain, cross-centre stage, had its attendant chorus gentlemen, arranged as villagers.

Beyond the curtain the orchestra was reaching the final bars of the overture. The stage-manager looked over his artistes and rounded them as a shepherd rounds his flock.

"Now, come along, ladies. The overture's nearly over. Put down that knitting, please. This isn't a tea-party. Miss Young, look at your tights. They've laddered. See Mrs. Green as soon as you come off. . . . Now, Harry, swing those lights back of the shop. . . . Come along. . . . come along. . . . Ready? . . . Stand by."

He ran to his corner and, as the orchestra broke into the bars of the opening chorus, pressed a button in his box. The beautiful velvet tabs parted . . . scurled back. The village maidens poured into Cheapside, gambolling and laughing. They broke into song:

> "In Cheapside, in Cheapside,
> In dear old London town,
> You buy a hat, you buy a mat,
> Or buy a wedding gown.
> Never worry, never flurry,
> Never wear a frown,
> It's cheap to buy in Cheapside
> When you shop in London Town."

The curtain was up. . . . The show was on.

The chorus ended—one never heard the words, of course; one never does, but the libretto is traditional—the stage filled up. On danced the wee Twinkle Belles; on came the Captain and his mate, just returned, they told the audience, from foreign parts, and looking for a crew. On came Idle Jack from the Fitzwarren store to joke about the work he never did. On came Alderman Fitzwarren and his daughter Alice, to explain their identities, and to mix with the company.

Presently the crowd dispersed on their day's business. In groups, and in singles, the company danced off, left and right, into the shops.

The stage stood empty.

The lights lowered to rose-pink and amber spots. The audience waited expectantly. From behind the market cross came a lonely figure, tired, and walking slowly.

Dick Whittington. . . .

The applause broke out.

The children in the audience saw only the fairy story of their books come to life; the grown-ups caught for a moment a remembrance of their childhood days, and remembered their first pantomime; a memory which never fails to revive the thrill of the first theatre expedition.

Miss Norma de Grey was a Dick Whittington worth seeing. Tall and slim and graceful, in scalloped leather jerkin, full, brown tights and thigh boots of soft kid, topped withal by the wee, jaunty cap with feathers, and carrying, of course, the stick with, tied to it, the bundle covered with the spotted red handkerchief, she stood bowing to the applause which came upon her like an avalanche over the footlights. It died away, to be succeeded by an even greater burst as, following his master into the view of the audience, came the Cat, Tommy, faithful friend and pet.

Again the clapping and the tumult died, and the audience settled down to listen to the story of Dick Whittington and his Cat.

Strange though it may seem, it *was* the story of Whittington. Mr. Henri de Benyat took pride in the fact that when he presented pantomime, it was the pantomime which came from the fairy stories, not from the 'gags' of artistes which, since the artistes had been doing them on the music-hall for at least twenty years, were already well-known. Henri de Benyat's pantomimes had a script, and the script was working along now, to the finale of the first half.

The audience saw Dick meet Alice Fitzwarren, saw him engaged in her father's store, saw him making love to Alice.

They saw—and the children greeted it with cat-calls—Idle Jack plant the shop's takings in Dick's pocket; saw the lad accused, and the crowd in the shop brand him in song, a la Grand Opera.

"He is a thief, and to prison he must go."

And Alice:

"Oh, father, spare him."

Alderman: "Leave my shop, I say."

And the reply:

Dick: "Good-bye, Alice. Remember me, I pray.
For I will return and claim you as my bride.
When luck has changed, and once more you're at my side.
Come, my faithful cat, some day we'll gain renown,
And they'll be glad to welcome us to good old London Town.
Farewell . . . farewell."

All: "Farewell . . . farewell . . . farewell"

The stage blacked out. The front cloth fell. The Dame entered in front of the cloth and began her beguiling of the audience—the routine to give the stage hands time to set the next scene.

* * * * *

Come behind the scenes for a few moments and remark upon the preamble to the tragedy that is so soon to fall on the heads of the company. As the curtain fell there was a hurried rush of principals and chorus from the stage. Girls dashed helter-skelter through the Green Room to the dressing-rooms to change for the second half, and to repair the ravages of heat and scurry on their make-up. Principals, with a little more time on their hands, made their way more slowly to a drink fetched for them by the dressers.

All but Dick Whittington. She stalked to the stage-manager's box and confronted that harassed executive.

"Tell that blasted stage-hand who changes the tree-trunks on the revolve to be more careful!" she snapped. "He damn near split my skull last night in the black-out, and those girls who stand up-stage are crowding in on me. I won't have it."

"All right, Miss de Grey, I'll see to it," William promised. He pulled her down-stage and dodged a ten-foot 'flat' which three stage-hands were moving across to set up. "You'd better go into the Green Room till we're set," he cooed, and piloted her out of danger. As he came back on the stage he caught up with a stage-hand setting the mossy bank on which Dick Whittington was soon to repose to hear the bells of Bow.

"Arthur, go steady in the revolve with those ground irons of yours," he said. "Miss de Grey says you nearly murdered her last night."

"Blasted good job if I had," was the reply. "She's been rocking again, I suppose. Properly got it on her tonight, ain't she? I reckon she's copped the brewer."

"Cut that out, Arthur," the stage-manager retorted sharply. "You do your job, and let it go at that."

"Orlright . . . orlright, guv. But somebody'll drop a counter-weight on that mess of peroxide one of these fine nights, and serve her blasted well right. Jes' listen to her a'rortin' to the Cat, now. . . . Blimey, he's walked out on her."

The Cat, swearing, swung angrily from the Green Room and turned towards the dressing-rooms. The stage-manager looked anxiously after him, and then the more pressing business of changing the scenery called his attention. He was to remember, later, the cat's disappearance at the head of the stairs. But now he turned to his staff.

"Come along, lads, we're letting it go a bit fine," he called. Down came the backcloth with its views of distant London. Down came the borders of tree foliage, and in went the 'flats' of oak and elm. Stage-hands carried on and arranged the mossy bank. The Highgate Hill scene, highlight of the pantomime, was ready. Ten minutes had passed since the black-out, and the

Dame had ended her front-cloth scene to sustained clapping and applause. She came off, wiping perspiration from her (or, rather, his) face.

The stage-manager gave the light cue. The electricians dimmed the stage, and stood by for their trickiest scene.

"Everybody ready?" asked the stage-manager, and looked anxiously round. His finger pressed a button, and the front cloth went up.

* * * * *

Dick Whittington, bundle and stick over his shoulder, walked on to the stage. A tired, and dispirited Dick. He came slowly into view, and approached the mossy bank.

"Come along, pussy, here's a bank.
We'll rest awhile."

There was a momentary pause. . . . The stage-manager jumped.

"Where's that blasted Cat?" he asked himself. "What the hell's he doing?"

He started out of his corner, but with a sigh of relief returned. A furry coat appeared up-stage, and slowly ambled towards Dick Whittington.

Miss de Grey saw it at the same time. To the stage-hands, watching her from the side, it was obvious that she was furious at the momentary delay. She fumbled her lines:

"The world is all against me. Only you are my friend
So we'll sleep awhile, and at break of day
To make our fortune we'll away.
Good night, Tommy."

Dick stretched herself gracefully at full length upon the moss of the bank, and closed her eyes. The Cat meowed and, to the delight of the younger members of the audience, washed carefully its fur and face, passing, of course, its paws round the back of its ears. Then, with a final stretch, he curled himself across Dick Whittington's legs.

Applause broke out, and subsided. From the wings came Fairy Bow Bells. Her wand extended over the sleeping Dick. She spoke her traditional lines:

"Sleep on, sweet boy.
Though fortune may frown,
Soon you'll return with wealth and renown.
Dream of the message that peals from Bow Bells;
Turn again, Whittington, that's what it tells.
Lord Mayor of London Town
Three times Lord Mayor.
Turn again, Whittington, life will be fair."

The soft music swelled to crescendo, and the sound of bells filled the theatre.

Slowly the stage revolved to a half-turn. Bells hung everywhere on this reverse side of the scenery. Girls dressed as silver and golden bells poised, and then broke into ballet for three minutes of sheer loveliness. The Belles appeared as in a dream.

Again the stage revolved, bringing the mossy bank and the sleeping Whittington once more to its original position downstage. The Fairy of the Bells sang her song—the cue for Dick's waking, and for his words:

"The bells, the bells; is it a dream?
I thought I heard the Bow Bells say:
Turn again, Whittington, Lord Mayor of London."

But no words came.

The Fairy Queen waited. The stage-manager, sensing something wrong, leaned forward and looked back along the stage. He saw Dick Whittington still reclining.

"What the hell's happened now?" he hissed. "God, she must have fainted." He turned towards the orchestra pit and waved frantically at the conductor.

"Go on, go on, for the love of Mike," he called in a loud whisper.

"YOU"—to the mesmerized Fairy Queen—"say it. . . . Say it, damn you!"

The Fairy took up the unspoken lines, the chorus joined in, and the audience, unaware that anything unusual had happened, applauded enthusiastically as the curtain closed.

"No call . . . no call," the stage-manager shouted, and rang down the fire-curtain for the interval.

He rushed to the mossy bank, as the Cat, free at last to move, got up and walked to the side of the revolve.

The stage-manager bent over the recumbent form of Miss de Grey. He shook her. "Miss de Grey . . . Miss de Grey," he called. "Are you ill?"

No answer came. He signalled a stage-hand.

"Carry her to the lounge in the Green Room," he said. "And get the first-aid man. Quick."

The first-aid man came at the run, his flask loosened and uncorked. He bent over the star and loosened her jerkin. He felt for her heart, and suddenly shrank back.

"Gawd A'Mighty!" he said softly. *"Gawd A'mighty, I believe she's dead."*

"What!"

The exclamation came from the house manager, breathless from his dash from the front of the house to find the reason for the stage *contretemps*.

"Dead? Impossible," he said.

"I reckon she is, sir," the first-aid man confirmed, after another examination. "You'd better get a doctor."

The manager, white-faced and trembling, waited for the fire-curtain to be raised, and then slipped on to the front of the stage, and faced the audience.

"Ladies and gentlemen," he said. "I regret to have to announce that Miss Norma de Grey has been taken suddenly ill. If there is a doctor in the house, the management would be grateful for his assistance."

His eyes searched the stalls and saw a man rise from the fourth row and acknowledge him with a nod. The manager hurried from the stage to meet him.

Behind the scenes consternation reigned. Principals and chorus were crowding the entrance to the Green Room, pushing and jostling in an endeavour to see the Principal Boy, still lying on the lounge.

"What's the matter with her *now*?" asked Idle Jack.

"'Nother tantrum, I reckon," retorted the Demon King. "The bloomin' Cat's scratched her tights, I shouldn't be surprised."

"Now, boys and girls, *please*," coerced the stage-manager. "You've got only five minutes." He jostled them clear of the entrance. "Off you go." He turned to the understudy.

"Miss de Grey won't be able to appear again tonight. You'll have to go on. Buck up and get dressed."

"Me? Bow Bells at last. Whoops! Well, I'll be damned! My chance at last." She dashed for her dressing-room.

"You've four minutes," the stage-manager warned her.

* * * * *

The doctor, escorted by the manager, came through the pass door, crossed the stage and, entering the Green Room, bent over the still figure of the star.

Beneath the powder and paint, the face stared out greyish-blue. The doctor sought for, and held, the pulse in the girl's left wrist. It showed no movement or beat. He lifted an eyelid and looked into a glassy, staring pupil.

Suddenly, he bent lower. Then, gravely, he turned to the manager and the stage-manager.

"I think you had better telephone for the police," he said. *"This woman has been poisoned."*

There was a shocked silence, broken by the voice of the stage-manager.

"Poisoned, sir?" he said. "But it's impossible. She was on the stage. I was watching her the entire time. Neither she nor anybody else moved a hand."

"I don't care where she was, sir," the doctor retorted, "she has been poisoned. She has had a dose of prussic acid, and must have died within a few seconds. I will remain here until the police arrive."

The three men looked at one another.

"The show must go on, of course." The manager looked at the doctor. "Can we move her into her own room? We have the company coming through here."

"I see no harm in that. She did not die in this lounge."

Gently, the body of Dick Whittington, for whom the Bow Bells would never again ring, was carried into Number One dressing-room, laid on the lounge, and reverently covered with a dust-sheet.

The stage-manager chivvied the call-boy. "Here, you, get them all down for the opening of the second half," he said. "And tell them to hurry."

A ring on his house telephone sent him back into his box. He lifted the receiver. "Hallo," he called.

"Front of the house calling, William. The kids are calling for the Cat. What's the matter with him?"

"The Cat? Isn't he out there? Gawd, what the devil is he doing? Haven't we got enough trouble without him causing more. . . . Call-boy! . . . *Call-boy!*"

"Yes, sir?"

"Go and see where the devil the Cat is."

It was the practice of the Cat, during the interval, to appear among the audience in the front of the house, gambolling along the gangways, playing with the children and walking along the plush front of the dress circle. For the kiddies it represented one of the high spots of the entire performance. It was the absence of 'Tommy' on this occasion that had led to the telephone call from the front of the house; and to the demand of the stage-manager to know where was the absentee.

Nor was it the children alone who enjoyed the perambulations of the Cat amongst them; the Cat enjoyed it—from a financial point of view. He usually carried a little bag into which patrons whose children were singled out for a lick and a meow, beneficently slipped in pieces of silver—and paper. A cat who knew his tiles, so to speak, could make several pounds a night by judiciously picking the right parents. And Mr. de Benyat's cat had done exceedingly well out of the Burlington audiences.

So William, the stage-manager, was as much puzzled as he was worried by the missing cat.

"Anyway, he can't do it now," he ruminated, "because the curtain is darned near due up. . . . Wonder if that understudy is going to be all right? She's—"

A series of piercing shrieks interrupted his soliloquy. He spun round, and out of the box on to the stage. "For the love of heaven, what the devil is going on now?" he called. "Dammit, they'll hear it in front."

The shrieks grew in volume as the operator of them came nearer. Doors of dressing-rooms opened, and scared girls in various stages of dress, or undress, peered out.

"Who is it?" roared the stage-manager. "Gag her, whoever it is."

The call-boy came into view at the far end of the Green Room, still shouting and waving his hands, and with a face as white as a sheet. William seized him by the collar, and shook him like a terrier shaking a rat.

"Shut up, you little devil, will you? What's got hold of you?"

"The Cat, sir . . . the Cat. . . ." He paused, panting.

"What's the matter with the blasted Cat?"

"He's dead . . . in his room . . . lying on the floor."

"What!"

The stage-manager stared incredulously.

"Dead. . . . On the floor." The boy gave one more shriek, and fell in a heap on the stage, unconscious. The first-aid man picked him up and rushed him off to the Green Room lounge only recently vacated by Dick Whittington.

"Lord, there's the orchestra finishing!" William ran his hands through his hair. He seized the telephone and dialled the orchestra pit. The conductor's voice answered.

"Bill, play the intermission through again, and then go straight on. We're holding the curtain—got to get hold of the Cat's understudy."

"Understudy? What's the matter with the Cat, then?"

"We think he's dead, too."

"What? Well, if that ain't the cat's whiskers. What are we playing tonight? *Whittington*, or *Sweeney Todd*?"

"I don't think that's funny, old man." William banged the receiver down. "Jack," he called to a stage-hand, "get hold of the Cat's understudy, and tell him he's got to go on. Room 26. Anybody taken the doctor to the Cat?"

"Yes, guv'nor. Manager's gone up with him."

"Right. Everybody down? Where's that call-boy? Crumbs, got to get an understudy for *him* now. Come along, ladies. Get a move on. We're late already. Stand by. . . ."

"What's the matter with Miss de Grey, Bill?" whispered one of the girls.

"Don't know, sweetheart. She can't go on. Stop talking." He turned to the Whittington understudy. "You all right, dearie?" he asked.

"What do you think, sonny—my chance."

"Right." He gave an anxious glance round the stage, noted the position of the chorus waiting, and counted them. None missing, he noted. He searched for, and found, the Captain and Mate waiting to follow after the chorus. . . . His fingers pressed the button once more.

The curtain went up.

The play went on.

The stage-manager breathed a sigh of relief and sat on his stool. A hand touched his shoulders.

"Can't find the Cat's understudy anywhere," announced Jack.

"Curses on him!" burst out the harassed man. "Here we're paying salary for a walking understudy, and when he's wanted he ain't here. Listen. The blighter will be in the Green Man, round the corner. Fetch him out, take him to his blazing room, and put him into his skin. Then come back and tell me he's there."

"Right, guv." Jack vanished on his Cat hunt.

The house manager, tip-toeing silently through the wings, edged his way into William's box. William eyed him.

"Dead?" he whispered.

"No. But damned near gone. He's on the way to hospital."

"What's wrong with him?"

"Poison, same as Miss de Grey. Got a police inspector here. Listen. After the finale, get everyone dressed quickly, and into the Green Room. They'll all have to be questioned. I've ordered coffee and sandwiches to be brought in. Heaven knows when they'll get away tonight. I'll try to get cars to take them all home afterwards. Nobody is to go out of the theatre. There's a copper on the stage door, and the door is locked."

"That means stage hands, too?"

"Yes, everybody."

"O.K."

CHAPTER III
THE COMPANY TELL THEIR STORY

AT 11.30 P.M. a hundred or more people gathered in the Green Room of the Burlington Pavilion Theatre.

They sat on the plush-covered lounges which lined the walls; they occupied chairs which had been carried from dressing-rooms. They eyed one another, talking in scared whispers, and casting now and again glances at the empty and silent stage shrouded in gloom as deep as the shroud of death which had descended over it during the evening.

Round a table at the exit end sat a little group of men talking among themselves. From amongst them one stood up—the manager of the theatre. He looked along the rows of faces, and spoke.

"Ladies and gentlemen," he said gravely, "I am sorry to have to tell you what some of you know already—that Miss de Grey is dead. . . ."

A shocked silence followed the announcement, broken only by a few sobs from the younger girls of the chorus. The manager paused for a moment, to regain his composure.

"She died on the stage, in the Highgate Hill scene," he continued. "Mr. Enora, than whom we have never had a better Cat, is seriously ill. Now some of you were on the stage at the time, and others were in the wings. Inspector Bradley here"—he indicated the man by his side—"wants to ask you a few questions.

He will not keep you long tonight. When he has finished, you will be taken to your diggings in cars, and I want to ask you not to discuss this tragic affair with anyone. The inspector assures me that it is most important that you shall not indulge in any talk. Now, Inspector."

Inspector Bradley leaned forward with his elbows on the table, and his chin cupped in his hands. He eyed the company pleasantly.

"I know that you are all tired after the wonderful performance you have given tonight. I think this is the best pantomime and company we have ever had in Burlington," he said. "I enjoyed it tremendously the other night, and I am sorry for the reason that I am here now, and also for the fact that I have to keep you from your suppers and beds."

He smiled slightly. "I've had a hard day myself, but I am afraid that I shall still be up when you are, at last, in bed." He smiled again at a company now more or less at its ease. They had feared a policeman; but felt that Mr. Bradley was an understanding soul. The inspector was a bit of a psychologist—a detective-inspector *has* to be—and he sensed the more comfortable feeling that had come over his audience.

"Now, the reason I asked you to be gathered here, is because some of you, as the manager said, were on the stage at a crucial moment, and others were near and around Miss de Grey and the Cat, and I want to get from you answers to a few questions while the happenings are clear in your minds, and before you have had time to think over the occurrence and imagine more than you actually saw."

He paused.

"Oh yes. You'd be surprised at the things people *say* they saw which they never did see. Quite clever and sensible people, too, who wouldn't exaggerate for anything on earth. What happens is that, in thinking about an action, they begin to wonder whether so-and-so *could* have been done, and when they are questioned twenty-four hours later, they put forward the ideas that have come into their minds as things which they really believe did happen. I've known my own policemen do it. So if we have a few questions now, before you have a night to think things over, we'll be on safer grounds.

"Now, firstly, will all the people who were on the stage in the Highgate Hill scene, please stand up?"

A number of the company rose to their feet. The inspector eyed them for a few seconds, and turned to the manager with a question. He listened to the reply, and nodded.

"I gather," he said, "that the tall ladies are the chorus, and the smaller ones the dancers—the Twinkle Belles," he added, with a little bow. "Would you all please sit together in your groupings, one group on either side of the room."

There was a general post round with chairs, and the inspector waited while order was restored. He turned to the single figure still standing. "You will be, of course, the Fairy Queen," he acknowledged. "Miss . . ." His voice invited an answer.

"Heather Low, Inspector."

"Well, Miss Low, where were you standing when Miss de Grey lay on the bank in the scene?"

"On the right of her, just off the revolve, sir."

The inspector looked puzzled. "Off the revolve?" he asked.

The manager came to his assistance. "We have a modern stage here, Inspector," he explained. "A large circular portion of it revolves. Thus, we can set a scene at the back part of the revolve while the scene in the front half of it is being played, and when the scene has to be changed, the stage is just turned round. It saves time, and also allows transformation effects as in the dream scene of Whittington. Miss Low means that she was standing just off the circular portion to avoid being carried round when the stage revolved. She had to remain downstage."

The inspector nodded. "I see," he acknowledged. "So you would be fairly close to Miss de Grey?"

"Quite close, Inspector."

"How close?"

The Fairy Queen considered the question speculatively. Before she had decided, however, the manager spoke. "I should say about six or seven feet, Inspector."

Inspector Bradley's eyes sought the darkened stage ponderingly. He appeared to be thinking introspectively. "Let me see," he said presently. "If I remember the scene correctly, Dick Whittington comes on followed by the Cat, and walks to the bank. The stage is otherwise empty. Is that correct?"

The manager agreed with a nod.

"And it is not until Whittington is asleep with the Cat that the others come on?"

"That is so."

"Where are you, Miss Low, before you come on?"

"In the wings, waiting, Inspector."

"For your cue?"

"Well, it is not exactly a cue. The lights change, the stage revolves a half-turn, and then I enter."

"So I gather that you would be facing across the stage in readiness, and looking at the progress of the scene?" He paused for any correction, and none being forthcoming, proceeded. "Whittington, I suppose, came on the stage from the side opposite to you. Did you see her come on, or was there any obstruction to your view?"

"Oh no, Inspector; there was no obstruction. I saw her walk into the scene, as I always did."

"Ah! Now will you tell me, Miss Low, in your own words, just what you saw on this occasion. How Miss de Grey came on, what she did, and how she did it. Think a moment first, and describe it exactly as it happened."

The girl stood for a few seconds, her brow wrinkled. Her eyes wandered to the stage, and the inspector, watching, saw them turn right and left, following her mental acting of the scene. Finally, they looked straight into his own.

"Well, sir, there was nothing different to the usual," she replied. "I went to my place, down-stage in the wings. Miss de Grey was waiting on the other side. She was buttoning her jerkin and straightening her cap. The front cloth turn came off. Then the lights dimmed, the front cloth went up, and Miss de Grey walked on, as usual."

"Did she say anything?"

"Of course. She said her lines, 'Come along, pussy, here's a bank. We'll rest awhile'. Then the Cat came. She laid down, said her good night lines, and closed her eyes. The Cat did his stuff and laid down with her. Then the revolve came, I made my entrance, spoke my lines waving the wand. Then the second revolve came, and I went back into the wings. . . ." She paused.

"Then what?" asked the inspector.

"Well, Miss de Grey did not wake up as she should have done . . . and . . . and . . . I said her lines, and the curtain came down."

"Now, Miss Low, did Miss de Grey do anything different at all on this occasion—anything that she had not done before?"

"Definitely not, Inspector."

"You did not see her eat or drink anything before she walked on, or while she was lying on the bank? She didn't, for instance, seem to slip a sweet into her mouth?"

"Not that I saw. And I think I should have seen it had she done so."

"Did she move at all after she laid on the bank?"

"No . . . I . . . don't think so."

"But you aren't quite sure, eh?"

"I wasn't watching her *that* closely, of course."

"Did she speak at all—I mean, outside the lines in the script?"

"No . . . well . . ." Miss Low paused. There was embarrassment in her voice.

The inspector seized upon it quickly. "She *did* say something," he questioned sharply. "What was it?"

The Fairy Queen faltered. "Well, it wasn't really very much," she replied. "She just said, in a loud whisper to the Cat: 'Don't stick your damned claws into me, and get off my legs. You laddered my tights the other night.'"

"Did the Cat make any reply?"

"He said something, but I couldn't hear what it was."

That concluded the questioning of Miss Low, and the inspector turned to the Twinkle Belles ballet girls.

"You little ladies danced round Dick and the Cat while they lay sleeping, didn't you?" he asked.

A chorus of shrill "yes's" answered him.

"You went closer to her than the Fairy Queen, didn't you? Did you see Miss de Grey do anything unusual?"

"Oh no!" Another chorus of reply.

Inspector Bradley scratched a worried head. He paused a second or two in thought—and evolved a brainwave. "Was there anything that she didn't do that she usually did?" he asked.

Nine voices sounded another concerted "No". The quick eyes of the inspector noticed the puckered lips of the tenth. He pointed a finger at her. "What is your name, my dear?" he asked.

"Mary Lee, sir."

"I think, Mary, that you are not so sure as your friends. Did you see something missing in Miss de Grey's actions in the dream scene tonight?"

"I . . . I . . . I don't really know, sir," was the hesitant reply. "Only Miss de Grey generally watched us dancing, and sometimes winked at us when we passed her. But she didn't open her eyes at all tonight."

The inspector's face lost its amiable softness. An alertness came into them, and they sought the face of the dancer and held it. "She did not open her eyes at all?" he asked. "Not once?"

"No, sir. I looked at her each time I passed in the ballet, and she kept them closed."

The chorus ladies, next to be questioned, collectively, could throw no further fight on the death scene, nor could any of the stage-hands who had been waiting in the wings for the change of scenery. The inspector looked at his watch. "There is just one more person I want to see—Miss de Grey's dresser," he announced.

A plump woman rose in answer to the request, and faced the officer. "And you are?" he asked.

"Helen Brough, sir. And it has nothing to do with me. I know nothing whatever about Miss de Grey, or her life. I was engaged to dress her, and I knew my place. I do not want to be mixed up in the business at all."

She stopped for breath, and the inspector was able to get a word in.

"Nobody is saying that it has anything to do with you, Mrs. Brough," he apologized. "And I can understand your desire to have nothing to do with the business. But, unfortunately, you cannot do that. After all, you dressed Miss de Grey, and knew more of her than most people in the theatre. What we want to know is something about Miss de Grey's actions just before her death. Did you, for instance, go down to the stage with her for the Highgate Hill scene?"

"No, sir, I did not," was the reply, "although, as a rule, I did go down, and stayed there until Miss de Grey went on in the scene. I generally used to put a last few touches to her costume and make-up."

"Then why did you not do so on this occasion?" asked the inspector.

"Because Miss de Grey had asked me to get her a glass of stout and some sandwiches ready for when she came off. She said that she would manage her costume herself for the scene."

"And you got them?"

"They are in her room still," the woman answered.

"Had she drunk anything before going down for the scene?"

"Not a drop—at least, not while she was in the theatre this evening."

"Or eaten anything?"

"No, nothing."

"Any sweets, for instance?"

"No. Only throat lozenges, which I got from Mr. Perkins, the chemist, on Monday."

"Where are those lozenges?"

"On the table in the dressing-room."

The inspector turned to his sergeant, who had been taking shorthand notes of the questions and answers. "The room's locked?" he asked.

"Yes, Inspector. The keys are in my pocket."

"Then I think that is all for now, ladies and gentlemen," he announced. "Thank you all very much. But I shall want you all here again tomorrow morning—say at eleven-thirty o'clock, so that we shan't interfere with your lunch."

The company made for the stage door. The inspector turned to the manager.

"I am going through the dressing-rooms of Miss de Grey and the Cat," he announced. "And I think you had better be present."

The manager led the way; the inspector and his sergeant followed.

CHAPTER IV
MYSTERY ON MYSTERY

TWO O'CLOCK A.M. chimed before Inspector Bradley and the sergeant left the stage door of the Pavilion, and they had little to show for their search of the dressing-rooms of the two stars. True, their departure was accompanied by several packages tied up in paper and carefully guarded; but the inspector had collected them more as a matter of routine than as likely to provide any clues. He said so to the manager and the sergeant.

"We must not let anything go by us," he commented, "though I don't think there is anything lethal about the lozenges, the powder, or the lipstick. Still . . ."

The articles thus designated had been taken from dressing-room Number 1, in which Dick Whittington had queened to visitors of both sexes who sought introductions via the stage door. The visitors, it was disclosed, were mostly men of varying ages, and chiefly local men with money to burn on glamour. The manager had known most of them. None, he insisted, were likely to have had any reason to kill Miss de Grey, and, anyway, they were certainly not on the stage when it happened. Nobody was allowed on the stage except the company and the stage-hands.

Miss de Grey's room had presented a fairly tidy appearance as dressing-rooms go, because it was the Principal Boy's custom to have one or two visitors during the interval; and the dresser accordingly usually cleared away articles of clothing in readiness. The lozenges, powder, and lipstick had been on the dressing-table, quite openly, alongside her make-up box. The table itself, with large mirror and swinging side-mirrors was covered with a clean cloth and a chintz covering ran round it, dropping to floor level. A straight-backed chair was set in front of the table, and an armchair and another straight-backed one, were set near by. There was, as well, the long lounge, also chintz-covered, and on which the body of Miss de Grey had been laid.

"Miss de Grey's furnishings, or the theatre's?" asked the inspector.

"Ours," was the reply. "We like to make our artistes comfortable."

It was the sergeant who had suggested taking the powder and the lipstick for analysis. "Suppose, sir, the poison is in either of them. Ladies of the stage like to pat their faces with a powder-puff, and put on a bit of rouge before they go on. Mebbe she did so while she was waiting her cue, and . . . well, there you are."

"And how do *you* know all these habits of ladies of the stage, Sergeant?" the inspector asked, interestedly.

"Well, sir. I used to do a bit of stage-door haunting at the old Majesty's before I was married."

The inspector smiled. "Oh," he said. "Nevertheless, the idea is a good one, and we'll take the stuff. But after what the doctor said about the time of death, I don't think we'll get much from it."

Inspection of the bathroom, which was curtained off from the dressing-room, disclosed nothing likely to assist in the investigations; and with a last look round, the company left, the sergeant again locking the door behind them.

The Cat's room provided even less in the way of possible clues. It was a small room at the end of a long passage. Though clean and comfortable, it had no chintz coverings, no armchairs or other trimmings. A tin of vaseline and another of cold cream stood on the dressing-table, together with a watch propped up against the mirror. The skin of Whittington's Cat lay crumbled and forlorn on a settee; as crumpled and shapeless as if it, too, had given up its life with its master Whittington. The inspector looked at it, and then placed it in the wardrobe which he locked, handing the key to the sergeant.

The Cat's ordinary coat, waistcoat, and trousers, and his shirt and undervest lay over a chair. Hanging from a hook behind the door was another, and dirty, combination undergarment. The inspector eyed it dubiously.

"His spare garment for the skin, Inspector," the manager explained. "It's pretty warm working in that skin, you understand, and the wearer perspires copiously. He generally changes after a scene, and then at night the suits are washed through and left for him next evening. He was, of course, wearing the other set when he was taken to hospital."

The inspector nodded. "Quite," he said. "Well, I'd like both these rooms kept locked and sealed. My men will come along later for any finger-prints there may be going. And when we've got a bit more from the doctor, we may have to make a more thorough search. Perhaps we'll have a bit more to go on."

Fixing a string and seal to the door, the three men retraced their steps to Number 1 room, and with this, also, sealed, passed through the stage door. The theatre echoed to the bang of it; they left the stage silent for the ghosts of the dead to play again their roles on the darkened boards. Who shall say what unseen miming the spirits of Thespis display when the silent hours come upon the stage, and the watchman is beyond seeing or hearing on his rounds?

Inspector Bradley's hopes that the doctor's report would give him a little more definite line on which to begin his investigations were quickly realized. It was hardly ten o'clock when the police surgeon was awaiting his arrival at the police-station. He greeted his police colleague with something like enthusiasm.

"This is a darned interesting corpse you've sent me, Inspector," he suggested.

The police chief stared. "Interesting?" he asked. "How? Doctor McBane said it was a simple death from prussic acid."

"Prussic acid, it certainly was, Inspector. And there isn't anything unusual in that. Lots of people have died from the effects of prussic acid. Photographic dark-room people have taken it in mistake for water, and people have inhaled the gas of it. There have been wrong prescriptions such as potassic cyanide instead of potassic chloride, and there have been people who tried a powder with the tip of the tongue, and found out too late that it was hydrocyanic acid. Oh, there's nothing unusual in prussic acid poisoning, accidental, suicidal, or murderous. But what *is* unusual in this girl's death is this: in every case of prussic acid poisoning I have known the stuff has been taken by the mouth, either drunk in liquid, inhaled as gas, or swallowed as crystals. But . . ."

He paused.

". . . *This girl had a dose injected with a hypodermic syringe.*"

"What!" The inspector let out a startled exclamation.

"Hypodermic injection. I've never heard of that before. I found the prick when I made the post-mortem."

"Then that disposes of any accident, Doctor?" the inspector asked.

The doctor grinned. "Unless the lady made a hobby of running round with a syringe charged full of the stuff—yes. Seems to be a stupid way of carrying it when a little bottle is easier and safer."

Remembrance came to the inspector. "What about the man?" he asked.

"He had a dose, too, but diluted. He'll pull through, I think. Doctor McBane gave him strychinine and washed him out with sodium thiosulphate and potassium carbonate. I couldn't have done better myself. It was a near thing, but he'll do. It will be some days before you can see him, however."

Inspector Bradley sat silent in his chair, his brow creased in thought. A startling idea had come into his mind. He was considering how to propound it to the doctor without presenting it in the form of what counsel call a leading question. He wanted the doctor to make an assertion of something he himself feared. "Supposing, Doctor," he said at length, "supposing for some reason Miss de Grey *did* carry a syringe of hydro—hydro—"

"Hydrocyanic acid," the doctor encouraged.

"Yes. And supposing that, while she was lying on the stage, the needle pierced her skin, and killed her. Could the stuff in any way have overcome the cat who was lying across her, and have only taken effect on him when he had left the stage and reached his own room?"

"I thought you would come to that," was the doctor's reply. "The answer is 'no'—*because the man drank his dose*. And if he had drunk the same stuff that was in that syringe, there would have been two corpses on the stage instead of one. Damn it, Inspector, I reckon she had five grains pumped into her."

"And the Cat?"

"Don't know yet. Doctor McBane kept some stomach content. He's sent it to your analyst. He thinks it was taken in beer."

"Where was the syringe mark, Doctor?"

"Ah, now, that's another very interesting feature, Inspector. It was on her left thigh." He chuckled at the inspector's expression.

"I'm going to see the Colonel," the policeman said abruptly. "I don't like the sound of it." He picked up his cap and left.

Colonel Lovelace, the chief constable, after he had grasped the points of the doctor's story, and the questioning of the theatre company, agreed that neither did he like the accumulated evidence.

"You see, sir," the inspector emphasized, "in the scene the Cat lies across Dick Whittington's legs, and they are both there for about three minutes. He could have needled her left thigh. Then, when the curtain came down, and he left the stage, he could have run to his dressing-room and taken the poison."

"Any substantiating evidence, Inspector? Any reason for it?"

"No, sir. Not at present—" He stopped suddenly, and an ejaculation broke from him. "I wonder if there is, sir?" he said.

The Colonel eyed him—waiting.

"The Fairy Queen, who was standing in the wings when the couple laid down on the stage, said that Miss de Grey said in an angry whisper, 'Don't stick your damned claws into me'. Now, sir, might not that claw have been the prick of the needle felt by Miss de Grey? Everybody agrees that she did not move again."

Colonel Lovelace digested this piece of information. "It might be so," he agreed. "But what motive? Why should the Cat go round killing his Principal Boy, because that is what you are suggesting, Inspector, isn't it? There were other people on the stage, and in close association with Miss de Grey."

"Tell you what, sir. I am having the company on the stage again at eleven-thirty o'clock. Would you come along and witness an experiment I want to try out?"

The experiment was obvious to the company when they arrived on the stage at the hour named, for, in response to a telephoned message, the Highgate Hill scene had been set. Inspector Bradley, sitting the chief constable in the front row of the stalls, addressed the crowd.

"I want you all to go through the scene exactly as you did last night," he announced. "Two of you not usually in it can play Dick and the Cat. I want to watch it through."

"Have we to dress, sir?" asked the fairy.

"No. That will not be necessary."

The inspector, sitting with his sergeant alongside Colonel Lovelace, gave the signal for the shadow performance to begin. He watched the pseudo Dick Whittington walk on, followed by the Cat, say her lines, and lay on the bank. At the moment of the lying he interrupted.

"Now, was that exactly as last night?" he asked. "This is most important. If anyone sees the slightest difference will they please say so?"

A reflective silence, followed by a general nodding of heads, was broken by the voice of the stage-manager.

"I don't know whether it is of any importance, Inspector," he said, "but there is a slight difference. Last night the Cat did not at once follow Miss de Grey on the stage. He was a few moments late. I remember getting the wind up in case he had missed his entrance, and I leaned round to look. He was just coming on from the back of the stage."

"Away from his usual entrance?"

"Certainly. He should have come on with Miss de Grey from there." The stage-manager indicated an opening between two flats.

"And Miss de Grey was *flaming*," called out one of the chorus. "She fluffed her lines."

"Right." The inspector acknowledged the explanation. "Proceed."

The stage made its half revolve, and the Ballet was mimed to the end. The Fairy Queen spoke her lines and the revolve returned.

"This is the stage at which Miss de Grey should have awakened," the stage-manager called out "She did not do so, and I rang down the curtain. We carried her off—"

"Who carried her off?"

Three stage-hands stepped forward. The sergeant recorded their names for future questioning. Together the chief constable and Bradley climbed on to the stage.

"What happened to the Cat after you rang down the curtain?" asked Inspector Bradley.

The company looked at one another in perplexity. The stage-manager scratched his head.

"Blessed if I know, sir," he said. "I suppose he went to his room. He usually ran there to get ready for his front-of-the-house act. But I can't say that I saw him go last night. I was too concerned over Miss de Grey."

"Did *anybody* see him leave the stage?" The inspector addressed the question to the company at large. There was a general shaking of heads.

"When did you first miss the Cat?"

"When the front of the house telephoned to ask why he was not doing his act for the children," replied the stage-manager. "I sent the call-boy up to his room."

"All right, ladies and gentlemen. Just one more question, and you can all go home," the inspector announced. "Had there been any unpleasantness between Miss de Grey and the Cat?"

An audible chorus of sniffs greeted the question. It was the Demon King who ultimately expressed the views of the crowd.

"There was disagreement, laddie, between Miss de Grey and everybody," he announced grandiloquently. "She was a difficult woman to get on with. She had not the troupers' spirit. The Cat . . . er . . . got too much applause to suit Miss de Grey. She resented applause except when it was directed towards her own performance."

"Her and the Cat had an 'ell of a row just before the scene, mister—in the Green Room," said a voice from the back of the stage.

The inspector peered through the gloom. "Who are you?" he asked.

"Arthur Black, stage-hand." He came forward. "They was a'rowing over something she said the Cat had done the previous night. I says to the stage-manager, 'Just listen to her rortin' to the Cat now.' Then I says, 'He's walked out on her.' And he had, too. Left her talkin' to herself."

The inspector looked for confirmation to the stage-manager.

"I remember Arthur saying that," was the reply.

It was as the company was breaking up that the chief constable said his first word. He had watched the reconstruction intently, and had listened intently to the interrogation of the people on the stage. It had given him an idea, which he now proceeded to implement.

"Have any of you seen anywhere an article like a glass tube?" he asked. "About four inches long"—he indicated with his fingers the length.

There was a chorus of "Noes."

"Has the stage been swept this morning, Mr. Stage-Manager?"

"No, Colonel. We decided not to touch it until you gentlemen had finished."

The chief constable nodded dismissal. He stood by the side of Inspector Bradley until they were alone by the footlights. Then:

"You see the point, do you not, Inspector?" he asked. "If Miss de Grey was poisoned on the bank with an hypodermic syringe—where is the syringe now? The point is important because—"

"Because, sir, only one person could have done it, and he hadn't the syringe on him, and I saw no sign of it in his room."

Colonel Lovelace regarded his executive searchingly. "Theory—or fact?" he asked.

"Fact, sir. If the scene we have just re-enacted was exactly as played last night, then the only person who was near enough to Miss de Grey to stick a needle into her was the Cat."

"Proof?"

"The doctor said that she would be dead within ten seconds of the prick. She had had rows with the Cat. She was heard to say 'Don't stick your damned claws into me'. The Cat vanished without attempting to give any assistance to her, though he must have known by her silence that she was ill. He never even tried to give her the cue which she missed. And within a few minutes he is found himself poisoned with the same stuff."

"I must acknowledge that you have strong case for suspicion, Bradley," the chief constable agreed.

The inspector turned to his sergeant. "I want a couple of plain-clothes men at the Cat's bedside," he said. "They are not to leave him until relieved by two others. They will make a note of everything the man says. Tell the hospital authorities that he is to be moved into a private ward. After you've arranged that, I want a dozen men to search this stage, and every inch of the way from it to the dressing-room of the Cat, as well as the dressing-room itself."

"And outside—underneath the windows," the chief constable put in. "He may have disposed of it by throwing it through the dressing-room window."

CHAPTER V
SCOTLAND YARD HEARS A STORY

THE HIGH STREET in the Lincolnshire town of Welsborough was resting quietly under a cloud-filled sky as the clock struck eleven-thirty on an October night. Welsborough was a busy town enough during the daytime hours, particularly on market days and on Saturdays. Farmers and their cowmen, their horsemen and their labourers, floated into it with their womenfolk and girl friends, to do the week's shopping, and to experience the only bustle of life they were likely to encounter until the end of the following week.

The High Street was, of course, the shopping street of Welsborough. You needed not to leave its length to procure anything the farmer required from seed to sow for his crops to a cultivator, plough or a harvesting machine to harvest the said crops. And his womenfolk could purchase in the same confines a thread of cotton or a separator for the milk in the dairy.

But at night-time the High Street of Welsborough was usually deserted after the old church clock had struck its cracked notes of eight o'clock. The permanent residents were conservative people, in habits as well as in politics; and the pubs had found no space in which to intrude themselves in the shopping centre—they were in the adjacent side streets. So at 11.30 p.m. the High Street was deserted. Well, not quite deserted. A solitary figure walked swiftly down its length. At the bottom it turned into Kitchener Road (not named in honour of the General), and walked half-way down to where the Dog and Gun was sleeping off the effects of the evening's libations. There it stepped into a small two-seater car; and presently the motor-car started up, and was driven away in the direction of Lincoln.

The High Street resumed its silence. At 12.15 a.m. Police-Constable Castle wandered down the street on his beat, trying carefully the fastenings of each door. Thus had he pursued his way for thirty-two years, so that his feet walked, as it were, an unseen groove in the pavement. Never, in all that time, had he found a door unfastened; and he would have been puzzled into confusion had he suddenly come upon a door that gave to his hand.

So, proceeding down the High Street on this October night—or rather, morning—he reached the shop of the London Fashion Modes, Ltd., a comparative newcomer to the town; it had appeared in all its glory in the old shop which had previously housed the drapery business of Mr. Franks, now defunct.

London Fashion Modes, Ltd., had taken over the premises and filled them with frocks and 'underneaths' which, the advertisement said, were straight from the great fashion houses which had the distinction of clothing from skin to fur coat the leading ladies of society—who would, be it said, have rather been found dead than seen in the Royal Enclosure at Ascot in such garments. Trade with the L.F.M. had been brisk in Welsborough; the result had been some peculiar pastoral fashions in the farmyards, the dairies, and among the chickens of the countryside. Business, however, had slackened off considerably of late.

London Fashion Modes, Ltd., differed in one regard from all the other shops in Welsborough. Alone of the business houses it wisely prepared itself against prowlers. Each night at seven o'clock the manager put up the shutters, hiding the wares in the windows from the possibility, however remote, of their desirable qualities so seducing the women of Welsborough from the path of rectitude, that they would remove with violence the garments in the dark hours of the night.

Police-Constable Castle reflected on this inferred insinuation against the reputation of Welsborough as he passed the shuttered windows of London Fashion Modes and stepped into its doorway. His hands had just found the fastenings secure when he paused and sniffed.

A pungent aroma wafted itself on the chilly air.

"Somebody's chimbly afire, blow it," he said.

He stepped back, and from the middle of the road inspected the heavens; no cloud obscured or darkened the grey of the sky.

The constable's nose led him again into the doorway of London Fashion Modes; the smell, he decided, must emanate from there. He pushed open the letter-box and peered inside. A reddish glow rewarded him.

"Dang me, the place is afire," he said; and ran to the house of Mr. Dingwall, the plumber, who was also the chief of the voluntary fire brigade of Welsborough. When, half an hour later, the members of the brigade had been assembled by a messenger on a bicycle and steam had been got up in the forty-year-old engine, flames had burst through the roof of the shop and stockrooms. Another half hour, and the fashion hopes of Welsborough's femininity were laid low; the creations of Bond Street (£3 10s., or 10s. down and 2s. a week) had dissolved into ashes.

The managing director, and principal shareholder, Mr. Jabez Montague, stood in front of the debris and wrung his hands at the doleful sight. He had been fetched from the neighbouring village, where he had a furnished house. He could not account for the fire, he said, unless it was from a cigarette left by one of those damned cigarette-smoking women. He had had to ask two only that morning to keep their cigarettes in their mouths or extinguish them, instead of putting them on show-cases while they tried on his confections.

"Insured?" Of course he was insured, he told the inspector of police. But only for £6,000. It would cost him double that figure to replace the stock he had, at today's prices. Three months later Mr. Montague collected the sum of £5,550 from the Provincial Insurance Company. Welsborough saw him no more; there was no other shop in the place which could house his wares and do justice to them, he said.

The next stage in the affairs of the London Fashion Modes, Ltd., had its setting in the room of the Assistant Commissioner (Crime) at Scotland Yard. Sir Edward Allen sat at his desk in the horseshoe-shaped chamber overlooking the Embankment and the Thames. His right hand fingered a monocle, attached to a thin black silken cord. Yard men would have recognized by the fingering that Sir Edward was perturbed; had he not been so, the monocle would have been held, precariously, in his perfectly good left eye.

His eyes, under a furrowed brow, looked thoughtfully at a card that lay on his desk. It read:

JOHN REDWOOD
Solicitor
Lincoln's Inn, London, E.C.4
Nat. Assn. of Insurance Societies

From the card the eyes turned to the man sitting in front of his desk—Mr. Redwood himself, in black coat, lavender waist-coat and striped trousers—a strictly legal-looking personality. For half an hour Mr. Redwood had talked. He now waited silently for the reply from the Assistant Commissioner.

"And you think—?" Sir Edward queried.

"That we are being defrauded. We think that these fires are being deliberately caused for the purpose of collecting the insurance."

"I do not see the sense of it, Mr. Redwood," retorted the Assistant Commissioner. "They would apparently do as well, if not better, by not purchasing the stock at all rather than by buying it, setting fire to it, and collecting the insurance money. It is true, of course, that they collect a trading profit on the insurance value, but—"

He ceased in puzzled silence.

His visitor smiled grimly.

"But supposing the stock is not in the place when the fire occurs?" he suggested. "Suppose it has, or the more valuable part of it, has been removed. What then?"

Sir Edward Allen stared. "You mean that the stuff was there and was taken away before the conflagration, Mr. Redwood, and that, as a consequence, they have both the material and the insurance value?"

A grim smile ran its way over the face of the insurance companies' legal adviser.

"We do not know that, Sir Edward," he answered. "If we did, then we shouldn't be worrying you. It may be so, or it may be that the stuff was never there in the first place. All we can say is that we have a feeling that we are being defrauded, and on a pretty big scale."

The Assistant Commissioner toyed with his monocle, his eyes on the face of his visitor. He remained thus for perhaps a minute. Then he appeared to make up his mind.

"I have here a colleague who has a very suspicious mind, Mr. Redwood," he said. "And he has a mind perhaps more acute than any other mind in the country. I would like him to hear your story and give an opinion on it. Have you any objection to that?"

"None whatever, Sir Edward. My association would welcome it, I am quite sure of that."

Sir Edward rang his desk bell. To a sergeant who answered he said, "Will you see if Doctor Manson is in his laboratory, and ask him to spare me a few minutes."

Chief Detective-Inspector Harry Manson entered the room five minutes later. He looked from the Assistant Commissioner to the visitor and smiled.

"Trouble?" he queried. And seated himself at an angle from which he could keep his gaze on the stranger within the gates.

Doctor Manson's degree was in science, not medicine, though his knowledge of the latter was in advance of that possessed by most doctors. He was, in fact, the scientist in charge of Scotland Yard's Science Laboratory; he had, indeed, founded the laboratory and built it up into the criminal-catching organization that it had become. His advent to the Yard had been a device of the Assistant Commissioner, who disliked his staff having to depend upon civilian scientists for expert opinion, and for aid in harnessing laboratory methods to the catching of criminals. For some considerable time now it had been unnecessary for the Yard to seek any outside expert aid; and the results of the experiment had been outstanding in the number of crimes solved by Scotland Yard.

Sir Edward effected the introduction to his visitor. "Mr. Redwood has come here with a very curious story which I should like you to hear," he announced. "He asks for aid from us to prove certain suspicions which he entertains. I will say no more until you have heard what he has to say."

Doctor Manson looked across at the solicitor. "Just one point before you start, Mr. Redwood," he said. "I have a very tidy mind, and I like to hear all the facts in their chronological order. I shall be glad if you will start at the beginning, and try to omit nothing, however small and unimportant it may seem to you. Even an insignificant detail may fit in somewhere in any subsequent investigations which may prove to be necessary."

He settled himself down in his chair. For a quarter of an hour he listened without speaking to the recital of his woes by the representative of the societies whose combined assets represented upwards of £250,000,000. From time to time he jotted down notes on a pad borrowed from the Assistant Commissioner's desk.

Mr. Redwood, at the end of his tale, wiped his brow with a large silk handkerchief, and looked anxiously across at Doctor Manson. So did Sir Edward Allen. The scientist had not moved in his chair. But the fingers of his right hand were beating a tattoo on the arm. That, to the men at the Yard, was as expressive a signal as is the beating of the war-drums to the tribes of Central Africa. Added to it was the fact that the scientist's brow was furrowed, and there were crinkles marking the corners of his eyes. Sir Edward, seeing them, cursed softly to himself. "He's seen something," he said under his breath. "Curse his suspicious mind."

Doctor Manson, coming at last out of his reverie, spoke to the solicitor.

"What I would like to know, Mr. Redwood, is what grounds do you think you have for suspicion? You have given me the details of seven fires which have taken place in the last few months, and on which you have paid out a sum running into six figures. Now, in that same period there have been, I suppose, three or four hundred fires up and down the country; and you have nothing to complain of in the others. Why are you suspicious about these seven?"

Mr. Redwood nodded. "That is precisely the point that brought me here," he said. "In most of those other outbreaks there was very considerable damage to the contents of the buildings. There was also a quantity of stuff by which we can assess just how much loss has been caused. Stuff, for instance, which we can handle and value. Now in each of these seven particular fires, all carrying heavy insurance, the contents of the buildings were a total loss. There was nothing saved."

Mr. Redwood paused. He corrected himself. "I am not quite right," he added. "In each case the receipts for, or *the invoices of the stocks were not only safe, but practically unsinged.*"

Doctor Manson regarded his visitor appreciatively. "That, Mr. Redwood, is an exceedingly odd circumstance," he agreed. "Now, suppose we run through those seven fires and see whether we can arrive at anything else equally odd. Shall we have them put down in nicely tabulated form? It looks tidy and we can see the position at a glance."

Mr. Redwood agreed. Half an hour's labour produced the following list:

(1) Messrs. Fines and Howards, drapers and outfitters, Sheffield. Stock insured for £12,000. Converted by fire into total loss. Claim settled for £9,800. Had previously been insured with non-combine company, who had refused to pay out on a theft claim. The firm had, therefore, ceased to insure with them further and had taken out a policy with Merchandise Assurance Company. Earlier insurance had been for £9,000.

(2) International Fur Warehouse, High Pavement, Nottingham. Stock insured for £35,000. Total loss settled for £28,000, by Commercial Insurance Corporation, after some criticism that there should have been a watchman on the premises, this being a warehouse. Fire brigade could make no suggestion as to how the fire started.

(3) Fancy goods shop in the Arcade at Burlington-on-Sea. Unusually large stock which was investigated before policy was issued for £12,000, after estimate had been given by company's assessor. Fire occurred two months later. Claim settled for £10,500.

(4) Silks, Ltd., Hanover Street, London. Original insurance was for £12,000 but was increased to £21,000 on purchases for summer trade. Fire occurred six weeks later. Total loss claim of £21,000 paid.

(5) Bric-à-Brac shop, Birmingham. Stock insured for £12,000. Mostly expensive antiques. The business had been lately purchased by the new owners, and value raised. Previous owners (three in number) had relied on a sprinkler safeguard. Shop next door had been taken and plumbers had been extending the sprinkler installation. As the two had not been connected the water had not been turned on. They would have been joined next day.

(6) Paris Show Rooms, Liverpool, packed with fashion gowns. Insured for £35,000. Insurance reduced a month before the fire to £28,000, due, the firm stated, to heavy sales having depleted the stock. Fire brigade view was that the fire was due to the fusing of an electric cable.

(7) London Fashion Modes, Welsborough, a new business. Stock insured under £5,550 policy. Settled in full.

The list completed, Doctor Manson studied it in silence. When he looked up and across at the Assistant Commissioner his brow was again furrowed, and the crinkles had returned to the corners of his eyes.

"There are one or two points, Mr. A.C., which I think should be looked into," he said. "There is a certain similarity which I do not like about these fires. I would suggest that I have a few inquiries made and communicate with Mr. Redwood again, later."

The Assistant Commissioner nodded agreement. "As you like, Doctor," he said.

"There is, however, one thing which I consider important," the scientist added. He turned to the solicitor. "Would you impress upon the members of your association the importance of making a list of all the firms who have stocks of a highly combustible nature and in which the insurance is a cause of inquiry, either because it is a new insurance, or an increased or decreased insurance. That is point one. The other is to have close contact kept so that you may be informed at once—I emphasize at once—of any fire. You should then take immediate steps to acquaint the police that a special investigation is to be made of the fire and the premises, and that the premises or its contents, however damaged they may be, should not be interfered with until such investigation has been undertaken. And you should inform me at once."

Mr. Redwood agreed with enthusiasm.

The Assistant Commissioner, his visitor departed, cast an anxious glance at the scientist.

"Something in it, Harry?" he asked.

In the privacy of their own company the two were Edward and Harry to each other, fellow clubmen and strong personal friends. Discipline, which made them Assistant Commissioner and chief detective-inspector, was waived.

The scientist in reply to his friend's query smiled that enigmatical smile that never told anything.

"You know that I never speak without facts to go on, Edward," he chided. "Redwood told you as much as he told me, and as much as I know. He said that in all these fires the premises were completely gutted. Fire brigades in places like Birmingham, Liverpool and Nottingham, to say nothing of London, are pretty efficient. If places were burnt completely out, then it can mean only one of two things."

"And those things, Harry?"

The scientist smiled again.

"Think them out, Edward," he suggested.

CHAPTER VI
SURPRISE FOR AN INSPECTOR

A WEEK had passed since Dick Whittington, for the first time in history, had failed to turn again but had, instead, died in full view of the audience in the Pavilion Theatre. The stricken company had moved on to fresh fields, and a new company had played, nightly, the musical comedy *The Lotus Blossoms*, to the usual crowded audience.

Sixty miles away *Dick Whittington* was performing to similarly crowded houses. The understudy to the late Miss Norma de Grey was making the most of her chance, for which she had waited many years, and was striving to please Mr. de Benyat. 'Principal Boy to Mr. Henri de Benyat', she worked out, would look well on her business note-paper on which would have to be written applications for a 'part' when the run of the pantomime was finished.

Had she known, she need not have spent much mental worry, for Mr. de Benyat had in any case been unable to find another Whittington. The only two ladies 'resting'—the theatrical euphemism for out of a job—who were in any way suitable declared, emphatically, that they weren't taking part in any company in which 'Boys' and 'Cats' were poisoned while on the stage.

The understudy Cat was meowing his way to fame with the new Dick; and the cast agreed, unanimously, that though the loss of Miss de Grey may have been a misfortune for Mr. Henri de Benyat, it was a distinct gain to his company, to which the old comfortable working conditions had happily returned.

At Burlington, the police waited, more or less patiently, for the poisoned Cat to recover. Enora—or, to give him his real name, Jimmy Martin—had had a narrow squeak, and there had been moments when the doctors despaired of saving his life for the inspector. Despite the accepted medical dictum that chemical antidotes serve no purpose in cases of hydrocyanic acid poisoning, the house doctor had insisted on injecting at intervals a solution of cobalt nitrate under the skin of the poisoned man. He maintained, later, and wrote a letter to the *Lancet* that this, combined with injections of sodium sulphocyanide, undoubtedly neutralized the prussic acid, and were the means of saving the artiste's life.

Now the patient, though still very weak, was on the way to recovery. So far he had spoken only a few sentences, the purport of which had been to inquire what was the matter with him, and how the show was doing.

To this the nurse, instructed by the police, had replied that he had been taken suddenly ill, and that the company was doing extraordinarily well, though suffering considerably from the loss of their invaluable Cat, and now he must not talk any more, but lay quiet and rest and get better.

This inquiry as to the reason of his bedridden state, conveyed to the inspector, caused the latter to scratch a puzzled head. No inkling of its possible meaning occurred to him, however. His two watchers, waiting, and bored from their hidden vigil, had no message to give; the Cat, they said, just lay either asleep or meditating on his fate. At any rate he said nothing.

Meanwhile the inspector's search for the hypodermic syringe had proved unavailing. The stage had been gone over as though by a tooth-comb; corridors, corners, and dressing-rooms had been searched, and so had the streets in the neighbourhood of the dressing-room windows. Even the council refuse dump had been gone carefully over, in case the syringe had been thrown into a dustbin, or had been gathered up and thrown away with the refuse of the theatre or the street bins. The baskets of the *Whittington* company had been searched before they were packed for removal to London. The Cat's props and clothes had been probed—all without result; no sign was to be found of the weapon which had put curtains to Miss de Grey for ever.

It was on the Sunday of the following week that the doctor informed Inspector Bradley that he might, if he so desired, have a few words with the sick man, who was now in a fit state to be questioned. The inspector did so care; he entered the room and sat down by the bedside.

The Cat looked up at him with interest.

"Hallo," he greeted. "Are you the other doctor? When the hell am I going out of this place?"

The inspector stared.

"I am not a doctor," he announced slowly. "I am Detective-Inspector Bradley of this town, and I want to ask you a few questions about Miss de Grey."

"Miss de Grey." The Cat echoed the name. "What's the old battle-axe been doing that you are interested in her? Murdering somebody?"

Had the dead Whittington risen, picked up her bed and walked, it would not have occasioned the inspector more surprise than the rejoinder to his announced identity. Although the voice was low, for Enora was still weak, the tone of it was sprightly, and without trace of the concern that the man should have shown at his position. The inspector's eyes roved over him speculatively for a few silent seconds.

"No," he said. "No, she hasn't been murdering anybody." He spoke slowly, watching the Cat as he spoke. "Why *should* she want to murder anybody?"

The Cat grinned slightly. "I reckon as she always looked at us as though she would like to," he rejoined. He thought for a minute and then added, with a chuckle, "Though I don't say, mind you, that it isn't more likely that one of us would murder her."

For the second time in the brief interview the inspector started in surprise. And for the second time he turned an inquiring and a puzzled gaze on the sick man. He thought for a moment before he put the next question. When he did speak it was with a disarming smile. "Anybody ever threaten to murder her?" he asked.

The Cat chuckled again. "Not *threatened*," he made answer. "Just *hoped* that somebody would do it."

"Yourself, for instance?" the inspector said.

"Me, particularly," was the response. "I'd have done it cheerfully, if I thought I wouldn't be found out." He laughed. "It would have been a bit of a sensation, I reckon. 'Murder of Dick Whittington. No turn again for the Lord Mayor of London.' Eh?"

"Found her unpleasant to get on with, eh?"

"Unpleasant? Listen, Mister Inspector. I've played Cat for twenty years and more, and never to such a cow of a Whittington as this one." He paused. "Anyway, what's all this got to do with me? If you want to know anything about Miss de Grey why not ask her? Why d'ye want to see *me* about her?"

The inspector shifted a little uncomfortably in his seat. He was in an uncomfortable position. He was treading on dangerous ground, and he knew it. It was against judges' rules to question a suspect without first warning him that he need not answer any questions unless he liked, and that he could have a solicitor present if he cared to do so. So far the inspector had not informed the Cat that Miss de Grey was dead, let alone that she had been poisoned. It was all strictly irregular. The inspector took such refuge as he could in the thought that he was not really regarding the Cat as a suspect. It was a bit thin, he knew. But the fact remained that there was no trace of the hypodermic syringe which the doctor said had been used to despatch Miss de Grey, and apart from suspicion there was no evidence that he (the inspector) could bring against the Cat. He was quite sure that the Cat had done the deed—that was evident—but he had no evidence whatever. He decided to chance his luck with judges' rules and question the Cat, not on Miss Grey but on himself. Something might come to light through that process.

"The fact is," he announced to the waiting man, "Miss de Grey had a similar illness to yours. Since it was so sudden we have to find out all about it. Now, you were with Miss de Grey on the stage. How did you feel?"

"How did I feel? I felt all right on the stage. I walked off all right."

"And Miss de Grey, did you notice anything unusual about her?"

"Only that she was in a worse temper than usual. The old so-and-so was rowing with me when we came off."

Inspector Bradley started in surprise for the third time. "She walked off with you?" he asked.

"Of course." The Cat looked up. "What the hell would you expect her to do when the stage was being set? Turn a ruddy somersault, or something?"

The inspector mentally ran over the scene as it had been described to him, and as he had had it re-enacted on the following morning. As he remembered it, Miss Grey did not leave the stage until the curtain had been dropped, and she had been carried off by stage-hands and laid on the lounge in the Green Room. Yet, here the Cat said that she walked off with him and at the same time was rowing with him. Had the illness of the man affected his memory? He decided to let him continue the story.

"Well, what happened then?" he asked. "On the stage, I mean," he added.

"We walked off on the prompt side and went into the Green Room as usual. But she started up another argument so I just told her to get to hell, and walked out on her."

"What was the trouble?"

"Oh, the usual story that I was masking her."

"Masking her?" The inspector looked puzzled.

"Getting in between her and the audience," the Cat explained. "Generally does happen to a blooming Cat in the shop scene."

"Then what did you do?"

"I went off to my dressing-room to get a drink."

Inspector Bradley passed a puzzled hand across his forehead. They seemed, he thought, to be talking at cross-purposes. They were not in the same scene. He tried another tack.

"What was going on on the stage then?" he asked.

"The Dame was doing his chorus act."

"You mean the Captain and Mate."

"I don't mean anything of the kind. That's after the Highgate Hill scene."

The inspector roused himself. "Now," he thought, "we are coming to it." Aloud he said:

"Now, that's what I want to get at. You come off after the shop scene, you have a row with Miss de Grey, you dash off to your dressing-room for a drink, and then there's the Highgate Hill scene. Now, what happened in that scene? That's what I want particularly to know."

"How the devil do I know what happened in the Hill scene?" The Cat was getting a bit peeved, and showed it. "That is when I was ill."

The inspector nodded. "Yes, I know that, Enora," he agreed. "But what made you ill? And what made Miss de Grey ill at the same time? We've been waiting for you to recover in order that we could find out."

The Cat stared at his questioner in exasperation.

"How the devil do I know what made Miss de Grey ill?" he demanded. "Dammit, I didn't know that she was ill. How should I know? I wasn't with her and she wasn't with me."

"Not with you? Miss de Grey not with you?" The inspector echoed the words.

"For the love of Mike, Inspector, of course she wasn't with me."

"Now take it easy, Enora." The inspector spoke quietly, and soothingly. He realized that the Cat was still a sick man, and must not be unduly aroused, lest he slipped back into sickness again. "Think carefully before you reply. You say that Miss de Grey was not with you at the time you were taken ill. I was told that she was with you. If she wasn't, then who was with you in the Highgate Hill scene?"

"The Highgate Hill scene?" The Cat scratched his head. "I don't know who the devil was in the Highgate Hill scene. *I* didn't play in it."

There was a silence. The mouth of the inspector was open, the bottom jaw dropped in a surprise that invested it with an appearance of comicality.

"You didn't play in the Highgate Hill scene? Then who was the Cat that was playing?"

"I suppose my understudy was. That's what he was there for. If I'm not on the stage he takes my place."

"Well, when did you last see Miss de Grey?"

"I've already told you. When we came off the stage after the shop scene, and we had the row. I walked out on her and went to my dressing-room."

"That's the time that you say you had your drink, is it?"

"That's right, Inspector."

"What happened after you had the drink?"

"Blimey, Inspector, that's what *I* want to know. I'm waiting to hear that from you."

The inspector considered the point. Enora, he felt bound to admit, seemed perfectly open in his answers. And he was not at fault in giving them. He proceeded with his questioning.

"What drink was it?" he asked.

"A pint of bitter, same as I usually had."

"You were all right when you went up to the room, and you drank the bitter. Then what happened?"

"I just went all queer. Felt as if the top of my head had gone. *All* light-headed, I was. And the next thing I knew was waking up here."

"And, of course, you don't know anything of what happened on the Highgate Hill scene?"

"Not a darned thing. You said that Miss de Grey was taken ill at the same time as me?"

The inspector nodded. "Don't you worry about that now," he adjured. "I'll come and see you again soon. You've talked enough for one day."

The inspector left. He wandered, a very puzzled man, back to the police-station. "He sure talked enough for one day," he said to himself. "What do I do now?"

He sat himself down in his chair and wrestled with the problem. It looked as though he had jumped too quickly to a conclusion. Not that he could really be blamed, he argued to himself, in his own defence. The doctor had said that the woman must have been doped on the stage itself, and he had convinced himself that only the Cat was near enough to her to have done it unnoticed. Enora had played the cat from the start of the show up to that very scene. Nobody had suggested that he was not the Cat in the Hill scene. They surely would have done if the understudy had been on. Was there any way in which the understudy could have taken the part unknown to the stage-manager and the company?

The inspector proceeded to work it out. Supposing that there had been an arrangement between Enora and the other Cat for the deputy to take that scene. Supposing there had been a monetary arrangement, in order that the deputy could poison Miss de Grey. Only one other person would know who the Cat was, and that was Enora. If Enora could be put out of the way at the same time with poisoned drink, then it would be assumed, as in fact it had been assumed, that Enora was the assailant. Was this the explanation of the strange story of Enora? If it was, the inspector realized that he had made a bad blunder, for the deputy Cat was with the company still, and would have had time enough to dispose both of the poison and of the syringe for which search had been made without result.

He decided that no time must be lost in inquiring closely into these possibilities. In the meantime the doctors must be urged to keep Enora in hospital as long as possible.

With this end in view he called upon the police surgeon and put his request.

"You need not worry, Inspector," was the reply. "He won't be able to leave for at least another week. He'll find that out when he tries to stand up."

"There's just one other thing, Doctor," said the inspector. "You stated that Miss de Grey must have had the poison administered to her while she was lying on the bank in the Highgate Hill scene?"

The doctor nodded.

"Now is that absolutely certain? I don't doubt that you believe it to be a certain, but a curious situation has developed in my inquiries, and I want to be sure that I do not go wrong. Is it absolutely impossible, in any conceivable circumstances, for the poison to have been taken by her before the particular part of that scene, though, perhaps, in the scene itself?"

"What are you getting at, Inspector? Suppose you put it a little more detailed."

"Well, Doctor. Miss de Grey stood in the wings before she made her entrance. There she stood surrounded by people—by stage-hands and members of the company, particularly the chorus. Can you say that there were no circumstances in which any one of such people in passing could not have pricked her with the needle as she was on the point of going on? I reckon, roughly, that there was no more than a minute or so, before Dick Whittington lies on the bank."

"I see your point," the police surgeon said. "There is one circumstance which would allow the lapse of about a minute before the poison took effect. Hydrocyanic acid, Inspector, as you know, is about the quickest-acting poison we have. But if the dose was *very considerably diluted*—very considerably diluted—then collapse might not occur at once. The patient would feel decidedly groggy, but under such will-power as would be necessary to an actress actually on the stage, she might stave off collapse for a minute. But no longer."

"Then . . ." began the inspector.

The doctor waved a hand to silence him.

"But there is no such possibility in this case, Inspector," he said. "The amount of prussic acid in the body of Miss de Grey does not admit the possibility of even the slightest degree of dilution. She would have been dead within seconds of the needle penetrating the skin. Of that there is not the slightest shadow of a doubt."

The inspector left. "Then it was the damned deputy Cat," he said.

He hurried to the railway station and took a first-class ticket for Waterloo. His next talk must be with the manager of the *Dick Whittington* company, who had now reached the Metropolis in their travels.

CHAPTER VII
STALKING A CAT

AT THE TIME that Inspector Bradley was interrogating the Cat in the hospital at Burlington, the company of *Dick Whittington* were gathered at the Old Sussex Theatre, in the area of the Elephant and Castle, in London. If the neighbourhood of the Elephant was not exactly salubrious, that of the old theatre was even less so. The Fairy Queen stood in the gloom of the pilot lights which were swinging high above the flies and trying, vainly, to illuminate the cramped stage. The stage staff having erected what part of the scenery they could get on the apology for a stage, had blacked out and 'gone for one' before band call started.

"Dreadful! Horrible!" cried the Fairy Queen. "How *could* they send us to such a place after Burlington"; and with a sound like a sob, she turned back into the passage and made for the dressing-rooms.

"Heavens, what will *they* be like?" she asked of herself, as she began the climb up the filthy stone stairs. The walls had once been distempered a bright pink. But that was probably in the days when the theatre had begun its career. The distemper had long ago crumbled into a dirty, depressing state of dilapidation. Up three flights of stairs toiled the Fairy Queen, the foetid smell of the dirt of years becoming more and more pronounced. She halted at a door marked in white chalk:

> Miss Low.
> Miss Peg Roff.
> Miss Harlington (understudy).

She paused inside a room measuring ten feet by ten feet. Stage baskets line up one side; on the other was a small waist-high bench on which stood a cracked mirror. Let into the bench was a cracked and stained bowl, which leaked its filthy contents on the dressing-room floor. Two rickety chairs comprised the furniture. The once white-washed walls were now embroidered with greasepaint drawings, and a large notice proclaiming to all and sundry that to deface the decorations would bring down retribution on the inhabitants.

For a couple of minutes the Fairy Queen gazed at the room. Then, near to tears, she ran down the stairs, down the dirty passage filled now with prop baskets, and out of the stage door into the dirty side street heaped with the discarded cabbage leaves of green-grocery stalls. She turned in at the doors of a cafe, there to drink tea and to adjust her ideas of theatrical fortune.

Yes, the Old Sussex was ancient, and horrible, all right, she reflected, as a tear dropped into her cup. But then, one had to have experience, and the Academy had sort of hinted that her voice wasn't strong enough for Opera. But she had not thought that it would bring her to places quite so awful as the Sussex. Still, it was only for two weeks, and she would then be out of work altogether, so one should not grumble. Besides, it was near the West End where one could go for auditions. Thus consoled, she made her way back to the theatre.

The company were beginning to assemble for the band call of the new date. The new ones took the appearance of the place in various degrees of indignation; the old stagers regarded it complacently as being all in the day's work; they were only too glad that any kind of a stage door was open to them.

In the absence of the stage-doorkeeper, who also stoked the boilers, artistes helped themselves to letters from the rack. Miss Prue took her correspondence and moved towards Dressing-room No. 1, which she now shared with the new Dick Whittington. After one revolted glance she took off her coat and, opening her trunk, took out soap, cloths and disinfectant and was in the midst of a little spring-cleaning when Dick Whittington arrived.

"Oh, Peg, what a hole," was the Boy's greeting. "Chuck me a cloth and I'll have a go, too. Perhaps it won't be too bad when we've got our bits out. But have you seen the stage and the augmented orchestra, my dear? Fred Karno's own. Heaven help us on a night like this."

"Freddie keeps telling me that Lottie Collins made her big success here. Gee, what stamina those old pros had. I'm sending out for some aspirins. We'll need 'em to pull the show through this."

Later came the performance.

"Overture and beginners, please. All down on stage."

The squeaking of the violins, the banging of drums, the shouting of stage-hands, as the company took their places and faced the stunted auditorium of faded gilt and red plush, the worn carpet showing between the broken seats, the dilapidated electric light shades dangling forlornly from the boxes on each side of the stage. The reek of years of stale smoke from cheap tobacco, of oranges and humbugs, mingled together in one foul broth came over the footlights.

"Oh God, I'll fail," said Dick. "Who could help it here. A fairy is funny in this rig-out. Who could believe in fairies here? . . . All right. Damn 'em. It's ten pounds a week, and a chance next year. . . ." And there's your cue, and you walk into the limes centre-stage and look forlornly into a sea of faces; hungry, tired, dirty little faces, and a gasp of awe comes up to you as you realize they are seeing their childish hero, Dick Whittington, perhaps for the first time, and you smile at them. Then the applause breaks over you, and you know that you haven't cheated them; they believe in you. If you had shattered their illusion, you would have murdered hundreds of little souls. That is your reward.

And as the warm glow of their happiness swirls round you, you bend and scratch the head of pussy—that's not in the script, but you've got to do something; you can't let the world see that Dick Whittington is crying. . . .

It was into this atmosphere of pride and prejudice that Inspector Bradley intruded, two nights later, after he had fortified himself first with a substantial meal in a neighbouring hotel. His appearance was greeted by the company with a demand for news of the Cat.

"He's getting better," was the reply. But to inquiries as to how he was proceeding with the case of the dead Whittington, he made no reply. Instead, he approached the stage-manager with a request for a short talk.

"Sorry, Inspector, can't arrange it now. The show is on, you know, and I can't be away from the stage—not this ruddy stage, at any rate. Now, if you like to hang round a bit until the interval, well, I'll be able to have a breather then, and we can talk. Sit in my cubby-hole. You'll be able to see the show from the wings."

So for the first time Inspector Bradley saw a performance from the back of the stage, instead, as was his wont, of from the audience. What is more, he found with no little interest that he was watching the very scene in which Miss de Grey had died at Burlington. It might well be that the scene could cast a new light on the mystery; some commonplace might have the effect of causing a change of attitude on his part towards certain members of the company. He watched closely all the movements of the artistes as they assembled in the wings, and as they took their appointed places on the stage. He noted, too, all those who came into contact with Dick Whittington. But at the end, when the tabs dropped, he found nothing which seemed to assist him in his investigations.

It was then that the stage-manager, wiping perspiration from his brow, for it was hot under the lights, came across to him.

"Now, Inspector, I can spare about ten minutes," he said. "Come along to my room."

The two men, behind the closed door, lighted up their pipes, and puffed the smoke ceilingwards.

"Well, Inspector?" asked the stage-manager.

"Mr. Trimble, I want you to cast your mind back to the moment when you realized at Burlington that Miss de Grey was ill. There are one or two points upon which I want to assure myself. Now Dick was lying on the bank, and had not spoken her lines. The cat was, of course, with her. You rang down the curtain and rushed to Miss de Grey. She was carried into the Green Room. *WHAT HAPPENED TO THE CAT?*"

"I think you asked me that question at Burlington, Inspector. I really don't know what happened to him. I was too busy seeing what was wrong with Miss de Grey. As the Cat usually went up to his room for a rub-down and a drink at that time, I assume he did so on this occasion."

"In spite of the fact that Miss de Grey was unconscious? Is that the normal thing for anyone to do?"

The stage-manager shrugged his shoulders. "The Cat, Inspector, is an old trouper. With an old trouper 'the show must go on' is a golden rule. Enora would have gone on in the show even if Miss de Grey had been his wife and was still lying ill. He would go to his room because he was due in the front of the house for his act after he had rubbed down and changed his undervest, which was, you understand, generally saturated at this time. Acting Cat in a skin is damned hot work."

The inspector nodded. "I see," he said. "When you found out from the front of the house that the Cat was not out there, and then found him ill in his room, you got hold of his understudy. Where was this man?"

"Where he had no right to be—in the pub round the corner," was the reply. We sent for him, rushed him into his skin and put him on only a minute or so late for his next entrance."

"I'd like to have a word with him, if I may?" the inspector asked.

The stage-manager put his head round the door and called for the boy. 'Tell Mr. Lancy I'd like to see him for a minute when he comes in from the front," he ordered.

A couple of minutes elapsed before Mr. Lancy, still in his skin, and puffing from his exertions, entered the room.

"You want me, Bill . . . Oh," catching sight of the visitor, "Good evenin', Inspector."

"Good evening, Mr. Lancy. It is I who really wants to see you. You remember the night Miss de Grey died? Mr. Trimble tells me that you were in the pub round the corner. It's quite off the record, of course, and the company won't hold it against you—but how long had you been in the pub that night?"

The Deputy Cat grinned, sheepishly. "Well, as a matter of fact, Inspector," he said, "I'd been there since the show started—as soon as I'd made sure that Enora was in his skin."

"And you did not leave the congenial company at all?"

"I did not."

"Thank you very much, Mr. Lancy," said the inspector m dismissal.

The stage-manager looked inquiringly at the inspector as the door closed behind the Cat.

"What is the point, sir?" he asked.

The inspector sat silent for a moment or two, thinking. He seemed to make up his mind to a course of action, for, after a glance at the closed door, he leaned forward, and, speaking softly, said: "This is strictly between ourselves, Mr. Trimble, and it must not be as much as whispered outside these walls. It would have a very serious effect on my investigations." He paused, and then continued:

"What would you say if I told you that Enora was taken ill in his dressing-room *before* the Highgate Hill scene? What would you say if I suggested that he was never on in that scene?"

He sat back, and eyed the stage-manager.

Mr. Trimble stared at him incredulously.

"I should say that you were crackers," he rejoined. "Dammit, you couldn't play the scene without the Cat, and do you suppose that I shouldn't have seen that the blasted cat wasn't there?"

"Nevertheless, Enora swears that he did not go on in Highgate Hill," the inspector insisted. He detailed his talk with the sick Cat, and the circumstances in which the man said he had been taken ill.

"Now, can you say whether or not it was another Cat, Mr. Trimble?"

The stage-manager gazed in bewilderment at the police inspector. "But, Inspector," he said, "we've only got the two of 'em, and Lancy was in the pub. Blast it all, we had to fetch him out."

"I know all that, Mr. Trimble," was the retort. "But suppose for an instant that Lancy was actually on the stage, could you have told the difference between him and Enora?"

"I don't suppose that I would—then," the stage-manager decided, after a moment or two of thought. "I had never seen Lancy; he had never been on for Enora. And, of course, the 'business' would not have told me because it runs mostly according to the script and rehearsals."

"You can't see the face, of course?"

"No. The face is blacked up below the mask. The make-up would be the same to look at whoever was on."

"Would he wear the same skin?"

"Lordy, no. Every cat has his own skin, of course. And great care they take of them, too. They cost a mint of money, do good skins."

"Would there be any difference in the skins?"

Mr. Trimble jerked into recollection. "There would, yes," he replied. "Enora's skin is black and white, and Lancy's is dark brown and white. I've only known that, of course, since he's been playing cat in place of Enora."

"You can't recall seeing any difference on the night of the tragedy?"

"'Fraid not, Inspector. I wasn't looking for it, you realize. But perhaps one of the people on the stage would have noticed it."

The inspector made a gesture of dissent. "No, not a word about it to anybody, yet," he insisted. "Later on, perhaps, I'll have to ask them a few questions. There is just one other point," he added, after a pause. "What time elapsed between your sending for the Lancy cat and the affair on the stage?"

"I'll have to work that one out, Inspector," the stage-manager replied. He sat for a few moments in thought "The fairy spoke Dick's lines, and we rang down the curtain. We carried her into the Green Room. First-aid man said he thought she was dead, and we got a doctor from the audience. Then front of the house rang to say the cat wasn't out there. I sent the call-boy for the cat . . . he ran down saying the cat was ill. Sent him to tell Lancy he was on . . . said he couldn't find him . . . sent him to the pub . . . say about five minutes in all, Inspector. Lancy got into his skin, and we had held the curtain back for three minutes while Miss de Grey's understudy got dressed."

"Can the Cat get into his skin by himself?"

"Crumbs, no. He has to have a dresser."

"Company's dresser?"

"No. Usually engaged locally. The theatre generally has a list in waiting."

"Right." The inspector stood up. "That will do me for the time being. I'll probably come again after I've made some inquiries." He stepped towards the door, and paused before opening it. "Remember, Mr. Trimble, not a word of this to anyone."

"As you say, Inspector."

It was a silent and thoughtful Inspector Bradley who made the return journey to Burlington. He sat in a corner seat of a first-class carriage, and, ignoring his travelling companions' attempts at conversation, smoked his pipe throughout the journey. The result of his cogitations was put into operation next morning.

It started at the Green Man. The little public house was a pleasant enough hostelry, living a gay Bacchanalian life 'neath the shadow of the Pavilion walls. In truth, the theatre was the chief contributor to its existence, for the proprietor was an old pro himself. Dave Henley had been a popular comic of his time. Never a top-of-the-Bill, but popular with his audiences; and he had chosen this house to buy at the end of his career, with that knowledge in view.

His lounge bar had its walls decorated from ceiling to panelling with signed photographs of stage stars past and present, and there were few nights when pros of both sexes appearing at the Pavilion failed to drop in for a quick one between acts, or after their night's work was done. This touch of the glamour of the footlights had attracted a steady clientele, from whom Dave derived a far better Treasury than ever he had done from the other side of the footlights. However, he deserved his popularity; there is a great deal of truth in the statement that it wants a good pro to make a good pub.

It was to Dave Henley that Inspector Bradley carried his troubles as soon as the house opened for the morning custom.

"A talk, Inspector?" echoed Dave. "Come into the back parlour. Nothing wrong, is there?"

Nothing, Dave. I want to see if I can get any help out of you. This Pavilion job," he added, as the door closed behind them.

"Nasty job that, Inspector," commiserated Henley. "I knew most of the parties concerned in it. Used to come in here quite a lot."

The inspector nodded. "Yes, that's where I'm hoping you will be able to help," he announced.

Henley pecked an inquiring look at his visitor. Inspector Bradley acknowledged it.

"It's Lancy, the Cat understudy, you know. I'm told that he was fetched from here after Enora had been found ill in his dressing-room. Do you know if that is correct?"

"Quite," responded Henley. "One of the stage-hands came dashing in, grabbed him by the arm and said he was wanted at once to go on for Enora. He went. I was just serving him with another pint."

"How long had he been in before that happened?"

"He came in a few minutes after we opened."

Inspector Bradley leaned forward in his chair, and emphasized his next question with a wagging finger. "Can you say, Dave, whether he went out of the place at all?" he asked. "And if he did at about what time. And how long he was away?"

The inn-keeper hesitated. Inspector Bradley, noticing it, supplemented his inquiry with an explanation. "What I'm trying to get at is whether it would have been possible for Lancy to be out of here for about ten minutes and then return—little enough time, in fact, for his absence not to have been commented upon."

Henley whistled softly. "Like that, is it?" he said. "Well, I wouldn't like to be sure of it. I was pretty busy in the two bars, you know. But Lancy was here every time I looked round the parlour. Tell you what, though, Harry Jenkins may know. He was sitting with him all the evening. If he was away Harry would remember it. He'll be in about six o'clock."

The inspector digested the information with a frown. "I don't want to make any inquiries among the public at this stage, Dave," he announced. "It's a bit awkward." He looked at the inn-keeper, hopefully.

Henley responded, with a grin. "You mean you would like me to find out, eh?" he queried. "All right I'll have a go. Look in about seven o'clock."

Fortune, however, turned her face from the inspector. His appearance in the lounge shortly after seven o'clock was greeted by

Henley with a nod in the direction of the back parlour. To there he adjourned, followed after a few moments by the innkeeper.

"It's no go, Inspector," the latter announced. "I've seen Harry and he says that Lancy never left the place until he was fetched. Sat in the lounge all the time telling stories and bemoaning the fact that he hadn't had a chance to show he was a better Cat than Enora. Harry is quite positive about it."

"Then that's that," commented the inspector. "Thanks, Dave, for the help."

But he had not yet shot his last bolt. There still remained, he thought, one chance. *Dick Whittington*'s stage-manager had said that the cat would be bound to have a dresser in order to get into his skin. He meant to explore every avenue, and the dresser was his next obvious step. He turned in at the front entrance of the Pavilion, and sought the manager.

In the office he explained his predicament, still under the seal of silence.

"Yes, that would be Bennett, I expect, Inspector, but I'll make sure. Do you want to see him?"

The inspector nodded.

The manager dialled a number on the house telephone, and spoke to the stage-manager.

He replaced the receiver with a nod at his visitor. "It *was* Bennett," he announced "The stage-manager is bringing him along "

Again, the inspector was doomed to disappointment. Bennett was equally confident that Lancy had not been in the theatre at all between the time that he left after the curtain had gone up on the first scene, and the time that he was fetched from the Green Man to play his part. He could not have used his skin without his (the dresser's) knowledge.

"How comes that?" asked Bradley.

"Because his skin was in his dress basket, and I had the key," was the reply. "He'd given me the key that morning when he came for his mail. I had to get his dirty laundry out and put the clean clothes in. I forgot to give him back the key when he came in in the evening, and they had to fetch me when he wanted the skin. Anyway, I had to help him into it, whenever he used it."

"That," said Inspector Bradley, as he wandered homewards, "that puts the kibosh on that." He carried the news next morning to his chief constable. That official greeted the negative results with a portentous frown.

"Then it means, Bradley, that you are no nearer a solution than we were on the night of the girl's death," he said.

"Afraid that is so, sir," was the despondent reply.

"It's bad—very bad. What do you propose doing with Enora? You can't keep him in the hospital indefinitely. He's been spoofing you, of course."

"Afraid that is so, sir. But on the evidence I've got I can't charge him. No magistrate would commit him. I don't think they would even give me a remand. I can't produce any evidence except that of opportunity."

"Then we'd better call in Scotland Yard, Bradley. We can't let anybody get away with this, you know."

"Just as you like, sir. We haven't had much experience of murder here, and the company is in London now, anyway."

* * * * *

Thus it happened that the following morning Superintendent Jones, the weighty and ponderous figure of the C.I.D. headquarters, toiled up the steps of the Embankment building to the horseshoe room of the Assistant Commissioner of Police (crime). He entered, and sat down with a grunt.

"Trouble," he announced.

"Trouble it is, Jones," was the reply. "Burlington wants our help."

"Burlington? That Jane job?" The superintendent had a habit of lapsing into American in moments of stress. "They've . . . had it . . . a week . . . cold . . . mutton now."

"I'm afraid that's so, Jones. But you'll have to tackle it."

A snort from Jones.

"Gimme Kenway?" he asked.

The Assistant Commissioner smiled. He knew Jones by this time. The staccato tones, the annoyance, was only a cloak for the enthusiasm of the man-hunter. So was the demand for Kenway.

The combination of stolid fact-searcher Jones and the volatile imaginative Inspector Kenway was a powerful one. That was why the A.C. smiled.

"Yes, Jones, you can have Kenway," he said.

CHAPTER VIII
ENTER DOCTOR MANSON

DOCTOR MANSON pulled up his big, black Oldsmobile outside the police headquarters in Waingate, Sheffield. He got out, stretched his long legs and his back, cramped with its sojourn in the bucket driving-seat, and after a sniff and a glance at the pall of smoke that hung in the sky above the great blast furnaces, stepped into the station.

For five hours the sleek car had purred along the hundred and sixty seven miles between the C.I.D. headquarters on London's Embankment and those in the steel city. Doctor Manson had driven himself, and he had driven alone, his eyes noting only physically the changing scenery—the heights of Hertford, the downs of Bedford, through Huntingdon and Rutland, through the county of Dukeries, on to Worksop, and then, finally, the run through to the city of steel. Hour after hour he had urged the car along on its hunt. His eyes saw but not his mind; that keen, analytical pigeonhole of knowledge and reasoning was detachedly preparing a plan of investigation which would start active operation in Sheffield. The Yard scientist was following the trail of the Fiery Cross.

He had listened with a keen, if undemonstrative, interest to the story of the conflagrations told by the insurance societies' legal adviser. In point of fact, Doctor Manson had, before the visit, cast a curious eye on the very fires which had been the object of the talk. A man with a suspicious mind, he had noted the curious incidence of *total* loss, and had filed away the various reports which had appeared in the Press. That was a performance which to him was routine work in investigation.

"You never know" he had once told the deputy scientist, Sergeant Merry, "you never know but what at some time you may require such material, and if you have not filed it away, the assistance it could have rendered is not at hand." His dictum, and method, had been justified on several occasions; a little heap of soil stored away because it was curiously unlike any other soil in the neighbourhood had, most unexpectedly, helped to hang Silas Levy months afterwards.

The insurance lawyer's more detailed information had changed his curiosity into something like suspicion. He had told the Assistant Commissioner that the complete destruction of the shops named, could only be explained as due to one of two things; it was in search of the correct answer that he had made the journey to Sheffield.

The scientist had asked that an appointment with the chief constable should be made for him. It was, however, the superintendent, six feet in height and broad in proportion, who greeted him. The chief constable, he explained, was on sick leave, but he, the superintendent, was under instructions to render all the help that it was possible to give. And, he added, he would be glad to do so to so distinguished a visitor.

To the scientist's explanation of his visit he replied with a little whistle, and a raising of the eyebrows.

"Fines and Howards' fire, eh?" he said. "Hum. Now, I never felt comfortable about that business at the time."

Doctor Manson looked up sharply. "Do you mean that you suspected that it was not accidental?" he asked.

"Not suspected, exactly, Doctor. The thought just crossed my mind."

"Why?"

"Well, Fines and Howards were in the main street. It's a very busy centre, a promenade at all hours of the day and night. Even at midnight there are quite a number of people passing up and down its length. When the firemen reached it, not three minutes after the alarm was raised, the place was a blazing inferno, with no chance of saving it. It seemed queer to me, if you follow what I mean."

"I think I see the point, Superintendent. You mean that one would have thought in such a promenade that some sign of flames should have been seen before they reached such proportions?"

"That is exactly what I do mean."

"Any reason why they should not have been seen?"

"The shop window and door shutters were up."

"That usual?"

"No. But the manager explained it by saying that the windows were stocked with expensive material, and they did not want the place smash and grabbed. In point of fact I did ascertain that the shutters had been put up each night for a week."

"I take it that as you were thus disturbed you made other inquiries into the blaze?"

"That is so. I saw the fire chief, and he said—"

Doctor Manson interrupted him. "If you don't mind, Superintendent, I would rather the fire brigade superintendent told me himself what he thought. I like my matter at first hand. Now, what standing had the firm?"

"They were at one time a very prosperous business, doing the best trade in the city in their line. But of late years their stock had gone down considerably. One or two London firms had opened up in the city, with more fashionable stuff, and cheaper, too. They had a burglary some months before this fire, and their claim for insurance was refused by a company. I had to make some inquiries into it."

"On what grounds was the claim contested?"

"On the grounds that in view of the kind of stock they were selling, and had been selling for some time, it was highly contestable that they had such goods as were claimed for on the premises. In the end they did not fight the company but allowed the loss to stand. Their explanation of the stock was that they were trying to get back their former trade, and were consequently stocking better and more expensive material in order to compete with the London firms."

"What happened afterwards?"

"They seemed to drop back into the middle-class line again. That was why I was surprised at the sudden window display of the higher-class goods—and one reason why I looked anxiously at the fire and the loss."

"They haven't opened up business again, since the fire?"

"No. In fact the partners have left the city altogether."

A more detailed description of the fire was given to the scientist by the fire brigade superintendent. He stated that only a little flame could be seen from the building when they arrived, and it did not appear at first to be a serious outbreak.

"A conclusion that did not last for long?" suggested Doctor Manson.

The brigade chief nodded. "As soon as the door was broken open, I was astounded at the hold which the fire had obtained," he said. "The place was a mass of flames. There was never any chance of saving it."

"They were, of course, hidden by the shutters?"

"That is so."

"I think the police superintendent mentioned certain doubts he had on the outbreak. Did you do anything as regards that?"

"Yes. I examined the place carefully after the fire had been extinguished—that was on the following morning. I could see nothing untoward. You have to remember, of course, the very inflammable nature of the contents. It was all very combustible."

The final visit of Doctor Manson was to the office of the Fire Salvage chief. That official announced that the brigade superintendent had passed on to him the remarks and suggestions of the police superintendent. But he had been unable to find any evidence of incendiarism. He could not account for the fierceness and extent of the blaze, but pointed out that the contents were highly imflammable. The fire, he said, had apparently broken out in the middle of the premises where there were the salons for trying on gowns which were usually demonstrated first on mannequins.

"Had the management any theory as to the cause of the fire?" asked Doctor Manson.

"They could only say that from the appearance it had started in the salons," was the reply. "They suggested that it might have been caused by cigarette ends put down by customers and which had been unnoticed. In point of fact one of the girls in the salons remembered that two ladies who had spent some considerable time in the salons shortly before closing time, had been smoking cigarettes."

"I see." Doctor Manson paused and reflected for a few moments. "There are only two other points," he said at last. "You mentioned just now the combustible nature of the contents. I gather that the stock was declared a total loss. Now, the firm were drapers as well as ladies' outfitters. Would there have been any bales of cloth in the place?"

"Yes. There were a number in the shop just in front of the salons."

"And in what state were the bales. Were they, too, destroyed?"

"Practically burnt up, yes. And what wasn't burned was, of course, ruined by water."

"Secondly, was any chemical analysis made of the dust or woodwork after the fire?"

"Chemical analysis?" The salvage chief looked up in astonishment. "No, sir, not that I know of. What kind of chemical analysis are you suggesting?"

The scientist dismissed the subject. "Never mind," he said, "I gather you do not go to such extremes in the city."

The following morning found the scientist in the city of Nottingham, where the second of the listed fires had destroyed the stock of the International Fur Warehouse, on the High Pavement, at a loss of £28,000. There again, much the same story was told of the fierceness of the outbreak, and lack of any information as to its cause. The explanation of the absent watchman was simple: the firm expected that he would have been there. He usually came on duty at dusk, after the employees had left. The man had a key, and let himself into the building. He had been taken suddenly ill on his way to the warehouse—in fact, shortly after he had his usual drink in a hostelry in the Poultry, and he had had to be taken home. Nothing suspicious in the fire had been noticed by the salvage brigade.

The scientist's inquiry as to whether any chemical tests had been made after the fire was greeted again with surprise. "What sort of tests were you thinking of, sir?" the salvage chief inquired.

Doctor Manson made no reply. He did, however, rub his chin with a hand—and in thoughtful mien.

Birmingham and Liverpool produced much the same story. The only difference was that whereas the other fires seemed to have had their origin in the heart of the buildings, the Liverpool blaze had apparently started at the rear in a room used as a workshop for altering and finishing off gowns. The workshop looked out on to a high wall which formed the back of premises in the next, and parallel, street. The wall had no windows overlooking the workshop, and a wooden partition divided it off from the front part of the premises. The partition was a recent innovation.

In each case the scientist had visited the scenes of the fires. The visits, however, were of little value, for the debris had been cleared away weeks before. At Liverpool, however, he did cut away a portion of charred wood which was more sheltered from the elements than other of the wreckage. This he placed carefully in an envelope, and transferred to a pocket.

From the great transatlantic port Doctor Manson drove back to London. Garaging his car, he walked from the Yard to the scene of the Hanover Square fire of Silks, Ltd. After inspecting the remains of the premises, he proceeded to the Salvage headquarters, where he remained talking to the chief officer for some time. Finally, without being much the wiser for his efforts, he retraced his steps to the Yard, and walked up the stairs to his Laboratory.

The deputy scientist, Sergeant Merry, was engaged in a tête-à-tête over the centre table with Inspector Kenway. He looked up as the door opened.

"Here *is* the doctor, Kenway," he announced. "Wants a bit of help, Doctor," he intimated. "He's got a corpse—or at least he's got a buried one."

"And darned well stiff and cold, Doctor, like the damned case," the inspector announced gloomily. "Been stiff and cold a week or so."

"And he's like a cat on hot bricks over it," put in the deputy scientist, with a grin.

Doctor Manson sat down. Merry produced glasses and a decanter.

"Tell me from the beginning," said the doctor.

"Well, it seems," began Kenway, "it seems that Dick Whittington was lying on Highgate Hill with his Cat—"

"Did you say that you had a corpse a week old, Kenway?" asked the scientist. "You don't mean a hundred years old, do you?"

The inspector saw the joke. "No, Doctor," he said, "this is not the original Dick Whittington, but the annual one. Now, when Dick should have turned again for London, he—or she . . ."

Lucidly and slowly the inspector told the tale of the Burlington-on-Sea pantomime . . . of the Cat who had been seen on the stage, who said he had not been there at all; of the complete alibi of the second Cat and the complete failure of the Burlington police to find out how Dick had been injected with the poison, and how the Cat had also been poisoned . . . in fact of the entire absence of any sound clue.

At the end Kenway looked hopefully at the scientist. His faith in his powers was that of a disciple looking, without question, for a miracle.

Doctor Manson sat silently until he had pigeonholed the details in his brain. Then:

"What has Jones done with the Cat—what did you say was his name?"

"Enora, Doctor."

"Enora. Well, what has happened to him?"

"Nothing—as yet. The superintendent wanted to have him arrested, but the Burlington inspector took the view that there wasn't even sufficient evidence on which the beak could hold and remand him." Kenway smiled. "Jones had to agree. But something has to be done soon, for they won't keep him in the hospital much longer."

"Is the pantomime company still at Burlington?"

"No, Doctor. As a matter of fact they're in London, down at the Old Sussex."

"Well, Kenway, I can't offer any suggestions until I have seen the setting. I've no doubt that you have given a true and accurate account of the stage setting, and of the scene at the time of the tragedy, but I must see it myself. Now, I suggest that you and I go along to the Old Sussex tonight and witness the performance. Then, if need be, I can go further into the matter with a visit to Burlington-on-Sea. As a matter of fact that will suit me perfectly, for I have in any case to visit the town on another matter, and I can in that way kill two birds with one stone. Will that satisfy you?"

"Suits me to a T," replied Kenway, making a gallant effort to disguise his delight at the suggestion. It was in the hope of getting the scientist to make the journey to Burlington that Kenway had journeyed to Town, and waited in the Yard Laboratory.

It was a bit of luck, he said to himself, as he went to arrange for a box at the theatre, that the doctor had business at Burlington. He wondered for a moment what the business could be in the one-eyed town that needed the presence of the scientist. But he did not pursue the thought; it was sufficient for him that he had induced Doctor Manson to look into the affair of Dick Whittington. Of the fire inquiries Kenway knew nothing. The investigation was still secret except from the Assistant Commissioner and Doctor Manson.

Thus it was that at 7.30 p.m. the Doctor and Inspector Kenway sat in a box at the Old Sussex Theatre and waited for the pantomime to begin its course. Together they watched the shop scene played through to the end, and the Highgate Hill scene take its place.

By a fortunate chance the police officers had been accorded one of the lower stage boxes, and, still more fortunate, that on the Opposite Prompt side of the stage. They could thus, by craning forward, actually see into the wings of the stage, where there could be obtained a glimpse of Dick Whittington waiting to make his entrance, and walk to the mossy bank on which he was to lie and hear the bells calling him to return to London.

Kenway, bending towards the doctor, whispered that that was identical with the position which the ill-fated Dick Whittington had occupied while she waited on the night of the death to make her entrance.

The doctor nodded, and eyed intently the position and that of other artistes. He followed with equal interest the entrance of Dick, the movements to the bank, the process of her reclining, and the attitude adopted by the cat.

"Is this exactly as on the night, Kenway?" he inquired in a whisper.

"As it has been described to the superintendent and I, Doctor, yes," was the reply. "That is, so far as the positions are concerned. I don't know whether this Cat has any different pose to Enora, of course."

"I should imagine not, Kenway," was the reply. "Most of the directions are marked in the script of these pantomimes."

The Ballet Scene followed, with the dance of the Bow Belles, twirling round and round the sleeping Dick and the Cat.

"This is a bit different from the Burlington scene, Doctor," the inspector pointed out. "The stage at Burlington was a revolving one. It made a half-turn, throwing Dick farther back, or up-stage as the Profession term it."

The dance ended, the Fairy Queen spoke her lines, and Dick stirred in his sleep.

"This is the moment, Doctor," prompted Kenway.

Dick rose to his feet, and spoke his lines:

> "The Bells, the bells. Is it a dream?
> I thought I heard the Bow Bells say:
> Turn again, Whittington, Lord Mayor of London."

"Those are the words Miss de Grey never said," announced Kenway. "The stage-manager rang down the curtain, and they found Miss de Grey dead."

"Then we need not spend any more time here," announced the scientist, and rose from his hard chair in the uncomfortable box. They left the theatre and boarded a bus in the main street.

"Well, Doctor?" asked the inspector.

"I'll ponder it during the night, Kenway, and let you know what I think tomorrow morning. Suppose we start for Burlington at nine o'clock? That suit you?"

"Down to the ground," the inspector agreed.

CHAPTER IX
TWO THINGS ARE MISSING

INSPECTOR BRADLEY arranged four chairs round a table in his office in the Burlington police station. From a drawer he produced a considerable sheaf of papers. These he proceeded to sort out into separate heaps.

"That's Enora," he said to himself . . . "and that's the other blasted Cat."

He evolved another pile:

"Miss de Grey . . . depositions on . . . the dresser . . . stage-manager . . . Mary Lee . . . she's important, I reckon . . . Miss Low . . . . he'll want that bit about the claws . . . Albert Black, stage hand . . . heard row between the two of them."

The inspector ran his glance through the remaining sheets of the papers. "Reckon I can mark this miscellaneous," he decided.

The piles anchored in position and safety, with paper weights, Inspector Bradley sat down in one of the chairs and awaited the coming of Doctor Manson. The latter had asked particularly that the local inspector should be present at the talk arranged for that morning. He had also asked to be made available all the statements taken in connection with the case.

Doctor Manson, with Superintendent Jones and Inspector Kenway, arrived at eleven o'clock. Inspector Bradley explained his array of paper. "I thought, sir, that as we talked we could refer to each of the people concerned more easily in this way."

"An excellent arrangement, and well thought out," was the reply. "But first, if you don't mind I would like to glance through the statements in order to get the hang of the investigation so far."

"Then I will make some coffee, sir," announced Bradley—a suggestion which found general support with the company.

A quarter of an hour passed before Doctor Manson put down the last of the papers, and turned to the inspector. "There is one point," he said. "Can you get the police surgeon here for a few moments?"

"I'll ring him, sir," was the reply. "He's only across the street. He can be here in a couple of minutes."

He was. Doctor Murdock, entering, greeted the scientist enthusiastically. "Often wanted to meet you, sir," he announced. "Pleased to be of any help . . . very peculiar case. What do you want to know?"

"You conducted the post-mortem, of course. What dose of hydrocyanide do you think Miss de Grey had?"

"I made a comparative analysis, Doctor, and I should say that there was not less than five grains in the body."

"So that death would undoubtedly occur within . . ."

"Within a few seconds, I should say."

"And the man?"

"Not very much. He drank it, you know. I found alcohol in the body, probably beer. At least that is what I took it to be."

"And you think that the hydrocyanide was in the beer?"

"It seems reasonable to assume so."

Doctor Manson nodded. "I agree," he said.

"There is one point which may be important, Doctor. That is, can you say how long the man would be conscious after he had drunk the amount of hydrocyanide you suggest he had taken?" Doctor Murdock hesitated. He consulted his note-book, and reflected for a considerable time before he replied. "That, Doctor Manson, is a very difficult question, as you will know better than I," he said. "Let me put it this way: the dose would not, I think, knock him out right away. I think he would have felt very queer, and would probably have sat down to prevent himself falling down. I should say that his head would swim round, as the saying is, and that he would gradually relapse into unconsciousness. Say within a couple of minutes."

Doctor Manson nodded. "I should have said much the same time myself. Thank you very much, Doctor."

The door closed behind the police surgeon, and Doctor Manson settled himself in his. chair. "Now," he said, "we will look at the *facts*."

"Only looks at . . . facts . . . does Doctor," Superintendent Jones explained to the Burlington Inspector. "Hell . . . row . . . if you . . . start tellin' . . . what you think."

"The facts are simple," the scientist explained. "Kenway and I saw the performance of the company in a London theatre last night, or, at least, all of the performance that was necessary. We saw the Highgate Hill scene. We saw Dick Whittington standing in the wings waiting to walk on to the stage. We saw her walk on. From the time she entered to the time she lay down on the bank was exactly two minutes. We can, I think, assume that the same time was taken by Miss de Grey, because all these scenes have to work to a time-table, as the show also works to a time-table.

"Now, she was alive when she lay down. She had had no dose of prussic acid then. We know that . . ."

"How?" asked Superintendent Jones.

"Because collapse from the dose would have occurred practically instantaneously," was the reply. "And additional proof is the fact that the Fairy Queen, according to Inspector Bradley's dossier of her here"—the scientist pointed to one of the piles of paper—"heard her talking to the Cat after she had lain down and after the Cat, too, had got down beside her, and he, you remember, had done his little washing business.

"The next fact we know is that within a minute or so she was dead. You see that?" He looked round at the company.

"Can't see it," said Jones.

"I do not follow it, sir," agreed Inspector Bradley.

"Well, let's work it out, then," retorted Doctor Manson. "I think it is possible to work out the time of death to within half a minute if we see another performance of the pantomime and time this scene with a stop watch—or rather, time each section of it."

He reached forward and picked up one of the arranged papers. "Now, this," he said, "is the statement made to Inspector Bradley by Mary Lee, who is one of the Bow Belles." He read it out:

"'Miss de Grey generally watched us while we were dancing, and sometimes winked at us when we passed her. But she didn't open her eyes tonight at all.'"

"As I had not, last night, seen this statement, I did not time the dancing of these little girls in the performance I saw with Inspector Kenway. I do remember, however, that the dancing started as soon as the Fairy Queen had said her lines, 'Sleep on, sweet boy.' Those lines would take less than half a minute. Thus we can say that Miss de Grey died between the time that the Fairy Queen heard her speak to the Cat as they were reclining together, and the time that the dancers first passed the pair of them, because Miss de Grey's eyes, which were always open, were on this occasion closed. Shall we say that a timing of the performance will fix the time to half a minute?"

Inspector Kenway interposed. "We could, possibly, knock it down to even less, Doctor."

Doctor Manson turned a questioning look on the inspector.

For reply, Kenway picked up the statement of Miss Low, the Fairy Queen. "The Doctor started his timing by saying that the Fairy Queen heard Miss de Grey talking to the Cat after they had lain down. Therefore she was alive then. But what did Miss de Grey say?" He read from the statement. This is Miss Low's question and answer examination:

"Did she (Miss de Grey) speak at all—I mean outside the lines she had to say?"

"No . . . well. . . ."

"She did say something. What was it?"

"It wasn't much. She just said in a loud whisper to the cat, 'Don't stick your damned claws into me, and get off my legs'."

Inspector Kenway replaced the paper on the table. "If we can assume that the *'damned claw'* stuck into her was the hypodermic needle, then we've only a quarter of a minute to the start of the dance—just the time the Fairy Queen's lines take—before the Bow Belle saw Dick *with her eyes closed*, that were usually open."

Doctor Manson beamed. "That is perfectly true, Kenway," he said. "I had missed that very important point!"

He paused to marshal the facts in his mind before summing up.

"Now you see where all these facts lead us," he said. "There is not the shadow of a doubt that Miss de Grey died on that stage, that she died at a time we can place to within a quarter of a minute, that the only person who was within even an arm's length of her at the crucial time, and who, therefore, must have been the murderer, was the—"

"The Cat," broke in Superintendent Jones. "Which is . . . what . . . said . . . from start."

"The Cat," agreed the scientist. "There is no doubt that the fatal prick which killed her was administered by the Cat."

"And the Cat says he wasn't on the stage, sir," put in Inspector Bradley. "And the other Cat is accounted for, and also could not have been on the stage. Yet there was a cat there."

"One thing at a time, Bradley," chided the scientist. "Let us keep strictly to our facts. It is always the best way. Now the fact, the one fact, we have at the moment is that there was *a* cat at the feet of Miss de Grey. The stage-manager saw him. The Fairy Queen saw him; the audience saw him—and if he hadn't been there the scene could not have been played. Therefore, we can say definitely that there was a cat on the stage. The only point at issue is—which cat *was* on the stage?"

Superintendent Jones chuckled, until the bulk of him quivered. "Thank Heavens . . . only . . . two . . . of 'em," he said. "Can't . . . be . . . much trouble . . . there."

"Both of them have alibis," said Bradley. "Enora says he wasn't on the stage, and the other one is proved not to have been there."

"Alibis are made to be broken, Bradley," retorted Kenway. "The doctor always mistrusts an alibi. Nine times out of ten the fact that anyone has an alibi pretty nearly proves them the person who did it. An innocent person seldom has an alibi. He doesn't need to go round making one, or looking for one, because he doesn't know one is likely to be wanted."

"You . . . talkin' . . . like . . . doctor," said Jones. "Couple of you at it . . . now."

Manson smiled. "Nevertheless, Jones, it's sound sense," he said. "Now let's look for a moment at these alibis. Take Enora first. What are the facts we know about him. He was on the stage at the opening of the performance. All the company can provide proof of that. He was on the stage in the shop scene. The company can prove that, and he says so himself. What's next?"

Inspector Bradley took up the recital. "He was on the stage at the end of the shop scene," he said. "That carries it a bit further. He came off with her?"

"Proof?" barked Jones.

"They had a row in the Green Room, which was heard by a stage-hand. He knew Enora."

The inspector picked out the statement of Arthur Black from amongst those on the desk. "Here it is," he said, and read:

"She and the Cat had an 'ell of a row. They was a'rowing over something she said he had done the previous night. I says to the stage-manager, just listen to her rorting to the Cat now. Then I says, he's walked out on her. And he did, too. Just left her talking to herself."

"The stage-manager agrees that there was a row and that the Cat did walk out."

"Right," said Doctor Manson. "Then we have the fact that the Cat was Enora at, and for some minutes after, the end of the shop scene, and just prior to the Highgate Hill scene. We have him leaving Miss de Grey in a fury. Where did he go from there?"

"He says that he went to his dressing-room for a drink and a rub down," said Inspector Bradley.

"Any *facts* in regard to that?" asked Manson.

There was no answer.

"Urn!" Doctor Manson looked at each in turn. "Let's see if we can find any. Was it in any way unusual for Enora to go to his dressing-room for a drink at that interval?"

"I think not, sir," replied Inspector Bradley. "He told me that he always had a drink at that time, before going on for the High-gate Hill scene."

"Have you checked that?"

"No."

"Can you get hold of the dresser?"

"Bennett, sir? Yes. He works in the 'pop-shop' round the corner."

A constable sent for the man, produced him in a matter of two or three minutes. Bennett eyed the formidable-looking company in some alarm. It was Doctor Manson who questioned him.

"Bennett, I understand that you looked after Mr. Enora during the pantomime. We are interested in one particular time in the pantomime—that interval between Enora coming off the shop scene, and returning for the Highgate Hill scene. What did Enora usually do during that interval? Do you know?"

"I do, sir. He went to his room for a drink. I always put a glass of bitter on his dressing-table ready for that little wait. He hadn't much time, and he always wanted it there ready."

"Did you put a drink there on the night that Miss de Grey died and he was taken ill?"

"I did, sir, same as usual."

"When did you go to the room again?"

"I never did, sir. One of the lads found the Cat ill, and a crowd got in there. Next I knew, the door was locked and the key gone."

"But you are sure that you yourself took a bottle of bitter to the room?"

"Yes, sir. I took it all right."

"That is fact number two," said Manson, after the dresser had gone. "Now, Enora says, according to this statement, that after he had the drink he went all queer, became light-headed, and the next thing he knew was waking up in hospital. That seems to tally with the view of Doctor Murdock that anyone drinking the dose which laid out the Cat would feel dizzy, probably sit down to save himself falling, and would go out of consciousness within a couple of minutes."

"Then, if that is the case, it was *not* Enora who was on the stage," said Kenway.

Doctor Manson made no response. He was reading from the papers on the desk those relating to the Cat. Presently he looked up, and across at Inspector Bradley.

"I have just been reading, Inspector, the contents of Enora's dressing-room. They consisted of a tin of vaseline, one of cold cream, a watch, a suit of clothes, collar and tie, underclothes, a dressing-gown, a towel, soap, ashtray, a tablecloth, a brush for the cat-skin, a make-up towel, a make-up glass, a combination undersuit and his cat's skin, which had been taken off him when he was found, and before he was taken to hospital. Was that everything that the room contained?"

"Everything, sir, yes."

"Think carefully for a moment, Inspector, before you answer. Was there anything—even though it seems to have no connection with the matter at all—was there anything else in that room?"

Inspector Bradley puckered his forehead in the process of visualizing the Cat's dressing-room. He let a minute elapse in thought. Then:

"No, sir. There was nothing else," he said.

"Nothing else on the dressing table, for instance?" insisted the scientist.

"No. I am quite sure of that."

"Doctor!"

Superintendent Jones leaned forward.

Manson looked at him. "Well, Super?" he asked.

"If I . . . wanted . . . murder . . . Whittington . . . and get 'way with it . . . stick needle . . . in her . . . run like hell . . . to room . . . drink prepared dope . . . be out to world when found . . . say I wasn't on . . . stage 'tall."

"I know, Jones. So would I. That is just what is worrying me."

He paused; then added:

"You see, *there are two things that ought to be in that dressing-room that are not there.* I am going to have a look at that room myself and at the contents, which I gather are still in the room, and still locked and sealed."

"What are the two things, Doctor?" asked Kenway.

"Think it over, Kenway, and you will probably find the answer," was the reply.

INTERLUDE I
TO THE READER

The practised Armchair Detective should, we think, by now be able to name one of the missing things mentioned by Doctor Manson. Maybe he can name them both.

Certainly any actor or actress will realize at once the second of the missing articles . . .

Or, at least, any actor or actress should *do so.*

The Authors.

CHAPTER X
A MINK COAT

THE FOUR MEN stood in the tiny dressing-room which had been the abode during theatre hours of Enora. The room was bare now, except for a large dressing-basket standing by the wall opposite the door. Doctor Manson, Superintendent Jones, and Inspector Kenway watched while Inspector Bradley broke the official seals on the basket, unlocked it, and laid out the contents on the dressing table.

Kenway ticked off each item as it was produced, using the Burlington police inventory for the purpose. The basket empty, Doctor Manson looked carefully over the exhibits.

There was the suit, the stained and dirty underclothes that were to have been sent to the laundry on the evening of the tragedy. There was the shirt, the collar and tie, the boxes of vaseline and cold cream. And there was the cat skin. His perusal over, the scientist peered into the wardrobe, the drawer of the dressing table, and every other crack and crevice which the room contained. He found nothing; and he said nothing.

He next turned his attention to the cat skin. "Well, there's one thing we need not worry over—finger-prints," he said. "We are not likely to find any on this sort of garment."

He opened the skin at the neck, turned back the folds, and with a lens taken from a waistcoat pocket examined the interior.

"Remarkable pieces of work these stage skins," he remarked.

The scientist was right. A skin is, indeed, a remarkable piece of work. The base is a woven net, like a thick stockinet. Into the holes of the net are woven hair, and it is this hair and its quality that gives the value to the skin. Sixty pounds is not at all a dear price to pay for the outfit, a hundred pounds would provide a good skin. The effect of the stockinet, thus woven, is that it stretches to 'fit' the wearer, thus avoiding the uncouth and ill-fitting appearance which a base of canvas or some other material would show.

"Yes, a remarkable piece of work indeed," the scientist added. He passed his lens over the netting, pausing now and again to make a closer examination of one or two spots. After two or three of these pauses he called to Kenway.

"In my overcoat pocket, Kenway," he said, "is a small case containing a pair of tweezers and some seed envelopes. Get them for me, will you?"

The inspector handed them over. Doctor Manson, again using his lens, searched the interior of the mask of the cat, and with the tweezers detached a small object. He slipped it into one of the envelopes, and proceeded with his search. Three times he carried out the operation, each time from a different part of the mask's interior. Then, apparently satisfied, he put down the skin, and sealing the envelopes, labelled them, and held them out to Superintendent Jones for his confirming initials.

"'Swat I like to see . . . Doctor . . . goin' all science," said Jones.

"And I want the skin wrapped up, too," the scientist retorted with a smile. "I'll take it back with me in the car."

From the Cat's dressing-room the company proceeded to that which had been occupied by Miss de Grey. This, too, had remained locked, and its contents were sealed in two dress baskets. Once again, the contents of the baskets were lifted out and laid on the dressing table, and on the lounge. They included all the costume changes required for her part of principal boy in the pantomime, her greasepaint, creams, and other toilet concomitants, her clothes, wraps, and the usual feminine contents of a well-supplied dressing-room of a star performer.

Doctor Manson, after a perfunctory glance at the toilet articles and fripperies, ignored them as not likely to pay for examination. He turned instead, to the clothes worn by Miss de Grey when she was using that identity, and not that of Dick Whittington. They contained two costumes and a fur coat. Each garment was wrapped in a silk dust sheet, which had enfolded them in the wardrobe, and in which the dresser had lifted them out and laid with them in the basket. The scientist opened the first of the dust sheets. It surrounded the garment in its entirety. In a corner was the name, in red lettering, 'Silks, Ltd.' The costume was a two-piece suit, of excellent quality, and so, too, was the second costume. From them, Doctor Manson passed to the fur coat. This, also, was enveloped in a dust sheet. It was shaken from its covering, and hung up on a hook behind the door.

Doctor Manson, looking at it, whistled softly. He felt it over, inside and out. Then, stepping back, he inspected it as a whole.

"You know anything about furs, Inspector?" he asked Bradley.

"Not a great deal, sir," was the reply. "My wife has one, but this strikes me as being a pretty good fur."

"It certainly *is* a pretty good fur, Bradley, and not one I should have expected to be found worn by an artiste in the second-rate pantomime class. It's mink, and would cost, I should say, about £1,200. You have not, I suppose, made any inquiries into Miss de Grey?"

"No. We saw no reason for it, Doctor. Mr. Henri de Benyat, the owner of the pantomime, said that as far as he knew she had no relatives. She had told him so and that she had come originally from Southampton, some five years ago. He attended the funeral, with the members of the company, but apart from that there were no other mourners."

The scientist slipped on his overcoat. "Well, I don't think you need deprive the theatre of their dressing-rooms any longer, Jones," he said. "But have the baskets packed again and taken to the police station, together with that in Enora's room. All that interests me is the skin of Enora and these dust sheets and the fur coat of Miss de Grey. Those I will take back with me."

The four men spent the next quarter of an hour in experimenting on the time taken to get from the Green Man to the stage door, and Enora's room and back again to the public house. At the end, Doctor Manson drew the superintendent apart.

"Get Kenway to find out all he can about Miss de Grey, Jones," he said. "Get it from the company, you understand. I'll attend to de Benyat myself. And now, I've a bit of personal business with Bradley." He called the inspector over, and, linking an arm in one of his, walked away.

The Burlington inspector stopped in surprise, and stared at his companion, when Doctor Manson mentioned the business on which he required the help of the police of the seaside town.

"Do you know, sir," he said, "I've had a bit of a doubt always about that fire. Never liked it."

"Why not?" from Manson.

"Well, for one thing, I did not like the proprietors. They were strangers in the place, and they were, to my mind, a shifty couple. They started off by making a large contribution to the police sports field and club fund. Now, the shop was taken over from a man who had found it hard to get a living out of it. You understand, sir, that trade here is purely a seasonal one. It does not last more than about three months. Half the people are 'broke' within a couple of months of the season ending. You've got to take enough money in the three months to last you through the winter. That isn't too bad when it's a trade like drapery, or outfitting, or ladies' clothes, because there are always the local people to eke out the off-season. But with a trade like these fancy goods, of the expensive kind, it's pretty hopeless. Now, this couple came here and paid a good price for the business. As a matter of fact, they paid £3,000, so the owner told me. They stocked it with more stuff than the other chap had sold in all the years he had been in business. It would have lasted them for years, and they wouldn't have seen their expenses back, let alone have made a living out of it.

"Then the fire came, on a Sunday night. I reckoned that too long had elapsed between the closing of the shop and the outbreak for it to have been an accident from carelessness of a customer or one of the couple themselves. After the fire the brigade chief and I had a good look round, but we couldn't find anything suspicious. Only that the entire place was burnt out. My experience of fires is that you can generally tell where an outbreak began. In this case there was no sign of the origin. I felt that if you had set fire to it in half a dozen places at once you would have got much the same effect. I don't know much about the properties of ashes and debris, sir, but I didn't think there was enough of it on the premises to account for all the stock which they had had in the place. And they must have done dashed well, if they had sold what to my mind was the difference."

Doctor Manson looked at his companion. "If I may say so, Bradley, that is an exceedingly valuable observation; an observation after my own heart. You have told me in a few words all that I came down to find out."

The Burlington inspector looked his gratification at the praise from the Yard scientist. "Is there anything phoney about the fire, Doctor?" he asked.

"That I do not know, Bradley," was the reply. "I am merely making certain inquiries for interested parties."

The talk with Bradley ended the scientist's interest in Burlington-on-Sea, and a few minutes later he left for London, taking with him in his car the skin of Enora and the fur coat and silk dust sheets of Miss de Grey. It was a thoughtful man who drove the Oldsmobile along the wide by-pass to the Metropolis.

On the following morning he began his investigations on the lines of the interviews of the last few days. And it was then that the scientist struck the first real clue in the trail that was to solve two mysteries. Accustomed as he was to unexpected results from the researches of his brilliant and analytical mind and reasoning, and his scientific tests of such findings, the clue that presented itself on this occasion was such as to cause him to lose for an instant that habitual calm and placid acceptance that was a source of constant comment by his colleagues.

It began when, in the Laboratory at the top of Scotland Yard, he began a routine examination of the fur coat of Miss de Grey. Neatly stitched inside the interior pocket of the coat was a tab which proclaimed that the coat had been made by Jacob Wernheimer, of Aldgate, London. He knew Wernheimer to be one of the greatest fur experts in the world, and one who dealt only in the choicest of skins. Accordingly, wrapping the coat in a parcel, he was driven to the Aldgate premises, and there was conducted to the private office of Jacob.

The dapper little Jew received him as an honoured visitor. He produced a bottle of wine and a box of cigars, and insisted on the refreshment being drunk and the cigars lighted before any business was talked. The ceremony in full swing he inquired the reason for the visit.

"And now, Doctor, what can I do for you?" he asked.

For reply Doctor Manson unwrapped the parcel and disclosed to view the fur coat. "This, Mr. Wernheimer, is one of your excellent products, I believe." he said.

The furrier took the coat. He ran his hands lovingly over it, examining the skins and the stitching. He nodded.

"It is, indeed, one of mine. A beautiful mink, Doctor. I sold it for . . . now let me see . . ."

He extracted a book from a shelf and turned over the pages, finally stopping at one about half-way through the book. After considering an entry, he turned an inquiring gaze on the coat which he again examined. Returning once more to the book, he ran again over the entry, muttering to himself.

Doctor Manson, watching him, had a queer sense of an impending something. "Is there anything wrong, Mr. Wernheimer?" he asked.

For reply, the furrier rang his desk bell. A girl answered the call.

"Miss Levison, will you bring me the correspondence file of our letters with the Commercial Insurance Corporation?" he asked.

The girl returned after a minute with the file. Mr. Wernheimer turned over the contents, finally taking out one of the letters and his firm's reply. He examined them with some care, and then turned to the scientist.

"This is a very strange affair, Doctor Manson," he said, quietly. "Is it permitted to ask how you came into possession of the coat?"

"It was the property of a young lady who died in circumstances which make it necessary that some inquiries should be held into her end," he said.

The furrier spread his hands. "Oh dear, oh dear, this is a bad business," he said, softly. "You see, Doctor, while it is true that we sold this coat, it is also true that it no longer exists. We sold the coat to a Nottingham firm called the International Fur Warehouse. The firm had a fire and this coat was one of the valuable furs destroyed. We were asked by the Commercial Insurance Company to confirm that we had sent it to the firm and to confirm that its value was the purchase price paid to us of a thousand guineas—that is wholesale price, of course. We did so, and the company paid out the amount claimed."

Doctor Manson sat for a minute staring at the old man. Wrinkles had appeared across the broad forehead, and the crinkles that were always a warning to his brother investigators were set in the corners of his eyes.

"Are you sure there is no chance of a mistake?" he asked.

"None, Doctor. This is a beautiful mink. I recall it perfectly. And it is the only mink of its value that we disposed of at that time. There is no doubt at all."

"What would be its selling price, do you suppose?"

"I cannot say what the Nottingham firm would ask for it. Maybe £2,000, maybe £1,750. But not under £1,500, I can assure you."

The scientist rose. "We have no place in Scotland Yard that could store a coat such as this without the chance of ruining it, Mr. Wernheimer," he said. "Might I ask you to take care of it until I want it again?"

The furrier nodded agreement, and gave a receipt.

Making his farewells, the scientist departed.

He stopped his car outside a building in the Charing Cross Road, and entered the offices of Mr. Henri de Benyat.

CHAPTER XI
MISS DE GREY

IF YOU WALK ACROSS Trafalgar Square, 'neath the Shade of Nelson, skirt the National Gallery, and turn left you will arrive in the Street of Laughter and Tears.

That is not the name which appears on the street-plate, set high above the pavement; the name on there is Charing Cross Road.

From the Irving statue at the start of the road to the Hippodrome Corner is no more than a three minute stroll. Yet, in those three minutes of distance there is, for the actor and actress, the path from laughter to tears, from hope to heartbreak, which ends on that same Hippodrome Corner, the title of which in the Profession is known as Heartbreak Corner.

For it is along this stretch of the West End that the members of the theatrical profession who are seeking work—the euphemistic term for the condition is 'resting'—congregate, seeking that elusive light which will blazon their names above the theatrical edifice. Hopefully they pass through doorways, and into offices set inside the doorways. Too often, alas, they come out with a smile, but with that smile hiding a dread in their hearts, that they are 'done', too old, and that there is no place for them any longer. And so they go into the next office, and out again, and into the next and out again, and into . . .

The offices in this part of Charing Cross Road are, you see, those occupied by theatrical impresarios and theatrical agents;

those with jobs to offer, and those who can negotiate jobs. And at nearly all hours of the day Heartbreak Corner has its little coterie of sad and weary men and women. The stage has no glamour to the player on it.

It was into one of these doorways that Doctor Manson walked. After scanning the large board of tenants, he joined the procession of people towards the lift. At the third floor there were four occupants of the lift. An alert little man with the merry eyes of a jester opened the gates, sprang through and hurried towards an open door at the bottom of the passage. Doctor Manson followed more slowly. He paused before the door to read the inscription in letters of gold:

HENRY DE BENYAT ENTERPRISES, LTD.
10 a.m. to 5 p.m.

Manson hesitated only long enough to allow a very blonde young lady in fox furs to enter first. Inside he found a waiting-room, lined with seats which stretched round three sides, full of people.

The merry little man hailed a friend at the end of one of the rows, and then dashed to a window hatch in the far wall. The face of a harassed man appeared in the opening.

"Hallo, Charlie. Mr. de Benyat in?"

"Well, he's very busy, and you'll have to wait your turn, as you can see," was the reply.

"All right, Charlie boy. Just bung my card in. He might want me."

He moved off and joined the friend at the end of the row. His place was taken by the very blonde young lady. The face appeared again at the hatch. "Oh, Mr. de Benyat wants to see you, miss. Just wait, will you?"

Doctor Manson had hung back to watch the by-play. A student of humanity and psychology, these people of the world of make-believe interested him. He was, he said to himself, in no hurry. He gazed round at the walls of the office. Playbills proclaimed that Mr. de Benyat's stupendous *Rodeo Show* was at Scunthorpe; Mr. de Benyat's revue *Glorious Girls* was at Brighton; Mr. de Benyat's *Cinderella* was at Manchester; and amongst many others, that Mr. de Benyat's *Dick Whittington* company was at the Old Sussex Theatre, London.

Around him chatted comedians, soubrettes, acrobats,- *passé* opera singers, and samples of all the patient, persevering souls which it takes to make up the theatrical profession. The little comic's voice floated on the air: "Yes, old man. Did enormous business. Absolute riot . . . oh yes. Just having a rest now. . . . No, haven't fixed anything for the summer, but got plenty of offers, of course. Just sticking out for me money, old boy."

"Mr. Micawber," thought Manson.

The chatter died down into silence as a door by the side of the window hatch opened suddenly. A tall, white-haired man appeared outlined in the lintels. He looked hurriedly round the room, saw the little blonde, and pointed at her. "I'll see you, Miss French, in a minute." His gaze passed on over the company. "Sorry, ladies and gentlemen," he announced. "I'm only booking circus this morning." He pointed at a thin, handsome boy. "Go inside, Bert. I want you. . . . And you . . . and you . . . and you,"—the words accompanying a jab at the persons indicated. "No more until this afternoon. Sorry, boys and girls."

The little comic stood up and tried to catch his eye. "Oh, Harry—" he began.

"Sorry, old man, nothing doing today. Come up next week." As others pressed forward, he nodded to them one by one. "Nothing today, Horace, for you. Sorry . . . Not today, no. Circus only." His eyes caught Manson, and he looked as though he was searching to 'place' him. But the same answer came: "Nothing today, old man. Sorry." He turned on his heel and entered the sacred sanctum of the inner office.

Manson smiled delightedly. The unlucky ones began to disperse until only those singled out by Mr. de Benyat remained in the room. Charlie looked through his hatch, and saw Manson.

"Sorry, sir," he said. "But you heard. He can't see any more this morning."

The scientist moved forward to the window, and extracted a card from his case. "Will you present Mr. de Benyat with this card. I think he will see me," he announced.

Charlie took the proferred card, but without looking at it. "Now listen, old man," he begged. "You heard the Guv say he's up to his eyes in it, and it's only circus today. Unless you're circus I daren't go inside again."

Manson's eyes twinkled. "Well, I'm not exactly circus—yet," he agreed. "But . . ."

At that moment Charlie looked at the card, and then, like lightning, at Doctor Manson. "Cor blimey!" he said, and swallowed hard. "Sorry, sir," he gasped, "I didn't think . . ."

He disappeared from view to return almost instantly with a "Come this way, sir."

Inside he was greeted by the impresario. "Good morning, Doctor Manson. This is a great hon—" He paused, and stared.

"Good Lord, you were waiting outside. I thought you were a pro." He threw back his head and roared with laughter. Manson joined him.

"Well, we do owe you an apology. I'm afraid we were too overcrowded to show much courtesy. Do be seated and have a drink. We'll make up for the waiting."

He poured out a glass of whisky, placed a box of cigars at the side of the scientist, and then seated himself in anticipation.

"And now, Doctor, what can I do for you? I suppose it's the Whittington thing, eh?" he asked, forlornly.

"Yes. I am afraid it is, Mr. de Benyat," was the scientist's reply. "What I want is for you to tell me all you know of Miss de Grey."

"Well, that won't take me very long, old boy. I know very little about her. I'm told that she was an artist's model some years ago. Then went on the stage in the chorus, got to be a show lady, had a part in a small revue, and then understudied a small part in musical comedy. An agent brought her round to me last summer. I wanted a boy. She was a good looker with a good figure, she sang quite nicely, and could do a bit o' dancing—not much, but enough—so I gave her Dick Whittington. That's all there is to her, old boy." The impresario sat back, threw out his hands and took a long drink from his glass of whisky.

Doctor Manson eyed the silver-haired, distinguished-looking impresario in some perplexity. "But, surely, Mr. de Benyat, that is not usual. I do not know much about the theatrical world, or its practices, but I seem to have heard that you are a purveyor of first-class entertainment to the Provinces. I gathered from that, that for a leading part in a Benyat production some person with a name, or at any rate some theatrical reputation, might generally be found. Am I then wrong?"

The theatrical magnate wriggled a little uncomfortably. He leaned forward, and spoke apologetically. "Well, as a matter of fact, Doctor, you are right, speaking generally. But in the case of Miss de Grey the pantomime was going to Burlington, where there is no opposition of any kind, to one more similar town and then to the Old Sussex, where any pantomime will go well. Get me, old boy? It's no good throwing money away on salaries where there is no competition."

He coughed.

"Then, as a matter of fact, old boy, Miss de Grey was a bit different. The agent who sent her to me said that she might be willing to put a bit of money in the firm. I've got a lot of the ready laid out in a string of shows, and I was ready to consider a bit of a sleeping partnership."

"And did she put up a bit?"

"She did—a couple of thousand, old boy. Mind you it was damned good investment. She'd have had a nice bit to come back on top of the two thou. And she wasn't a bad 'boy'. I'd have given her a run in a better show the next year."

"How much salary did she get? I suppose you paid her a salary?"

"Yes. Not so much as I'd have paid somebody with a name, mind you. She had fifteen of the best a week."

"Biggest salary she had earned?"

"Sure was, old boy."

"Well, I don't think there is much else, Mr. de Benyat. Who was the agent who sent her to you?"

"Old Joe Davis. Want to speak to him? I'll get him on the 'phone." He dialled a number. "What are you after? Where she got two thousand from, and so on?"

The scientist nodded.

A voice came over the 'phone. Mr. de Benyat answered. "Joe, remember that Grey girl? How did you get on to her?" Manson, listening in on an extension, heard the answer: "Oh, came up for an audition. Chorus job."

"What! With all that money?"

Joe chuckled. "Say, she hadn't any money then, laddie. Wanted a job badly, and didn't look as if she could get together a wardrobe. The money came later, see."

"Where's the gold mine, old boy?"

Another chuckle from Joe. "Haven't the least idea, old man. Wish I had. I could use some of it."

"All right, Joe. Thanks."

"That's all I can do, Doctor," said Mr. de Benyat.

The scientist thanked him, and made his way back to the street, and to Scotland Yard.

Having thus probed the mystery of Miss de Grey's mink coat and the source of the money which paid for it, Doctor Manson next turned his attention to a third point. The knowledge that the fur coat was one of the articles supposed to have been destroyed in the fire in the Nottingham warehouse, which he had investigated, made him turn his eyes on the dust sheet which, also found among Miss de Grey's possessions, contained the mark of another firm which had been the victim of a fire—namely, Silks Ltd. It might, he thought, be an advantage to know how that article had come into her possession, and whether it would take him further along what now seemed to be two cases in one, the fire sequences and the death of Dick Whittington.

In the hope that the salvage department of the fire brigade might be able to help, he telephoned the offices. He was, for once, in luck's way. Captain Fergus was able to give him the business address of the manager of Silks, Ltd., a Mr. Anstruther, who since the firm had not restarted, and did not seem likely to restart, had taken a position in a firm in the same line of goods, in Regent Street.

The man was able quickly to identify the sheet which the scientist unwrapped from the paper in which he had carried it. It was, he said, one of the sheets which was used to cover up the more expensive articles during the time they were awaiting a customer in the salons of Silks, Ltd. He was a little puzzled as to how the scientist came to be possessed of it, since they were not articles which the firm had ever offered for sale.

"That is just what I wanted to know," the scientist explained. "This particular one of some three or four was covering the dresses of a lady of the stage. How would that come about, do you think?"

The man confessed himself as quite unable to think of any explanation. He could not remember any occasion on which one had been sold to a customer.

"Did you ever have a customer named Grey—Miss Norma de Grey?" asked Manson.

"Norma de Grey?" The man thought hard for a few moments. "No, I can't recall the name. What kind of looking woman would she be?"

He failed, however, to recognize from the description supplied to him of the pantomime star any customer in the shop. Nor could he say that the proprietors of the business, Mr. James Barford and Mr. Andre Bessing, had any particular lady friend whom they supplied with goods from the premises.

Asked how trade had been with the firm, he said that he had been looking for another job for some time, as he did not think the firm could last very much longer. He would be surprised to hear, he said, that the fire damage was settled for £21,000. He thought that the owners had been trying to sell the business before the fire, and had failed. A tall, rather flaxen-haired gentleman had paid several visits, and had been shown round the premises by Mr. Bessing. He had come on several occasions, the last about a week before the fire. The cause of the outbreak, he said, was put down as due to an electric iron being left on an ironing board in the pressing department. This was rather a shock to him, because he had been quite sure that he followed his usual custom of turning off the electric current at the main switch before he left the place. That he always did because of the combustible nature of the contents of the premises, and because he had once before had a fire caused by that very means.

Pressed to think carefully, he said that he distinctly remembered walking out of the shop in the light of his torch—or thought he did. That was the reason he had been surprised to hear the official theory of the outbreak.

"That flaxen-haired gentleman, can you recall his name?" asked Doctor Manson.

"It was never given to me by the bosses," was the reply, "but I do remember Mr. Bessing on one occasion calling him Mr. Onslow. At least, what he said was, 'Shall I send it to Mr. Onslow?'"

With that, Doctor Manson had to be satisfied. Back at the Yard he spent the next hour in studying the results of his two days' visits. Finally, after telephoning Superintendent Jones at Burlington, he called it a day, and walked to his flat, and an evening meal.

CHAPTER XII
THE HAIRS OF A CAT

DOCTOR MANSON, arriving at the Yard next morning, went at once to his Laboratory, slipped on a white coat, and set up a microscope on the large middle table.

He whistled for Sergeant Merry, the deputy scientist.

* * * * *

At the same time Superintendent Jones, in a first-class compartment in the Burlington-Waterloo train, was eyeing Inspector Kenway in perplexity.

"What . . . suppose . . . he wants . . . a thing . . . like that . . . for?" he asked.

"Who's he?" asked Kenway.

"The doctor."

"And what is it he wants, anyway?"

"Some . . . Enora's . . . hairs."

Inspector Kenway said nothing, but just ruminated. The superintendent added to his wailing.

"Don't cut 'em," he says. "Pull 'em out. And put 'em in envelope. What's ruddy difference? . . . Hair's . . . hair cut or yanked."

"Point is, old fat man, have you got them?" asked Kenway.

The superintendent produced a white and labelled envelope. "In here," he announced.

Kenway chuckled.

The superintendent glared. "What's funny about it?" he demanded.

"Just thought of a joke." The inspector waited a moment for the inevitable question.

"Perhaps the doctor's started a hare," he explained.

* * * * *

Sergeant Merry and the scientist unwrapped together the cat skin of Enora and laid it out on the table. The fastening was unzipped and the skin opened out. Together, the two men examined the netted interior through their lenses. Now and then they extracted with tweezers one or two small fragments of fluff, each piece of which was carefully put under a watch-glass on a porcelain tile.

From the inside of the mask of the skin some dozen or so hairs were similarly retrieved and preserved. The outside of the skin was next examined, but seemingly without result.

The failure was not unexpected, for Doctor Manson, at the end of the examination, comforted himself with the reflection: "Well, I didn't expect we would get much from there. It does not, as you know, lend itself to results."

With his exhibits safely housed under separate watch-glasses Doctor Manson drew his microscope forward, fitted an appropriate eyepiece and prepared to make a detailed examination.

First taking the fragments of fluff he submitted each to a careful scrutiny.

"Seems to be a mixture of silk and wool," he said of the first two or three pieces, and made way for Merry. The deputy scientist, after peering through the instrument, agreed. At the next piece, however, the scientist, after what started with a cursory glance, developed a close attention. Twice he looked, and then, fitting another eyepiece stared at the exhibit again. He shot an inquiring glance at Merry. The sergeant, after himself examining the fluff, pronounced it as a mixture of cotton and wool.

"Exactly what I put it down as myself," said Manson. He took from the parcel which he had brought from Burlington the undergarment found in Enora's room, and examined it.

"This, too, is cotton and wool," he observed. "Now that is rather a curious circumstance."

Merry, who knew the signs, promptly proceeded to fix a mica slide over the exhibits, each on a separate microscope slide, and the Doctor prepared for his next examination.

This concerned the hairs that he had taken from the mask of the skin. With a diluted solution of glycerine he mounted each of them on a glass slide. When eight of these had been completed he called the Laboratory assistant.

"Now, Wilkins," he announced, "you may as well learn how to examine the hairs found on scene of any suspicious circumstance."

Wilkins was one of the men chosen by Doctor Manson for training in the Laboratory. The men were to form the nucleus of a body of skilled police scientific investigators to be distributed among the police forces all over the country. Wilkins stood by, expectantly.

"Firstly," said the scientist, "you should know that the examination of hairs in criminal investigation was made for the first time when the Duchesse de Praslin was murdered in Paris in 1847. An examination was made of a hair which was found clinging to the pistol used." He turned to the slides which he had prepared, and slipped one under the instrument.

"Now, the first thing we have to find out about a hair is whether it is animal or man. In this case, however, we need not worry; there is no animal involved. The next thing is to decide from which part of the body it has come. Look through the microscope and tell me what shape is the cross-cut section of the hair you see?"

"Round," replied Wilkins.

"Then it comes from the scalp," said Doctor Manson. "Only in very exceptional cases are head hairs anything but round. Hair taken from the beard is generally triangular, and from the torso kidney-shaped.

"Now," he went on, "we will measure the hair." He slipped a micrometer eyepiece on to the instrument. "This hair is 1/350 inch," he announced, "which means that in all probability it is from the head of a male. That, we can check by the medullary index." The scientist did so, and announced the result as 0.132. "In a woman," he explained, "the size would have been 0.148. We are now certain that the hair we are examining came from the forehead of a man. That is a scientific check, which would be accepted as expert evidence of the facts as we already knew them; the hairs were found on the inside of the head of a skin which is used by a man impersonating a cat in pantomime.

"It is necessary next to note the colour of the hair, which is light, or flaxen. Then we take the condition of the root, if there is one attached. In this particular hair there is a root. Now, where hairs are shown to have a dry root they have mostly fallen out by themselves. Not always, because, should they be mixed together with hairs with living roots, it means that hair has been pulled out by force, the live hairs taking the dead ones with them. But in this case we need not worry over that, because this particular hair has a living root. Also, if you look carefully, you will see that its sheath has been torn, indicating that the hair has been pulled by force out of the head. The probability is that the hair became caught in the netting base of the Cat skin, and was pulled out either when the head was forced into the mask, or withdrawn.

"Finally, Wilkins, we will examine the other end of the hair—the tip." The scientist looked through the microscope.

"Mark the fact that the tip of the hair, although seemingly cut straight across, is becoming rounded along the edges. We are entitled to say from this that in all probability the owner of the hair visited the barber some two days before this hair came out. A hair cut across by the barber's scissors begins to 'heal' within twenty-four hours, and is more or less rounded again within twenty days.

"Now, Wilkins, you test with Merry the remainder of the hairs in the slides, and be sure to mark each slide as you go along. In the meantime we will try to prove one of the probabilities we have arrived at. The hair we have just examined is a live one."

He telephoned the Burlington hospital and requested the matron to ask Enora if he had visited a barber a short time before he was taken ill, and if so, how long before?

The answer came within a couple of minutes. "Mr. Enora says he had his hair trimmed on the morning of the day previous to his illness," the matron announced.

"Which shows you what a microscope and a little investigation can tell you," the scientist announced to Wilkins. "How are you getting along?"

For reply Sergeant Merry handed the scientist a slip of paper on which was written the measurements of the hairs examined. The entries read:

1/350, 1/350, 1/350, 1/450, 1/450, 1/350, 1/350
1/450, 1/350, 1/350, 1/450, 1/350.

The sergeant made no comment on the tests, but watched the face of his chief. Doctor Manson read them through, and then, as if thinking that he had misread, went back again to the beginning. At the end of the two rows he looked at the face of his deputy, surprise written in his eyes.

"That is an extraordinarily interesting point, Merry," he said.

"So I thought," was the reply.

Before any further comment could be passed, the door opened and Superintendent Jones and Inspector Kenway entered. The fat superintendent passed over a envelope. "In here," he announced.

Doctor Manson passed it over to Merry, who took from it the hairs which Jones had acquired from the head of Enora, at once mounted them on slides and examined them. The newcomers watched the operation in silence. There were six separate hairs, and the slip on which Wilkins recorded the report of Sergeant Merry read 1/350.

Doctor Manson himself then checked up by a personal examination, and then examined carefully the roots of the hairs, and the medulas.

"You can mark the medullary index as 0.132," he announced. "I do not think there is any doubt, all things considered, that the hairs from the mask of the cat skin are those of Enora. In any case, we can say that there are no hairs from any other man to be found in the skin."

Inspector Kenway chuckled, and turned to the scientist. "All along in the train, Doctor, the super has been moaning about plucking the hairs of the Cat. He says what's the difference between a cut hair and one yanked out by the roots."

"None, Kenway," was the reply. "But no scientist worthy of the name will take other than a plucked human hair for the purpose of comparison, which is the reason I wanted Enora's hair. Besides, I wanted to see the roots of the hairs, because I have two or three hairs with roots here."

The superintendent subsided. "Got . . . go, now," he announced. "Got . . . Bradley . . . he's downstairs . . . Got . . . see A.C."

"I'll come along with you, old fat man," said Manson.

The main reason for the visit of Jones and Kenway was that they had been asked to report progress to the Assistant Commissioner at the Yard. The bringing by them of Inspector Bradley had been an afterthought of the two men, principally because the inspector could corroborate several things they had to report, and also because he had asked to come in order that he might be able to see the interior of the great headquarters. The A.C., always willing to welcome executive officers of the outside force, had agreed.

He now greeted his officers and their guest in the room where such conferences always took place; but noted with surprise the appearance of the scientist.

"Hello, Doctor," he announced. "Are you in on this, too? I thought you were busily engaged elsewhere?"

"So I was, Sir Edward," was the rueful reply, "but I'm deeply involved, I fear."

The Assistant Commissioner looked up sharply. He was about to ask the inevitable question, when he caught a warning glance from the scientist, and lapsed into silence.

The four men seated themselves in easy chairs in front of the desk of the Assistant Commissioner. The latter adjusted his ornamental monocle in his perfectly good left eye, and surveyed them.

"Now, let me have it!" he demanded.

For upwards of twenty minutes Superintendent Jones, with interjections from Inspector Kenway, and additional help from Inspector Bradley, detailed the results of the local and Yard inquiries into the death of Miss Norma de Grey. In his staccato, quick-firing phrases he took Sir Edward through the positions on the stage at the time of the death, through the investigations, and on to his conclusions. The Assistant Commissioner listened silently through to the end, and then commented:

"So you plump for Enora, in spite of his denials that he was on the stage, Jones?"

"I do, sir," was the reply. "Alibi . . . other Cat . . . too strong . . . couldn't do it. . . Doctor here admits . . . murder . . . done by Cat," he ended triumphantly.

The A.C. looked across at the scientist. Doctor Manson smiled, rather grimly.

"I did say so—and I still say that there is no possible doubt that the poison was injected into Miss de Grey by the Cat at her feet," he announced slowly, and very distinctly.

"Have you taken Enora into custody, Jones?" asked the A.C.

Before any reply could come from the superintendent, Doctor Manson broke in again.

"I was saying that there is no possible doubt that the poison was injected into Miss de Grey by the Cat at her feet," he said, *"but I did not say that that Cat was Enora. Nor, in fact, was it Enora."*

A startled silence followed the scientist's emphatic announcement. Superintendent Jones sat forward at a precarious angle for a man of his bulk, as though mesmerized. Inspector Kenway was cudgelling his brains in an effort to recall the details of the case they had made against Enora. Inspector Bradley looked as though he could not believe his ears. The Assistant Commissioner looked only at the scientist. He was under no illusions as regards the doctor's ability to justify to the full his pronouncement. He knew from past experience that the statement would not have come was he not able to prove it.

"Why is he not the man who administered the poison, Doctor?" he inquired.

"Were I Sherlock Holmes, Sir Edward, I should say the answer is perfectly simple," he began. "But, in point of fact it is not quite so simple. Enora's story is that he broke off a row with Dick Whittington, and went to his room for a drink, which he knew would be waiting there. The dresser tells us that he always took a drink to the room for Enora to have during that brief wait, and that he did so on this occasion. We checked up with the bar that the drink was fetched.

"So far we are all in agreement. Now, then, Enora says that after taking the drink he felt dizzy, went queer, and the next he knew was waking up and finding himself in hospital. The doctor and the police surgeon say that the man took the dose of poison in his drink, almost certainly in beer, the surgeon added, and that he would be unconscious within two minutes of taking it. Are you all with me, up to this stage?"

There was a chorus of "yes" from the company.

"Right." He turned to the A.C. "Would you ask your sergeant to fetch for me the cat skin from the Laboratory? Merry will know what I mean."

Sir Edward gave the necessary orders, and the scientist continued:

"Next, I want you to recall the things that were found in the dressing-room of Enora—the skin, his day clothes, an under-vest, vaseline, cold cream, a watch—and nothing else. I told Jones and Kenway that there were two things missing from the dressing-room, and that they worried me." He looked across at the officers. "Have you decided what are missing?" he asked.

There was a shaking of heads. At the same time the door opened and a sergeant walked in with the cat skin of Enora. Doctor Manson took it.

"I don't want to have to get into the thing. I think if I can just put it over my back loosely and slip into the head, that will be sufficient."

He did so. The mask came down to the nose and round the cheek-bones, leaving the mouth and lower part of the face of the scientist bare.

"You see," he said, "that in order to allow the wearer to breathe, and to speak distinctly, the mouth and that part of his face below the mouth has to be uncovered. Therefore, the wearer, that is Enora, has to make up his face to imitate the lower part of the face of a cat. He paused, momentarily, and then went on, quietly:

"There was no make-up in the dressing-room. The make-up box, or materials if he did not use a box, were missing. Yet they must have been there at the start, for Enora was made-up. I am not blaming Jones or Kenway, much less Inspector Bradley, for not realizing this; they are not, perhaps, conversant with the requirements of a stage artiste, particularly of the cat tribe.

"But that is not all that was missing. And I think all three of you ought to have seen the other articles. Enora has a drink. Within two minutes he is unconscious, and during those two minutes he is dizzy and lightheaded. *Yet, there was no sign when we examined that dressing-room of either the bottle or the glass from which he had drunk the beer*. Who removed the bottle, glass and the make-up from the room of Enora? And why?

"There is one other point of quite considerable interest in this connection which I am not prepared to divulge at present. It is, however, taken with the others I have just mentioned, quite conclusive proof that Enora was not on the stage during the Highgate Hill scene and could not, therefore, have murdered Miss de Grey."

The Assistant Commissioner was the first to recover from the surprise occasioned by the totally unexpected denouement of the scientist. He leaned forward in his chair and played with the monocle on its long, silken cord, that had not been near his eye for the last five minutes.

"I know your dislike of theorizing, Doctor," he said, "but I feel it would be of some help to Jones, here, if you could give him some idea of what did happen in that dressing-room."

Doctor Manson nodded. "I was about to do so, Sir Edward," he said. "There is no theorizing about it, not in the sense you mean. I have never objected to theorizing when there are facts on which to theorize; my objection is to theorizing and then looking for facts to fit the theory. In this case the facts are, to me, perfectly plain. Somebody doped the drink which Enora always had at that time of the evening. That somebody was very close at hand, for he entered the dressing-room within three minutes of Enora taking the drink. That somebody at once stripped Enora of his skin, if he had not already got out of it for his rub-down, got into the skin and made up the lower part of the face from the make-up box of Enora. Then that somebody, having locked the dressing-room door, played the Highgate Hill scene, left the stage in the excitement of the moment when Miss de Grey was carried off, returned to the dressing-room, stripped off the skin, partly replaced it on Enora, and left the room, taking the make-up box and the bottle and glass.

"The reason for taking the make-up box is obvious; it would necessarily have fingerprints on it. Why the bottle and glass I do not know, except that it may be the person was not sure whether their hands had not come into contact with it during the scurry."

"No idea, Doctor, who it could be?" asked the A.C.

A shake of the head. "None, Sir Edward. It must be obvious, however, that it was somebody who knew the part, and who knew just the moment to do the deed. *They had also access to the theatre, and knew the habits of Enora.*

"By the way, there is just another little corroboration of the fact that the Cat was not Enora. The stage-manager, in describing the scene on Highgate Hill, said that for a moment he had a shock when he could not see the Cat coming on with Miss de Grey. Then he saw him enter from a little farther back-stage. Enora, who had chosen his entrance and had made it at that spot every night throughout the pantomime, would not change it. No artiste would."

Superintendent Jones, recovered from his surprise, now spoke.

"Doctor's right . . . 'course . . . Ought . . . have seen it. . . Only one person fits . . . other cat . . ."

"His alibi," protested Inspector Bradley.

"Alibis are made to be broken, Inspector, as we know very well," said Sir Edward. "What are your views on the second Cat, Doctor?"

"No ideas at all, Sir Edward, I have nothing to show that it was the deputy Cat."

The Assistant Commissioner half rose in his chair. "Then that seems as far as we can go," he announced. "Have you any further suggestions, Doctor?"

Manson thought. Then: "Only one, Sir Edward, and that I have already mentioned—that I would like to know all the background story of Miss de Grey, especially who were her friends. I regard this as most important."

"Kenway . . . seein' . . . that," explained Superintendent Jones, and rose to depart.

At a sign from the Assistant Commissioner, Doctor Manson remained behind after the other officers left the room. The scientist eyed his friend, smilingly.

"This is a rum business, Harry," Sir Edward hazarded. "I notice you didn't mention anything about the fire, so kept silent myself. What is the connection between the fire and this?"

"A very queer one, Edward, and one I dropped on by sheer chance."

He recited the circumstances in which Jones had asked for his help, and the coincidence that he was actually going down to Burlington on that day. He recounted his astonishment on seeing the mink coat of obviously four figure value among the possessions of a provincial pantomime girl.

"Still, Harry, there are many ladies of the stage with similar treasures. I understand that some have gentleman friends who are prepared to fork out in order to associate with ladies of the footlights."

"That I know all about, Edward," was the reply. "But they do not, I take it, all have mink coats which have been reported as totally destroyed in a fur warehouse fire, and on which full insurance has been paid out by an insurance company."

"Good Lord—in the Nottingham warehouse?" asked the Assistant Commissioner.

"So. And what is more, she also had a number of silk dust sheets bearing the label, Silks, Ltd., which were never sold to customers, and which, also, were supposed to have been destroyed in the fire at those premises."

The Assistant Commissioner turned the matter over in his mind. "It might be, of course, Harry, that she, or her boy friend, bought the coat from someone to whom it had been sold by the fur warehouse. What I mean is that the coat might have been removed from the warehouse in preparation for the fire, sold, and then resold quite innocently by the vendor."

"That is precisely why I want to find Miss de Grey's boy friend, Edward. But I have my doubts on the probability of your theory; in fact I might go so far as to venture the opinion that it cannot hold water."

"Why not?"

"Because there was no label inside the coat. Now, if a firm deals in and sells £1,500 mink coats, they are only too proud to acknowledge the fact, and the name of the firm appears on a tag somewhere inside the coat, together with the name of the customer, for identification, and the date of the sale. You have a peep inside the breast-pocket of that handsome-looking coat of yours. Where do you buy your coats, by the way?"

"You've no idea where to look, I suppose?"

"Not the slightest, and I can't ask anybody without revealing the fact that we are making inquiries into the fire, which is just the thing we do not want to do at the present stage. I am relying on Kenway to give me a line."

He paused as though a sudden thought had occurred to him. The Assistant Commissioner watched him in silence for a few moments. Then: "Thought of something?" he asked.

"Yes," agreed Manson. "Yes, I have. A remark made by the manager of the late Silks, Ltd., has given me an idea. I think I'll set about looking into it."

CHAPTER XIII
MR. OPPENHEIMER'S FIRE

THE HAMMERSMITH Fire Brigade received a call at 11.30 on a dark night, and turned out with clanging bells along the road linking Hammersmith with Shepherd's Bush Green, and into the Uxbridge Road, as far down as the junction of that thoroughfare and Montmorency Road. There, round the corner, flames were just starting to shoot through the roof of a two-storey dwelling. Hoses were run out, a ladder pushed up and from above and below firemen played water on the blaze. Little by little the flames died down, until, at last, the fire was officially returned as extinguished.

Now, following the visit of Mr. Redwood, the insurance company's legal representative, to Scotland Yard, and the arrangements made by the Assistant Commissioner and Doctor Manson, the companies had presented to the police a fist of certain premises the contents of which were particularly combustible, and which for no reason that could be given a name the companies viewed with perturbation. Also a request had gone to the heads of the various fire brigades that any fire which broke out in any business premises should at once be notified to the police, without waiting for the extent of it to be ascertained. The report was asked for within as early a time from the call as was physically possible. Thus, at roughly a quarter to twelve on this particular night, Mr. Redwood was telephoned by Scotland Yard and asked whether any of his companies would be interested in a fiery beacon of two-guinea frocks now reaching to the sky through the roof of Modern Gowns, Ltd., of Montmorency Road, Shepherd's Bush.

Mr. Redwood replied that he was intensely interested, so much so that he would be obliged if Scotland Yard would put into effect the arrangements made between the Assistant Commissioner and himself. And he would present himself on the scene at, say, eight o'clock the next morning.

Thus it came about that a guard of the salvage corps was posted round the burned building and its contents, with instructions that nobody was to enter unless they bore a special permit issued by the Assistant Commissioner, or was known to be a police officer not below the rank of inspector. At 7.30 a.m. Mr. Izzy Oppenheimer arrived, having been informed of the fire by a policeman way out in the wilds of his Commercial Road, East, rooms, from which he had, unfortunately, been absent when that same policeman had called earlier in the morning. He was proceeding to enter the premises when a captain of the salvage corps barred the entrance, explaining that nobody was allowed admittance until the police had inspected the place.

Mr. Oppenheimer waved his arms at the captain. "But I am the owner isn't it?" he announced. "All my beautiful frocks have gone. I am ruined."

"Well, sir, you can't bring them back now, can you?" retorted the captain. "And they won't come to any more harm by waiting until the police come. In any case you aren't allowed to go in. And that's that."

Mr. Oppenheimer, dancing like a cat on hot bricks, perambulated up and down the frontage until 8.15 a.m., when there arrived in a black Oldsmobile car Mr. Redwood, Doctor Manson, and Detective-Inspector Makepeace. A second car followed bearing Sergeant Merry and Wilkins, the Laboratory chief assistant.

To this collective assembly Mr. Oppenheimer made his complaint. He did not know the extent of the damage and he had to make an early return to his insurance company according to the conditions of his insurance policy.

"Vy is it I vos not to go into my own shop?" he demanded.

"Nobody is stopping you going into your own shop, Mr. Op-penheimer," announced Mr. Redwood, "and as regards the in-surance, I am representing the insurance company and will take notice of the fact that you have been delayed by official action in making your return. After we have inspected the interior of the premises, you can enter and stay there to your heart's content. Meanwhile, you must remain outside until we send for you."

Leaving the proprietor still moaning his protests, Doctor Manson and Mr. Redwood proceeded to inspect the property from the outside. Its position was not without interest. It occu-pied the second position in the road. The first, or corner shop was empty, and had been so for some time. In consequence of its damaged condition, it had had all the windows boarded up. This, it was explained, had been partly on the request of Mr. Oppenheimer when he had taken the adjoining premises, for, he pointed out, access to this empty premises would make it quite easy for thieves to break through the party wall into his shop, and work their way unseen. The third shop, adjoining the gown shop, although not empty, was a lock-up, used as a laun-dry office. It closed at four o'clock each afternoon. Along the back of all this property ran an engineering works. Only a small yard, some twelve feet deep, separated the shops from the high, walled, back of the works. Doctor Manson surveyed the layout with lively interest.

"An ideal place for a fire to be burning some time before being discovered, Mr. Redwood," he suggested. "Empty prem-ises either side, and a blank wall of other premises unoccupied during the night."

Mr. Redwood agreed. "And a fire within two months of open-ing up in business," he suggested.

The outside survey completed, the two men, accompanied by the inspector, entered the burnt-out shop. Blackened walls sur-rounded them. The interior of the premises had been destroyed completely. The roof, though badly burned, had not fallen, except for a few slates, which had crashed to the ground. Black-ened beams represented all that was left of the ceiling and the room above the shop. On the floor were the ashes of the burnt frocks, with here and there a few pieces of twisted iron, presumably the hooks of the hangers which had held the dresses.

From appearances the fire had been fiercest at the rear of the premises, where the floor itself was badly burned. The fire salvage corps local chief, who had joined the party, expressed the confident view that the blaze had started at that spot. The least destruction was noticable in the large window, across which an iron shutter rolled down for the night protection of the stock. There, some couple of dozen frocks still hung on cardboard heads and shoulders. They were scorched, and bedraggled with water; in fact as much ruined as were those reduced to ashes.

It was at this stage that Mr. Oppenheimer was invited to enter his own ruins. He came in, a look of anxious enquiry on his face. Doctor Manson greeted him.

"Ah, Mr. Oppenheimer. Perhaps you can help us with a reconstruction of the premises," he said. "For instance, what part of the set-up was this little space?" He pointed to what it had been agreed was the original firing point.

"The vorkshop," replied Mr. Oppenheimer, promptly. "Vhere the frocks vas altered vhen they did not fit."

"Do we understand that it was just a part of the shop open to the gaze of the public, then?"

"No, No, No. That is wrong. It had a partition round it, so."

Mr. Oppenehimer drew a diagram on the floor showing where the wooden walls had been.

"I see," said Doctor Manson, thoughtfully. "The frocks were altered and made to fit in there. Were they altered in order that the customer might take them away at once?"

"Yes, yes!"

"So that they would have to be pressed, eh?"

"Pressed?" Mr. Oppenheimer started. "Zat damn' woman. She leave the iron. It make the fire. She left it before, I remember."

"Oh, there was an electric iron, was there?" The scientist carefully sifted through the ash below the burned floor.

Mr. Redwood took up the questioning of the businessman. "Now, about the damage, Mr. Oppenheimer. I represent the insurance company, you know. We have to be very careful of these fires. What stock had you here?"

"I had three hundred frocks wot I sells at two guinea each one. That is six hunderd pounds and six hunderd shillin. That makes—twice six hun—"

"That makes £630," put in Mr. Redwood, helpfully.

"And I had fifty rolls of ze best silk to make more frocks which it came only two day ago."

"Ah. And how much would that be worth a roll, Mr. Oppenheimer?"

"I pay the French firm fourteen pounds a roll and I must make a profit, isn't it?"

"So that is another £700. You did a good trade here then?"

"No. It was not for here I want the silk. It is for another shop I open. I make the frocks here."

"You can, I suppose, produce the evidence of the frocks and the silk?"

Mr. Oppenheimer looked pained, and at the same time agitated. Pained that his word should be doubted, no doubt. The agitation was relieved when he hurried over to a corner of the burnt-out premises and opened a small iron door in a part of the blackened wall. It revealed itself as a wall safe. From it he extracted two or three books and a bundle of invoices. A second helping revealed a sheaf of papers. All were slightly scorched, but otherwise unscathed. With a pleased smile Mr. Oppenheimer hurried back to the waiting company, and displayed them.

They appeared to be a full list of the frocks that had been in the shop the previous day, the invoices of a number of them, and of the silk, together with his day book and ledger. Mr. Redwood expressed some surprise at the very up-to-date list of frocks. "Rather a fortunate circumstance, is it not?" he inquired.

"No, no, mister," protested Mr. Oppenheimer. "I take ze stock each Friday. And then I make up the profits of the week. I take the stock yesterday, see."

"Then you'll show a nice profit this week, Mr. Oppenheimer," said Doctor Manson, brightly. "All the goods sold, so to speak, and no bad debts, eh? Now, about this woman who left the iron burning, or, at least, seems to have done so. Who is she?"

"Rachel Wherner, mister. She will be here on Monday. Her address I do not know."

The scientist looked across at Mr. Redwood, who shook his head. He had been glancing through the books and papers. He now put them into his attaché-case. "I will keep these and check them for the figures, Mr. Oppenheimer," he announced. "You can have them back when we have arrived at the insurable amount of the loss."

Detective-Inspector Makepeace, who had departed on some errand after a whispered conversation with Doctor Manson, returned as Mr. Oppenheimer hurried from the premises and started off down the street. The inspector answered the scientist's unspoken question with a nod.

"I spoke to the supervisor, Doctor, who is taking all calls there herself," he announced. "A police-constable is on the lookout, and will let us know."

Mr. Redwood looked at Manson. "Then you think there is something queer, Doctor?" he asked.

"I feel that the fire has the same characteristics as the seven we discussed some time ago, Mr. Redwood," was the reply. "There is the same fierceness of flame which has destroyed nearly everything. There is the same loneliness of position making it possible for the flames to get a very considerable—in fact, almost a hopeless—hold before there was any likelihood of discovery. Whether it is just chance or design I am not prepared to say, at present. But I propose to make one or two experiments, which may give me data on which to express such an opinion."

He turned to the salvage corps officer. "You know who I am, Captain?"

The man nodded.

"Well, I shall want your help. I want all this ash carefully sifted and weighed. Sergeant Merry, the deputy scientist, will take charge of the operation. Anything which is not definitely ash, but, say, fabric or thread, must be placed on one side, and preserved for examination. But Sergeant Merry will attend to that. What I want from you is a couple of reliable men to do the sifting and the weighing. Meanwhile, there are one or two things to which I will attend myself."

As the salvage officer left in search of his two men, the scientist opened out the Box of Tricks which Merry had fetched from the police car. From it he extracted a number of white envelopes made from druggists' surfaced paper, a sharp knife, and a medical scalpel.

With a hogs-hair brush, also taken from the Box of Tricks, he swept clear of debris a portion of the floor near where it had burnt through at what seemed to be the origin of the fire. From the edges he cut a number of slivers of the charred wood, placing them in one of the envelopes, which he at once sealed and labelled, obtaining the signature of Mr. Redwood as to the contents and the place from which they had been cut.

He then moved to another portion of the floor, where the same procedure was enacted, the slivers going into a separate envelope, also labelled and initialled. Finally, with the scalpel he scraped a quantity of the soot from the beams of the ceiling immediately above the burned floor, and a further quantity from each of the four corners of the shop. These exhibits, too, were sealed in the envelopes and a record made of their location.

He placed the envelopes in the Box of Tricks and was about to close the case when a thought apparently occurred to him. Taking a larger envelope he filled it with a quantity of ash from the floor. A pair of letter scales on which he weighed the package showed that it contained three ounces of ash.

"That can be added on to the weight of the bulk," he told Merry; and putting the envelope with the others, closed the case and carried it to the car.

Detective-Inspector Makepeace, who had watched these operations with no little interest, turned at a touch on his shoulder to find a police-constable waiting. The man whispered to him, and the inspector, with a word to the scientist, hurried away. He returned in a few minutes. Doctor Manson looked inquiringly. The inspector nodded.

"He made a call, Doctor," he announced. "Royalty 07765. He said, 'there has been an accident'. I'll get the subscriber from Royalty exchange, shall I?"

Doctor Manson nodded.

"There was one curious circumstance, however," the inspector added, "I don't know whether it has any significance. When he first answered the call for the number wanted, he said 'Royalty 05545'. Told there was no reply he said he was sorry, he'd made a mistake, and the number was Royalty 07765. That was where he gave the message."

Doctor Manson looked up with marked interest. "It may very well have a significance, Inspector," he said. "It looks as though Mr. Oppenheimer might have made a slip."

The scientist waited only long enough to see Merry and Wilkins begin their task of sifting the ashes, before leaving with Mr. Redwood and the inspector for the return to Scotland Yard.

Arrived at headquarters the inspector proceeded at once to contact the Royalty exchange. Royalty 07765 was, he was told, down in the telephone directory in the name of Mr. Raoul da Costa, who had a flat in Cumberland Court, South Kensington. The number Royalty 05545 was not connected.

"Then," said Doctor Manson, "it seems a good move, Inspector, to find out all we can about Mr. da Costa. Where is the flat now vacant situated?"

"Between Kensington and Knightsbridge."

"Perhaps we had better have a look at that place, too, and ascertain if Mr. da Costa was there at any time, and why he left."

CHAPTER XIV
SIX POINTS OF A RIDDLE

DOCTOR MANSON entered his laboratory. He placed the Box of Tricks on the table which was his own special part of the large main room. He took off his jacket and donned the long white coat which he usually wore when making a chemical analysis, a microscopic examination, or a forensic toxological experiment.

After a glance round the room—a satisfied glance as he saw the great laboratory which he had himself built up—he sat down to consider the problem with which the morning's work in Shepherd's Bush had provided him.

The scientist was a puzzled man.

For the space of a quarter of an hour he lay slouched back in his armchair, his eyes closed and his fingers beating a tattoo on the arms. They had not ceased their drumming when he pulled himself to an upright position, and, lifting a sheet of paper from a drawer, proceeded to tabulate his problem. That, in itself, showed the mental concern of the scientist, for he possessed an extraordinarily tidy mind, which grasped and retained in correct order of importance and sequence the points of any investigation upon which he was engaged. Rarely, indeed, had he recourse to any notes. Now, however, he proceeded to write a series of questions to which an answer had to be found:

(1) Was the fire at Shepherd's Bush accidental, or incendiary?
(2) Were the seven fires into which he had already inquired accidental or incendiary?
(3) Was there any connection between these fires in six widely-spread towns?
(4) What was the implication, at the Shepherd's Bush fire, of the telephoned message, 'There has been an accident'?
(5) What was the connection of Mr. da Costa with the Shepherd's Bush fire?
(6) What was the connection, if any, of the fires with Miss Norma de Grey, the pantomime star found murdered?

After considering his list Doctor Manson decided to scrap for the moment problem one, and start with numbers two and three.

Were seven fires accidental or incendiary and was there any connection between the fires in six widely separated towns?

Quietly the scientist reviewed the information gleaned during his visits to the towns, and the statements made by the officers of the police forces and fire brigades. It was, of course, true that the majority of the places had been burned completely out. That is what had attracted his suspicions even before he had seen any of the buildings. But that, in itself, was not proof that incendiarism was involved. The stock in all the shops was of a peculiarly inflammable nature. If a collection of silk dresses became involved in a fire, they would not only burn right out very quickly, but would feed the flames with combustible fuel. The same thing applied to a shop full of gowns.

Against this, the scientist put the example of the Sheffield fire which destroyed the premises and the stock of a drapers and outfitters. Now, included in the loss were a number of bales of cloth—dress lengths. These, the scientist was assured, were a charred mass. It was, he argued, a particularly efficient conflagration that could burn through wrapped bales of cloth; as efficient as one which could burn through rolls of paper. The exclusion of air from between the layers would have the effect of extinguishing the flames attacking the rolls; the first half-dozen of the layers might be badly scorched or charred, but not the complete bale. If, however, the bales had first been soaked in some combustible liquid—then there would be a different story to tell.

The doctor, however, had no evidence on which to go, since no examination had been made of the remains of the fire. The next suspicious aspect was the position of the buildings, and the fact that in each case the conditions of locality and the shuttering made it fairly certain that the fires in each case could not have been discovered from the outside until the flames had gained such a hold that there was little chance of them being extinguished, in view of the highly combustible nature of the contents.

Was this chance—or design? Imitation could not be left out of the reckoning, supposing that the fires were incendiary. None knew better than Chief Detective-Inspector Doctor Manson, that a successful crime of a particular nature, reported in the newspapers, will be copied up and down the country by other miscreants. And even if a fire is an accidental one, revelations of its success under certain conditions are invariably copied by someone who *wants* a successful fire.

Were these just copy fires, or were they deliberately planned as a scheme to take huge sums of money from the insurance companies? If so, were they to go on?

The scientist realized that such a conclusion necessitated the theory that there was some mastermind at work with a gang, for the fires not only needed clever organizing, but considerable capital to purchase businesses and stock. All the businesses which had been under investigation had changed hands quite recently—that is, recently in relation to the time of the fire.

That was one of the most suspicious circumstances in connection with the fires—that although the businesses had in the main been in existence for a number of years without any fire claim against the insurance companies, save in the case of one of them, within a few weeks of their changing proprietors there was not only a claim but a claim for total loss. It seemed straining coincidence to its limit to assume them as all of accidental origin.

The only other real point of suspicion he possessed was one which linked up with Miss de Grey, and that brought the scientist to the sixth point he had tabulated: What was the connection, if any, of the fires with Miss Norma de Grey?

Articles from two of the fires, and on which insurance had been paid, were in the possession of the pantomime star. One of the articles was of such value as made it virtually impossible for her to have purchased it from her earnings on the stage. Who had given it to her? How had he obtained it? Was he someone who had an active interest in the fires, and had contrived to obtain the fur coat before the fire in the knowledge that insurance would be paid out on its loss?

Doctor Manson, turning these questions over in his mind, came to the conclusion that they could not be answered until he had Inspector Kenway's report on the life story of Miss de Grey. He turned, accordingly, to points four and five: The telephoned message, 'There has been an accident', and the name of the man to whom the message was presumably sent—Mr. da Costa, who was the tenant of the telephone over which the message had been received.

At this stage of the proceedings, however, nothing could be gained by speculating on the mysterious message or stranger until something more was known about both of them. The scientist waited for the inspector's report on the flat in Cumberland Court, South Kensington, and into the strange request of Mr. Oppenheimer for another number—in a flat unoccupied.

That left only one of his tabulated points—the first one: Was the fire at Shepherd's Bush accidental or incendiary? At this stage Doctor Manson, for the first time, showed something like animation. Here, he said to himself, was something tangible. Up to now he had been, if not theorizing, at least doing something very near to it. All he had to judge from the other fires were *ex parte* statements; in Shepherd's Bush he had something more solid upon which to go. He turned to the solid now.

From the Box of Tricks he took out one of the envelopes which contained the slivers of wood cut from the floor of the shop in the Bush. Two of the pieces he slipped into a wide-mouthed flask. Corking the flask he put it into a container, and covered it with water. The container was then placed over a Bunsen burner, the flame of which was lighted.

Leaving the water to heat in the Bunsen flame, Doctor Manson next extracted from the Box of Tricks one of the envelopes containing the soot scraped from the blackened walls of the premises. He scattered a little on to a porcelain tile, and examined it under a lens. The inspection seemed to afford him no little interest, for presently he dipped a finger into the edge of the soot, and rubbed a fraction between finger and thumb, afterwards examining the stains on his finger.

It was at this stage that Sergeant Merry returned from Shepherd's Bush and his job of supervising the sifting of the ash contents of the burned-out premises. He carried over an arm the dozen or so frocks which had been left in the window. Bedraggled they were, and scorched, but not destroyed. The scientist eyed them, and nodded assentingly.

"I see you've got the idea, Jim," he remarked.

Merry smiled—and looked at the flask. "Any result from that?" he asked.

Doctor Manson slipped a clinical thermometer into the water, and examined the markings. It registered just over 70 degrees Centigrade. He lifted out the flask with a pair of wooden holders, and grasping it between the folds of an asbestos cloth, gently eased the stopper from the neck, and sniffed.

There was a faint, oily smell.

"Paraffiny?" suggested Merry.

Doctor Manson nodded. He marked the result of the experiment on the outside of the envelope containing the remaining slivers of wood, and then placed the envelope in his drawer in the laboratory table.

The second stage in the tracing of suspicions on the Shepherd's Bush fire began with the remains of soot which the scientist had already examined under his lens. A portion was now dropped into a small test tube and to it was added a quantity of distilled water, the mixture being shaken. The two scientists peered closely for a moment at the result. After a conference the tube was placed slightly above the light of a gas jet and gently heated, after which it was again shaken.

Satisfied at the result, Doctor Manson next filtered the mixture through a piece of pure filter paper into a second tube. Wilkins, the Laboratory assistant, who had now entered the room, stood with questioning glance at the test tube. Doctor Manson, looking up, caught the glance.

"Soot, which you saw me take from the walls of the premises, Wilkins," he explained. "We are testing it for what it can tell us."

"And what do you expect it to tell, Doctor?" was the query.

The scientist laid the tube aside, and turned to his assistant.

"It may tell quite a lot, Wilkins," he replied. "Certain substances—we won't specify for the moment what substances—contain various ingredients such as metals, gases, or other properties which chemistry can analyse. Now, when those substances are burnt, the properties in them are never destroyed—there is very little of anything that is entirely consumed by fire leaving no trace, which is what most criminals do not, thank goodness, know. Soot, for instance, can contain various elements which were in the substance the burning of which caused the soot to accumulate in the form of carbon on the walls. Soot left by the flame of a candle, for instance, will contain paraffin.

"Now this"—he held up the filtered mixture—"is a small quantity of the soot from Shepherd's Bush boiled up with water. I am about to divide it into three parts"—he did so—"and to one part I shall add a few drops of this hydrochloric acid. Watch it carefully to see what happens . . . well?"

"There is a small precipitate at the bottom," announced the assistant.

"So? Then the precipitate from this experiment must contain either one or more of three metals—lead, silver, or mercury. We must, therefore, identify it more exactly."

"How are we to do that, Doctor?"

For reply, the scientist poured off the liquid, leaving the precipitate, and then added a drop or two more of hydrochloric acid, shaking the mixture, and again dividing it from the precipitate.

"Now," he explained, "I shall shake the contents with ammonia, and one of three things is likely to happen—either the precipitate dissolves, in which case it is composed of silver chloride, or it blackens, indicating the presence of mercury, or it remains unchanged . . ." He shook the tube . . .

"Which it does," he added, and turned a serious face towards Sergeant Merry.

"And that means?" asked Wilkins.

"That the precipitate is in all probability lead," was the reply.

Wilkins looked inquiry, and Doctor Manson smiled, grimly.

"The point we have proved, Wilkins," he emphasized, "is that there is lead in the soot. Now, the only substance I can recall which would produce lead-laden soot is—"

"Petrol," put in Merry. "Because petrol contains in these days Tetra-Ethyl, and there is lead in that."

"Phew!" whistled Wilkins. "Then since this was a dress shop the petrol could only have been introduced for an ulterior motive."

"It looks that way, I agree," said Doctor Manson. "But it doesn't altogether follow. Mr. Oppenheimer might say, for instance, that he kept petrol for cleaning fabrics which became soiled, and that might well be a reasonable explanation. Perhaps we may know a little more about the petrol when you and Sergeant Merry have carried out similar tests of the ash debris we brought back with us. Try ash from the various parts of the building, Merry," he requested.

While the sergeant and Wilkins went to work on the debris, the doctor turned his attention to the day book and the stock sheets left by Mr. Redwood. He scrutinized the writing through a lens, taking entries from various pages. Not satisfied, he examined various of the entries through his microscope. Neither, apparently, did this bring any satisfactory explanation to his mind.

His next move was to take a pipette and, loading it with a solution of dipyridyl, he let a drop fall on one of the ink strokes of the writing at the beginning of the book. Allowing about a minute to elapse, he then recovered the reagent with a piece of filter paper. The filter paper he next placed on the stage of an Osborn comparison microscope, which was then fitted with Lovibond's tintometer glasses. Through this combination the doctor examined closely the filtered drop.

He repeated the experiment with filterings from various other parts of the day book and sheets, until he had made notes of some thirty entries. These he proceeded to tabulate on a sheet of foolscap paper.

It was at this stage that Sergeant Merry called him over to the small laboratory table, on which he and Wilkins had been carrying out the experiments with the ash debris. The table was littered with test tubes, all labelled and marked with the results of various tests. The sergeant stood regarding them with puzzled eyes. Doctor Manson regarded the furrowed brows of his deputy.

"Something wrong, Merry?" he asked.

"Something curious, Doctor," was the reply. He indicated his note-book.

"We have separated iron, wood ash, silk and textile, a variety of metals which one would associate with the contents of a destroyed interior. That is all well and good. But I've also found something else."

"What else?" asked Manson.

"I don't know. I can't separate it." The sergeant described the reagent used which had produced the precipitate, and then placed the latter under his microscope for the scientist to inspect.

Doctor Manson's examination, however, was no more successful than that of his deputy. At the end of an intensive search through the lenses for some five minutes, and comparison with preserved specimens of metals on slides taken from the cabinets in the laboratory, he confessed himself beaten.

"We had better put it through the spectroscope, Merry," he announced. "That may give us a clue."

Now, the spectroscope is the greatest detective known to man. It found helium in the sun many years before it was discovered on earth. It is the spectroscope that has enabled scientists to say of what matter the sun, the moon, and the planets are composed. The principle can be roughly described. Every metal heated to incandescence gives off its own distinctive colour, which never varies. Thus, a scientist who heated iron to incandescence and threw its rays through the prism of a spectroscope would see thrown up the colours of incandescent iron. If, on pointing the spectroscope at the sun, he saw reflected the same colours (among scores of others) he would know that there is iron in the sun. This is a very rough and ready explanation, but it will suffice to illustrate the experiments by which Doctor Manson hoped to identify the mysterious substance discovered in the ash debris from the Shepherd's Bush fire.

In the course of the years scientists have listed the colours of the various metals when thus heated, and it is (to a scientist) a fairly simple matter to identify any metal by heating it as described, and putting its constant spectrum through the spectroscope. There are, still, a number of colours, however, which have no known name—they are still unknown metals.

Accordingly the Doctor and Merry proceeded to test the metal precipitate. Heated as required for the test, it was projected through the instrument. *Two indigo lines showed up on the screen, as its characteristic spectrum colour,* and in a certain wavelength.

Reference to the compiled spectrum list revealed the metal to be indium.

"Indium?" queried Merry. "What the deuce is that? I've never heard of it."

He produced a book on metallurgy, and turning to its reference, read it out:

"Indium: a rare element occurring in certain zinc ores, is a silvery, very soft metal. It is unacted upon by air or boiling water, but burns to its sesquioxide when heated in air."

"Now how the devil does *that* stuff come in the place?" he asked.

"Blessed if I know," retorted Doctor Manson. He looked through the notes of his deputy, made during the tests. They showed the separation of a number of substances.

"Looks as if the stuff was mixed with petrol and oil. Does that convey anything to you, Merry?" he asked.

"Not a thing, Doctor. Incidentally, the mixture was dirty."

"Well, we'll have to find out something about it. Ring up a metallurgist, and see what he can suggest. Now, I think that is all, with the exception of one thing."

His eyes caught sight of the collection of frocks which Merry had brought back from Shepherd's Bush. "And that's it," he concluded.

Then followed what was to Wilkins a curious performance. The frocks were carried to the flat roof of the Yard and there placed in a large metal bin. Merry poured a portion of petrol mixed with oil over them, and they were then set on fire. When burnt out, the ashes were sprayed with water, gathered together and weighed.

The weight of the twelve dresses was compared, in quantitative analysis, with the weight of the ash representing the three hundred dresses which Mr. Oppenheimer stated were in the burned building, plus the bales of silk, and plus the debris from the burned interior. Doctor Manson regarded the figures with no little interest. And so did Sergeant Merry.

"We'll have to work out a ratio, Merry," the scientist announced, "but I don't like the look of it at the moment."

At that moment the door of the laboratory opened, and the head of Inspector Kenway appeared round the jamb, followed a moment later by the body of the same. He saw Merry. "Doctor in, Merry?" he asked, and then saw the figure of the scientist.

"Oh, there you are," he added. "Got something funny for you. You know I've been tracing the past life of Miss de Grey?" Doctor Manson nodded.

"Well, I got the address of her flat in Town, and on getting back a little while ago blew round to the address to see what I could hunt up there. Who do you suppose I found there?"

"Not the least idea," said Manson. "I'm a scientist—not a thought reader."

"Well, I found Inspector Makepeace there nosing round. It seems your Mr. Oppenheimer telephoned some number to give a message and there was no answer, the 'phone having been disconnected. Then he 'phoned another number, saying he'd made a mistake. Makepeace said he'd come along to see what connection the first number had with a Mr. da Costa—he's the gent Oppenheimer 'phoned to."

Manson nodded again. "I know all that, Kenway," he announced.

"Yes, but here's what you don't know. The flat I found Makepeace mooning into, the flat with the number Oppenheimer first asked for, was the one which Miss de Grey, of Dick Whittington fame, had occupied. And the janitor fellow didn't know a Mr. da Costa. See."

Manson stared.

"That's a very peculiar circumstance, Kenway," he said.

Chapter XV
FIRST CLUES

APART FROM his surprising announcement on Miss de Grey's flat, Inspector Kenway had not learned a great deal about the pantomime star's private life. And what he *had* discovered, it seemed to him, did not throw much light on the riddle of her death. He had searched in vain for anything that would link her with the second Cat (since Doctor Manson's pronouncement had wiped out altogether the first Cat as the murderer.) But nothing had come to light which provided any trace of association between Miss de Grey and the second Cat prior to their meeting at Burlington-on-Sea. On the contrary, Kenway had begun to doubt whether Miss de Grey even knew the second Cat at all. He had never appeared on the stage with her, and was hardly ever in the theatre once the curtain had gone up for the evening's performance, when he knew that he was not likely to be called upon.

The inspector had begun his backwards search with the *Dick Whittington* company, who were still at the Old Sussex Theatre. Notified of his intention to question them once more, the members of the cast had assembled in the Circle Bar of the theatre at the convenient hour of eleven o'clock in the morning. It was the last fortnight of the run of the piece and as they waited they talked among themselves of the not-far-distant future.

It is brave talk, this chatter of theatrical people when the 'notice has gone up' of the end of the tour, especially if the show is a pantomime, and the artistes are past the bloom of theatrical youth. *Pagliacci* is acted more often, and more poignantly, off the stage than it is *on* the Boards. For, when the curtain rings down for the last time on pantomime, there begins the tragic search for work of the little artiste that is heartbreaking in its hopelessness; for pantomime comes but once a year, and makes jobs plentiful even for those of little talent.

You would not think so from the words and the poses of the artistes in the company of their fellows on these last nights. The mask is on the faces; the make-believe in the care-free carriage. Nobody is ever going to be 'resting', the theatrical euphemism for being out of a job. The names of The Great in production are bandied around familiarly. The little knockabout, who is just terrible, will pat a pocket and announce that Jack Hylton has approached him with an offer. The chorus lady of fifty, haggard behind her paint, talks of Mr. Cochran. Nobody believes a word of it, of course, but nobody ever says so, save when, outside, some sympathetic soul will comment: "Poor little devil, she'll never get another part."

It was this way with the *Dick Whittington* company as they talked in the bar while awaiting the arrival of Inspector Kenway. The Mate stood by the Demon King. "Fixed up anything, old man?" he inquired.

Mr. Frederick Barnson straightened his tie, and examined the fake diamond ring on his finger. "Not exactly, old boy," he announced. "I'm not in any hurry. Reckon I'll take a bit of a holiday first. Got three good offers, mind you. Question which I'll take. Thank God I'm not one of the kind who plays panto, and for the rest of the year has to hang round Hippodrome corner waiting for somebody to drop dead." (He had stood on that heartbreak corner, and made the daily round of the agents' offices for three months before Mr. de Benyat had given him the Demon King.)

"I've a little part in drama," announced the manager, Mr. Castle. "Suits me. I used to do 'if its' in the Rhondda valley."

"If its? Whatever are they?" asked the Fairy Queen.

Mr. Castle smiled reminiscently. "If it comes in, you get it," he announced succinctly. "Fit-up was the real name. Sometimes we'd carry our own scenery and play *A Royal Divorce* at the town hall to £2 10s. gross, on which we'd send out for fish and chips all round, have a sumptuous repast in the throne-room scene, and sleep on the dress-baskets in the dressing-rooms. Then, next day, we'd walk or cadge rides to our next date, if any. Those were the days, laddie."

The Captain scratched a puzzled head. "Blimey," he said. "No legit, for me. Now, in my game you ain't never stuck. There's panto, halls revue, concert party with a bit of busking on the sands, circus, fêtes, all grist to the mill, me old china. Even done crowd work at Elstree? I ain't never been flat on me pat yet."

"You have 'em, if you likes." The words came from the wardrobe mistress. "I was born in a portable theatre—and one of the best of them, too. My mother was playing leading lady, providing four baskets of wardrobe, costume and modern, and doing six plays a week with a 'laughable farce' thrown in, for thirty-five shillings a week. Yes, indeed, she lived well and reared four children on it—and kept her wardrobe up to date from the second-hand stores, *and* saved five shillings a week. Had to. She wasn't always working. Oh yes, I played kids' parts at a shilling a night, anything from Poor Joe in *Bleak House* to *East Lynne*. I sold chocolates between the acts; used to make three shillings a week that way, so Mother saved my money, too.

"Mind you, we'd get diggings for us all at six or seven shillings a week, and food was cheap—rabbits fourpence and sixpence each, butter sixpence a pound, eggs twenty-four for a shilling, bacon threepence a pound, and stewing meat fourpence. Mother always saw to it that we had plenty to eat. She'd come from rehearsal and cook by the time we came home from school. Oh yes, she saw we had some schooling of sorts.

"Then, I used to write out her parts from scripts, so I could read and write and recite all Shakespeare's plays. We were happy, too. Little pleasures meant big things to me, such as a new hat or a quarter of sweets. Those were the days."

Alderman FitzWarren cleared his throat, and addressed the Fairy. "Of course my side of the Profession would interest you the most since you study music, my dear," he said. "The true art, if I may say so—Opera. Yes, yes, it's a long journey from this travesty of a theatre to the Opera House, Milan. The theatre crowded with famous people, with gay, sparkling women struck to awed silence as the curtain rises on *Tosca*. And on towards the end where Cavaradossi bids farewell to love and life and walks to his death. The curtain falls, and the house rises to its feet and acclaims the hero—'Cavaradossi, brava, brava'. That is success, my dear. Then one has lived, indeed."

"Oh, Mr. James"—the Fairy looked her adoration—"I had no idea you had sung Cavaradossi in Milan."

"I didn't, my dear. I was in the back row of the chorus."

The chatter was interrupted by the entrance of Inspector Kenway. He apologized for bringing them to the theatre in the morning leisure hours.

"The fact is," he explained, "we feel that the cause of Miss de Grey's death may lie somewhere in her earlier life. Perhaps some of you who knew her, or of her, may be able to help us. We would welcome any information of any kind." He looked at the Glee Brothers.

The Mate shook a head. "No, Inspector, it's no use looking at me," he said. "I never saw her before this show. And we didn't get much chance to know her, then. Nobody was very friendly with her. Right from the first rehearsal she showed us where we got off. Blimey, you'd have thought she owned the bloomin' show. In fact one or two of the lads still think she had some spondulicks in it. I think Mrs. Wilson, the wardrobe mistress, was in a show with her once, though."

The wardrobe mistress nodded. "Yes, that's right," she agreed. "I did know Miss de Grey before this show. She was playing a small part in the *Sunshine Girl*, and I was wardrobe mistress there, too. She wasn't liked in that show, either, because of her airs and graces."

"Did you know anything about her, Mrs. Wilson?" asked Kenway.

"Well, I don't like to speak ill of the dead. All I'll say is that she wasn't living on her salary."

"In other words she had a friend, eh?"

The woman smiled. "Yes, sir, she had a gentleman friend. He was dressing her up to the nines, as the saying goes."

"Did you know who he was?"

"No. I didn't know his name. I saw him, though, when he called for her at the stage door in Manchester. He had a big black car."

"What was he like?"

"Oh, tall chap, quite nice he seemed—too nice for my lady, I thought. He was a good-looking fellow, I should say he was a foreigner. Had light hair. He gave the stage-doorkeeper ten shillings to tell Miss de Grey he was waiting for her."

"Was that the only time you saw him?"

"Only time I saw him, yes. But he came to see her at several places. Once she got permission to travel to the next date by road instead of by the usual train call. She arrived on the Monday too late for the show, and got the push—you know, the sack. I was surprised to see her playing Boy for Henri. Shouldn't have thought he'd have taken her, though she was good-looking, and had a nice figure."

The wardrobe mistress added that she didn't have any trouble with Miss de Grey. The girl had her own dresser who looked after her, so she didn't clash with her. Pressed to recall anything else she might have known about the star, Mrs. Wilson remembered that a girl in the other show said that Miss de Grey had a mother living in Manchester, but nobody seemed to know much about Miss de Grey's private life more than that.

Miss Prue, questioned, could only add to the knowledge by stating that she thought that the gentleman friend mentioned by the wardrobe mistress must still have been a friend, because there was a photograph of a handsome gentleman on her dressing table at Burlington. "At least," said Miss Prue, "it was there the first week, then it vanished."

"Do you mean somebody took it?" asked Kenway.

"Oh no. If they had she'd have raised hell, sir. I mean she put it away somewhere. I thought at the time it might have been her husband, and she didn't want gentlemen visitors to know that she was married. I knew, of course, from the clothes she wore that she must have some private means."

"What about you, Mr. Lancy?" The inspector eyed the deputy Cat, interestedly. Here, he knew, was the principal suspect. Kenway was, indeed, at a loss to understand why it was that the deputy Cat was still at liberty. The Doctor had agreed that it was the Cat who had poisoned Miss de Grey. He had stated that it wasn't Enora, the Cat. Since there were only the two of them it was obvious that Mr. Lancy was the man. Why the doctor was waiting, he could not understand, unless it was that he had not any direct evidence sufficient to guarantee a conviction. It was true, of course, that if evidence lacking fact were given, then the accused man might easily be acquitted, and could not then be again brought up for trial even if fresh evidence were subsequently obtained. No man can be put in peril of his life twice on the same charge. Inspector Kenway, accordingly, waited with lively interest for anything that Lancy might say.

"Me?" queried the Cat. "Never heard of the bitch before this show. Never knew her even in this show. Never met her."

"Never met her. You're in the company."

"Mebbe, but I still say I never met her. I was only a walking understudy, and never appeared with her at all. And I don't want to be mixed up with her now, see."

The inspector started to make some reply, but changed his mind, and lapsed into silence. No other member of the company could add anything to the little he had gained in the interviews. He wished them good morning.

Kenway's next visit was to Mr. Joe Davis. Joe was a theatrical agent, with a small office in Soho. It was Joe who had sent Miss de Grey to Mr. Henri de Benyat, with the intimation that she could put a bit of money in any show for which she was engaged. Joe admitted the impeachment to the inspector.

"Sure, that's right, Inspector," he announced. "Money wasn't any good to me, cos I don't produce shows, see. But I had me ten per cent out of what Benyat paid her. How did I get hold of her?"

His story was straightforward enough. He had picked her out at an audition for show girls. She couldn't do anything but she looked good, and anyway, all he wanted were show girls at that time. He was engaging them for a revue in the provinces.

Asked where he communicated with her, he replied that he wrote to her at the Cats' Home.

"The Cats' Home?" Inspector Kenway looked bewildered.

Mr. Davis chuckled. "Name the Profesh calls a theatrical girls' club," he explained. "Place for chorus girls, really. They can live there pretty cheaply, and most of 'em use it when they're resting. Well, I sent her to Henri, and I haven't had much to do with her since."

The matron of the theatrical club could add little more. She believed that Miss de Grey came originally from Lancashire, but thought one of the girls now in the club might know more. She had been a bit friendly with Miss de Grey.

The girl, Marion Strange, a chorus lady, agreed that Miss de Grey had come from Manchester. She had, she said, run away from home to go on the stage, and had started in the chorus before becoming a show girl. Then she got a small part in a musical comedy on tour. She had appeared in several other little parts, and then, said Miss Strange, she met a gentleman friend. He had financed a small, but expensive, flat in Kensington for her. Since then, Miss Strange announced, she had not seen much of Miss de Grey, whom she had known as just Norma Grey. She had read that she was playing Boy in *Dick Whittington*, and wondered what kind of a job she'd make of it.

The problem of the Kensington flat gave Inspector Kenway a headache. He could find no Norma Grey in the telephone book. It was not until he telephoned Burlington police that he obtained a clue to it. The Burlington inspector visited the girl's diggings in the town. Where, he asked the landlady, had Miss de Grey written from when booking the rooms? After some searching, the woman was able to produce a letter giving a Kensington address. This the inspector telephoned to Kenway.

On arriving at the address he was staggered to find Inspector Makepeace already making inquiries at the block. He was even more surprised to hear that the inspector's inquiries were directed to a telephone call to a man.

"Sounds to me like the gentleman friend," he announced.

"Gentleman friend," echoed Makepeace. "What's all this about, anyway?"

After comparing notes the two interviewed the porter together. That worthy agreed that a Miss de Grey had occupied flat number 27. Very nice person she was, on the stage. He had heard of her death, and was very sorry indeed to hear it.

She had, he said, vacated the flat a week before the tragedy. The furniture had been removed on her written instructions. She had given written notice of her intention to give up the flat a week before that—in Christmas week, he thought—and then a van had come for the furniture, the driver of which had produced a letter from her. The van, he thought, came from Barings.

"Gentleman friend? Well, gentlemen, I do know that she had a gentleman caller sometimes. Rather foreign-looking gentleman he was, tall gentleman, and good-looking in a foreign sort of way, if you get me."

He did not know his name, said the man, never having heard it, and he had not seen him since Miss de Grey had left.

"Better go and see Barings, and find out what happened to the furniture," suggested Inspector Makepeace.

Inspector Kenway shook his head.

"I think perhaps not," he rejoined. "I think we'd better tell the doctor first, and see what he says about it."

"Why?"

"Well, as I see it, Makepeace, there's a link-up here. I come to this flat on a hunt into Miss de Grey. I find you here, on a hunt about a fire. I don't know whether you know it, but Doctor Manson is working on a series of fires. If we go messing about with the furniture in this flat we might be getting in his way. Apparently your man made a slip-up in asking for the telephone number of this flat first. The Doctor might not want the man to know that we are on to this flat."

Doctor Manson, told of the decision, nodded warm approval. "You did very well, Kenway," he said. "It would, as it happens, have been a fatal move. I do not know, as yet, how far Mr. da Costa is mixed up with the fire at Shepherd's Bush, and I do not know whether he is concerned at all with the other fires, but any inquiries into the whereabouts of the furniture would in all probability have put him on his guard. We can, I think, assume that the furniture was his, or at least he had paid for it, and that it has probably gone back to his charge, now that Miss de Grey is dead."

He thought over the points of the interviews which the inspector had had with the *Dick Whittington* company. "I should think that the pair had broken off their relationship," he said, "and that the break dated from the time Miss Prue missed the photograph of the handsome gentleman from the dressing table of Miss de Grey in the Burlington theatre. The date would seem to agree with the time that Miss de Grey gave notice to vacate the flat, if she had lost the financial support of Mr. da Costa, she obviously couldn't keep up the rent of the flat. Is there any other point in the talks you have had which suggests anything to you?" he concluded.

"Only one thing, Doctor. And that is Lancy, the second Cat. He was violently bitter against Miss de Grey. Called her a bitch. But what excited my interest was his saying that he had never known her, and that he had never met her in the show."

"What worries you about that, Kenway?"

"Well, Doctor, we know that Enora did not play the Cat on Highgate Hill that night, don't we? So Lancy *must* have been playing. . . ."

Doctor Manson regarded the inspector thoughtfully.

"Does it not occur to you, Kenway, that Lancy does not know that we are aware that Enora was not on the stage in the High-gate Hill scene; that he thinks we are under the delusion that he *was* on the stage? Nobody, except us, is aware that it was impossible for Enora to have been playing the part. The entire company knew that Bradley had stationed two plainclothes men at the bedside of the man, and I suppose they still believe that Enora is virtually under arrest, and will be arrested when he is able to leave hospital."

"You mean that the company are probably under the delusion that Enora poisoned Miss de Grey, and then dashed up to his room and tried to commit suicide by poisoning himself, and didn't take enough stuff?" asked Kenway.

Doctor Manson considered the question carefully before he replied. "I think it quite possible, Kenway," he said at last. "Except for one person, maybe two, but more probably a single one—*the one who removed the greasepaint and the bottle that had contained beer, and the glass that went with it, from the dressing-room of Enora.*"

CHAPTER XVI
INK AND ASHES

NOW, INK IS a weapon fraught with menace to bad men. The adage of a worldly father to his son, come of age, about saying what you like to a lady but never putting it into writing, is pro-verbial. But that refers only to the laws of evidence. That is the least of the perils of ink. There are also the gentlemen who tell your character from your writing. Unpleasant, sometimes, but not a menace. The peril of the use of ink is not so much in the writing *with* it as in the writing *in* it. For inked words in the hands of a forensic chemist can reveal all kinds of unpleasant things that the writer fondly hoped, and certainly expected, would remain for ever hidden.

The forger who takes out one figure and substitutes another is doomed; the ink will give him away. The fraudulent heir who maintains that the will under which he is benefiting was made six years ago is like to be gaoled by a learned man who talks to the judge and jury of the oxidation of ferrous iron in ink, or the diffusion of sulphates.

The point was well illustrated by Doctor Manson's explanation of certain proved facts to the conference which the Assistant Commissioner (Crime) called in order to learn what progress had been made in the crime at Burlington, and whether the apparent link-up with the fires had been strengthened, or disproved.

At the request of Doctor Manson, Mr. Redwood, of the insurance societies, had been invited to be present at the conference—a little unusual, Sir Edward had suggested, to be met with the reply from the scientist that perhaps it was, but he regarded it as worth while, and Redwood was a lawyer who would keep his mouth shut about facts that transpired about the murder side of the inquiry.

Sir Edward listened without much interruption to the reports of the officers who had inquired further into the death of Miss de Grey. The past life of Miss de Grey, so far as it had been made known, was related by Inspector Kenway. He regarded the inquiries as telling only that Miss de Grey had a gentleman friend, who was maintaining her flat, and that they had apparently quarrelled about a week after she had gone to Burlington, and at the time that his photograph had disappeared from her dressing table in the theatre.

The meeting of Kenway and Makepeace at the Kensington flat brought a raising of the eyebrows on the face of the Assistant Commissioner.

"Then you think that Mr. da Costa is the gentleman friend of Miss de Grey?" he asked.

"It would look that way," answered Kenway. "But we made no further inquiry pending consultation with Doctor Manson."

The A.C. nodded. He looked towards the doctor, for the first time in the conference. It was his custom to hear the scientist's views last of all. He liked to give that analytical mind time to coordinate the information gleaned by the other investigators and assess its possible value. He received an affirming nod from Manson, and then addressed the gathering.

"That," he announced, "brings us to another point in this inquiry which most of you know nothing about. It is in regard to this that Mr. Redwood is present at our conference. Mr. Redwood is the legal representative of a number of insurance societies. . . ."

Briefly, the Assistant Commissioner sketched the suspicions of the insurance societies, and the result of investigations which had been carried out by Doctor Manson. He concluded with the identification of Miss de Grey's mink coat as one which had figured in the claim of a Nottingham warehouse. "That," he said, "seemed to link up the pantomime star with the fires."

"But . . . nothing . . . links up with . . . murder?" suggested Superintendent Jones.

"Not that I can see," agreed Sir Edward. "Perhaps the doctor—" He broke off and waved Manson into speech. "I think that you should now hear what the doctor has to say on the fire investigations," he concluded.

The scientist began by answering Superintendent Jones's question.

"No, Jones, I have nothing to link the death of Miss de Grey with the fires. Only her life is joined in some way with the goods destroyed, or supposed to have been destroyed by the flames," he said. "At the moment, the two inquiries are a jigsaw puzzle with the key piece unidentified. I am wondering whether the

Shepherd's Bush fire is the key-piece. And I think it will be best if I explain what the Laboratory has discovered out of that fire."

Mr. Redwood, who up to now had listened with no more than a polite interest, now sat up and began to take notice. The scientist eyed him, smilingly.

"The first thing I had to probe was whether the fire was accidental, or otherwise," Doctor Manson began. "Mr. Oppenheimer, the proprietor of the business, suggested that a woman worker, whose job it was to alter and press frocks which had been sold, had left an electric iron burning, and that this might have set fire to material on which it was standing, and that this led to the place catching fire. It was a fact that the seat of the fire seemed to be at a spot which Mr. Oppenheimer explained was a part of the premises partitioned off by plywood and curtains for the purpose of making a small work-room. The floor was badly burned at that spot."

The scientist described how he had cut away some of the charred boards, and had tested them in the laboratory.

"It is a simple test, but remarkably efficient," he said. "It disclosed the presence of paraffin still in the charred fragments."

He looked across at Mr. Redwood.

"Now, if a candle standing on a floor burned down to its end, or was otherwise melted by heat, I should expect to find in the boards traces of paraffin wax. Paraffin is an exceedingly difficult thing to get completely rid of; it actually hangs about for weeks afterwards. And one way of starting a fire is to place a candle on, say a celluloid tray, so that when it burns down to the tray, the latter at once flares up and sets fire to any inflammable material that may have been arranged round it.

"So I had some grounds on which to base a suspicion that the fire which destroyed the shop was not accidental. Not, of course, evidence. Paraffin might have been spilt there. Fortunately, other material for tests, confirmatory or otherwise, was at hand."

The scientist next described the tests which he had applied to the portions of soot which he had taken.

"The presence of lead supposes the use of petrol," he explained. "Now, the spot from which I had taken this particular specimen of soot was over the area from which came the paraffin traces. It is worth noting that petrol gives a large burst of flame but not a lasting one; it burns out very quickly, unless fed by something else, by some other substance. Further afield, the soot samples that greasy appearance due to oil, and very little evidence of petrol."

Finally, Manson detailed the finding of indium in the ash debris.

"This was to me remarkably interesting," he announced. "Because whatever explanation there may be for the accidental presence of paraffin and petrol in the debris, I can imagine none for indium, which is a metal not only very rare, generally, but *exceedingly* rare in this country. I have come across it only on one occasion here, and that was in the laboratory of a scientist. He had sent to America for a few pieces of it for experimental purposes. There is no doubt whatever that the stuff was indium; its spectrum colour and its place on the wave band were quite convincing. I am hoping that a metallurgist of my acquaintance may be able to suggest some explanation of the phenomenon."

The Assistant Commissioner digested the explanation during a pause in the recapitulation of the experiments. He now spoke.

"I gather then, Doctor, that you think that what took place in that shop was something like this: Inflammable material was piled round a celluloid tray on which was stood a candle, lighted. The candle burned down to the tray, which then caught fire, igniting in its turn the petrol-soaked material, and this, by means of an oily trail, was conveyed to other parts of the interior."

Doctor Manson nodded. "That is exactly what I conjecture to have taken place," he agreed.

"Then that is incendiarism," said the Assistant Commissioner.

He considered the point for a moment or two. Then: "But it has a weakness so far as the investigations into the series of fires are concerned, and one that will have to be eliminated."

"And that is?" asked Doctor Manson.

"Who done it."

The reply came from Superintendent Jones. The fat man of the Yard leaned forward.

"Oppenheimer'll say . . . wasn't near Bush . . . miles away . . . old game . . . candle . . . give him time . . . get forty miles away."

Manson nodded agreement. So did the Assistant Commissioner.

"He can say . . . somebody broke in . . . stole something . . . set fire to place . . . can say . . . employee must have done it. Can you say . . . Oppenheimer . . . did it. If . . . can't . . . no link Oppenheimer or Bush . . . other fires."

The Assistant Commissioner turned his gaze from Jones to the scientist.

Manson grinned delightedly. "Excellently argued, Jones," he said. "Becoming quite imaginative, aren't you?" There was a ripple of laughter among the Yard men for the lack of imagination of the fat superintendent was something of a joke. He was the greatest hunter of facts the Yard possessed, but his usefulness generally ended there.

"The answer to Jones's argument is this," the scientist proceeded. "If I can prove attempts at fraud on the insurance companies by Oppenheimer, by which he would gain large sums of money to which he was not entitled, then I think we should be entitled to assume that the fire we have found to be incendiary was indeed contrived by him for the purpose of thus defrauding."

"Can you?" demanded Mr. Redwood.

"I think that I can," was the reply.

"How?" The query came from the Assistant Commissioner.

For reply, Doctor Manson produced the day book and the stock sheets taken from Mr. Oppenheimer. He opened the former and displayed its pages.

"The purpose of this day book," he explained, "is the purpose of all day books of business houses—to give an account of purchases and sales of each day. From it, and from the stock lists allied to it, the proprietors of the business can compute their stocks, their expenses and their receipts. The balance is, naturally, profit. The day book is, of course, made up from day to day. The stock list is compiled from time to time as goods are purchased, and as goods are sold. The stock list goes back to the day that the shop at Shepherd's Bush was opened—some six weeks before the fire. It shows—or it purports to show—what was destroyed in the fire, and that means the amount of the damage which Mr. Oppenheimer is about to claim from Mr. Redwood's company. Is that clear?"

There was general agreement that the facts were as the scientist had stated.

Doctor Manson continued.

"It is an old-established scientific fact that ink darkens with exposure to the air. The explanation is that the gallotannates of iron deepen in colour with oxidation. Because of this it is possible for an expert to tell if any expiry of time has taken place between the writing of any one part of the text and another. The time that has elapsed cannot be stated with any degree of accuracy; only the fact that it was not written at the same time, although in certain circumstances it is possible to say definitely that a period exceeding twenty-one days has passed between two entries. There is, for instance, the case of an Archdeacon some years ago in which he claimed that the words 'and wife', after his name in a hotel register, had been added some time after he had written his own name there. It was proved that the words were written at the same time, and by himself.

"Now, I took this day book and the stock sheets and tested them. The test is not a difficult one for an expert. From a dozen or so different entries I subtracted the colour of the ink with the aid of re-agent. These subtractions I compared through a comparison microscope and regulation tintometer glasses.

"*I could find no variation of any kind in the colour of the ink used on the pages of this day book. Neither could I find any variation in the colour of the inked entries in the stock lists, although those entries purport to extend over a period of six weeks.*

"*I am, therefore, of the opinion that the entries in this day book, and on the stock, list, were deliberately filled in all at the same time to show stock at one time, and are not, therefore, a day to day record of business.*"

Mr. Redwood rubbed his hands together. "That is something I can understand, Doctor," he said. "That will want a bit of explaining away."

Manson smiled. "There is just one other thing, and I have done," he said. "Mr. Oppenheimer claimed that there were in the shop on the night of the fire 300 frocks and fifty rolls of silk. Fortunately a dozen of the frocks were saved. These Sergeant Merry and I reduced to ashes, and watered them until they resembled the debris of ash in the building. We had the debris weighed. A dozen yards of silk—the bill for which will come to the Assistant Commissioner—was also destroyed, and the ash weighed. We then weighed the debris in the shop. A comparative calculation would give us what should be the weight of the debris of 300 frocks and bales of silk worked out on the weight of the dozen frocks and the yards of silk, reduced to identical ash. *The weight was a considerable amount under what should have been there*—and this notwithstanding the fact that it ought to have exceeded our estimate, for it should have included the ash of the plywood screens, the curtains and the fittings of the shop.

"I say there were not 300 frocks and fifty bales of silk on the premises."

Mr. Redwood, who had listened with the closest attention to the scientist's recital, now leaned forward and polished his spectacles with gusto. He addressed the scientist.

"That, if I may say so, Doctor Manson, is a remarkable piece of investigation," he applauded.

"It is really nothing of the kind, Mr. Redwood," was the reply. "Any forensic chemist would have done the same, and done it equally as well. It is mere elementary harnessing of science to criminal investigation."

"But does it link up with Mr. da Costa and Miss de Grey, Doctor?" asked the Assistant Commissioner.

"That, Sir Edward, is the next stage in the investigation," was the reply. "All we know in that direction is that Oppenheimer telephoned to da Costa a message that an accident had occurred, and that the number he first asked for, and did not get, was that of the flat in which Miss de Grey was living, and where she was visited by a foreign gentleman. Mr. da Costa sounds to me like a foreign gentleman. We want to know all about him, and his connection with Miss de Grey, and that is why I applaud Kenway's decision not to see da Costa until he had first seen me. I will, I think, interview Mr. da Costa myself on the question of the fire and the message. On what he says depends what further questions I put to him."

"Anybody . . . know . . . Costa's job?" asked Superintendent Jones.

"He is, I understand, a financier," replied Doctor Manson. "That covers a multitude of sins."

Sir Edward Allen looked round at his officers. "The Doctor is taking on Mr. da Costa," he reminded them. "Has anybody else any suggestions?"

There was no response to the invitation.

"You, Doctor?" he asked.

"Yes, Sir Edward. I want a lot of help from you, and fairly quickly."

"It's yours. What do you want?"

"Firstly, a photograph of da Costa, to see if Miss Prue, the pantomime lady, can identify it as that of the gentleman in the photograph on Miss de Grey's dressing table. Then, I want to know something of the activities of Mr. da Costa. We know where he is now living. I would like to know if there is another lady there, or at a flat provided elsewhere by Mr. da Costa.

"Finally, and this is very important, I want to find out from employees of the various shops and warehouses, the outbreaks of fire in which we are investigating, if any unusual circumstances were noted by them shortly before the fires occurred."

His mind went back for a moment to an interview he had had a couple of days ago.

"If any strangers were noted about the place, for instance. That is the case also in the Shepherd's Bush incident," he concluded.

INTERLUDE II
To the Reader

The reader may care to exercise his thoughts (or her thoughts) on the reasons for Doctor Manson's request for these items of knowledge.

They are all outlined in clues in the pages of the murder of Dick Whittington and the fire epidemic so far written—and, we hope, carefully read.

Chapter XVII
MR. DA COSTA

MR. RAOUL DA COSTA lived, or perhaps one should say resided, in one of a lined nest of luxury flats known as Cumberland Court, Kensington. They were, indeed, luxury flats, and the greatest care was exercised by the proprietors to ensure that only the best people were accommodated in their cosy depths.

By the 'best people' it must not be understood that the proprietors were guilty of the evil of snobbery. They were not. No lordship, or ladyship, would be accorded any priority when a flat fell vacant. In fact, the proprietors would rather not have any request from lords and ladies for house room. Usually, lords and ladies, it had been their experience, had little money, and no guarantor. And people without money, or without enough of it, were of little use to the Cumberland. By which, you will have gathered the kind of people the 'best people' were, in the view of the proprietors of the Cumberland.

Mr. Raoul da Costa had only recently aspired to Cumberland Court. This must not be held to imply that he had only recently come into the amount of money which, in the eyes of the proprietors, justified his acceptance; the reason, on the contrary, was that there had been no flat vacant for a considerable time. Mr. da Costa had always had quite a lot of money. Money talks, and the talking of the da Costa money drowned the comments of many people on the methods by which da Costa accumulated his wealth.

He was, in appearance, a tall slim man, with what in America are known as snake hips. They moved with the sinuousness of the serpent, when he walked. He had dark eyes, and a head of sleek straw-coloured hair. This was unusual, to say the least, for Mr. da Costa was accredited in London as a South American; and the people of those Latin races are generally sleekly topped with jet-black hair.

Just when he came to England nobody seemed to be sure. He had appeared in the night life of the West End some six years before this story opened, and there he had hovered ever since.

By day he frequented the City. Officially he was financier. A moneylender is a financier; but Mr. da Costa was not, so far as was known, a moneylender. He was known to have financed a few companies in his time, mostly shady companies. He had been known to do a little bill discounting, and to purchase promissory notes at a very heavy discount. It was also rumoured that a part of his financial dealings consisted of organizing gaming parties in houses where chemin de fer and baccarat were the games. There were other means of acquiring wealth which were whispered, but not proved.

The joint proceeds of these many ventures allowed him not only to live in Cumberland Court, but also to frequent the most expensive *caravanserai* in the West End, and spend money lavishly.

Doctor Manson had assimilated these details before he set out to chat with Mr. da Costa, and he ruminated over them on his way to Kensington. His ring at the flat door was answered by a deferential manservant.

The Doctor had not announced his coming, though he had taken the precaution of assuring himself that Mr. da Costa would be in his flat at the time he intended to call. The manservant admitted that his master was in, but had the gentleman an appointment?

No, the visitor had not, but he was an executive officer of Scotland Yard who would value the help of Mr. da Costa in some inquiries on which they were engaged. He handed over his card, and was shown into what seemed to be the writing-room.

A handsome Sheraton writing desk occupied a corner of the room. A large leather lounge was set along one side, and scattered around were club armchairs. Books lined the walls. Into this setting walked Mr. da Costa, dressed in a brown lounge suit, with brown velvet smoking jacket. He looked at his visitor.

Doctor Manson, eyeing him keenly, saw no sign of anxiety or alarm in his face. The introductions made, Mr. da Costa waved him to one of the armchairs, and sat himself in the chair behind his desk. He was at an advantage, and he knew it.

"And in what way can I assist Scotland Yard?" he asked. He pushed over a box. "Have a cigar?" he invited.

Doctor Manson declined.

"Whisky and soda?"

"I never drink on duty, Mr. da Costa."

"Well, if you don't mind, I'll have one myself," retorted the host. He poured out a glass of neat spirit. "Here's your health," he toasted. "And what can I do for you?"

"It is more or less a formal matter," replied Doctor Manson.

"There was a fire the other night in Shepherd's Bush. A shop was burned out. The stock was destroyed. The proprietor of the shop, a Mr. Oppenheimer, has claimed total loss from the insurance company."

Mr. da Costa put on a puzzled air.

"But what has this to do with me, Doctor Manson?" he asked. "I do not own the shop, I wasn't in Shepherd's Bush, I don't think I would care to be found dead in Shepherd's Bush. My game is finance, not dress shops."

Doctor Manson smiled slightly, but only for a fraction of a second. "Mistake number one," he said under his breath. Aloud, he retorted, looking at da Costa: "A dress shop? I did not say that it was a dress shop. But, as a matter of fact, it *was* a dress shop."

"That's queer. Must have read about it in the newspaper." Mr. da Costa drained his glass.

"I still do not see where I come in," he reminded his visitor.

"You come in in rather a curious way, Mr. da Costa," retorted Manson. "Scotland Yard is trying to reduce the number of fires in business premises. The result is that whenever a fire occurs an official investigation is made in order that some idea may be gained as to how the fire might have been caused. The idea, you understand, is to devise some greater safeguard in the future."

Mr. da Costa nodded. "Very interesting, and very commendable," he agreed.

"Now, Mr. da Costa, after we had viewed the scene of the fire, and assured Mr. Oppenheimer that his claim for total loss would be considered, he went to a nearby telephone and called up a number. To the person answering he said, just, 'There has been an accident.' That number is credited in the telephone directory as rented to you, Mr. da Costa. What do you know about Mr. Oppenheimer, and why should he telephone you, since, as you say, you are in finance, and not dress shops?"

Doctor Manson sat back in his chair and waited the reply with every sign of interestedness.

"Most unfortunate. . . . Most unfortunate," replied Mr. da Costa, running an embarrassed hand through his hair. "Wouldn't have had this happen for worlds . . . Make me a laughing stock if it gets out."

He bent forward to Doctor Manson, as if fearing that the walls, which notoriously have ears, might be listening and overhear his story.

"It's like this, Chief Inspector," he explained. "It is true, as I said, that I am in finance. Anybody in the City will tell you that, and they will tell you about my deals. But I'm not averse from making a few hundred pounds in other ways. Surtax is the devil these days, you know.

"I know Mr. Oppenheimer. He once did me a service. He wanted five hundred pounds to complete his capital for starting the shop in Shepherd's Bush, and he asked me for it. I don't lend money. But I was prepared to help him if he could show me that the business was one in which money could be made. He did that—showed me an estimate of costs of the dresses and the amount at which they could sell. I agreed to lend him the five hundred on condition that I stood in for a half-share, as a sleeping partner. There was, however, one other condition; my name was not to be mentioned. As I said, dress shops are small fry, and I didn't want to be associated with them, publicly. Have my City friends calling me 'Gertie' or something."

He looked anxiously at Manson.

"I trust that this will not go further," he entreated.

"I see nothing in your answers to necessitate it going further than Scotland Yard," replied Doctor Manson.

"Well, when he knew that the shop was a total loss, Oppenheimer did telephone me that there had been an accident. He used the words because he did not, of course, want to mention the shop over the telephone, as I was not publicly to be associated with it."

Mr. da Costa sat back in his chair and eyed the scientist, anxiously. "I hope that is satisfactory," he queried.

Doctor Manson ignored the query. He countered it with a question of his own.

"You said that your business was finance, Mr. da Costa. What exactly do you mean by that? That you finance businesses, and so on?"

"Oh, dear, no." Mr. da Costa smiled. "I refer to finance in its wider aspect—Stock Exchange, Bills, Discount, and company promoting."

"And you have no connection with the financing of businesses other than in this instance of Mr. Oppenheimer?"

"None at all. I should not have had that except that Mr. Oppenheimer, as I say, did me a good turn once."

"Did you know anything about the Shepherd's Bush business, the amount of stock he had, and so on? He is, you see, claiming a considerable sum of money for the loss."

"He had a stock list, didn't he?" Mr. da Costa inquired with some anxiety.

Doctor Manson nodded. "Oh yes, he had a stock list. But we have no means of checking whether the stock was in the place, you know."

"He kept a day book. I made it a condition that he should keep books properly. Nobody is going to swing anything over on me. The day book would show what he sold, and what was left over from the stock list would be on the premises."

"Yes, he has a day book, too," agreed Doctor Manson. "Then, I take it, you can give us your word that Oppenheimer is all right?"

"Definitely all right."

Doctor Manson stood up to go. He walked to the window and looked out over the street below. A table stood in front of the window, and his gaze wandered over the contents. There were copies of *Vogue*, and of *Woman's Own*. On a chair beside it lay a piece of needlework. A bowl of flowers stood near by on a pedestal. The scientist noted them with an interested gaze. He turned and walked back to his unwilling host, and bade him good morning.

On the way out he stopped at the porter's lodge, and put a peculiar question.

"Have you seen Mrs. da Costa come in?"

The porter shook his head. "No, sir," he replied. "She hasn't passed me."

"Perhaps I'll meet her. What kind of a person is she?"

"Nice little woman, sir. What the frenchies call *petite*, if you knows what I means."

"I understand it quite well," was the smiling response.

It was later in the day that the first reports of the officers of Scotland Yard detailed to inquire into the points raised by the scientist came in. Inspector Makepeace, who had started with the Shepherd's Bush fire, sought the Doctor in his Laboratory. He had, he said, questioned a constable who, on receipt of official intimation that any suspicious circumstance round the scene of the fire should be reported, had come forward with a story which sounded a little queer. The area was on his beat, and a few days before the fire, he had noticed a large car standing a few yards down the main Uxbridge road, just past the junction with Montmorency Road. The car was empty, and he wondered who would be leaving a car like that in such a neighbourhood at that time of night.

"It was 10.30 p.m.," Kenway explained.

"Did he take the number?" asked Manson.

"He did, but as nothing developed during the next few days, he did not keep it," was the reply. "But he says it was an SAS registration.

"Anyway," went on the inspector, "the constable says he crossed the road to continue his beat up the main street, and as he passed across the side turning, he saw a man and a woman walking along Montmorency Road. They were approaching the main thoroughfare, but on reaching the corner, retraced their steps, looking across at the opposite side of the street. After going about forty yards they again returned, on the other side, and stood for a moment or two in front of the buildings. They then walked to the car, got in, sounded a toot on the horn, and drove off in the direction of London.

"Did the constable give any description of the couple?"

"Yes. He said one of them was a tall man, in a heavy black coat, and the other a woman. He does not think he would be able to recognize them, except on general appearance if he saw them together in similar circumstances."

"And what buildings did they pass and then stop in front?"

"That is the point which made me come to you. As far as I can see the buildings were those in the centre of which is the Oppenheimer shop."

"It wasn't Oppenheimer, I suppose?"

"No, Doctor. The constable knows that gentleman, and he was quite certain that it wasn't him."

"H'm." The Doctor turned to Inspector Kenway. "What do you make of this circumstance, Kenway?" he asked.

The inspector scratched his head. "Well, Doctor, I remember that in a case some time ago of incendiarism, it was stated that before the actual fire there had been a rehearsal of the operation, and that candles were lit in the place they were to occupy on the actual event, while one of the confederates walked past the outside of the premises to see whether the light could be detected from outside."

"And you think that something of the kind was being done on this occasion?"

Inspector Kenway nodded agreement.

"It is certainly a possibility," said Manson.

"You saw da Costa?" the inspector queried.

"I did, Kenway." Manson gave the inspector the gist of the interview. "Did I understand you to say the other day that da Costa was a bachelor?"

"Yes, Doctor."

"Well, he has a lady in the flat. There were all the signs of a woman's presence. And there is, apparently, a Mrs. da Costa, who is a very nice and a *petite* person. You had better find out who she is."

"He seems to make a hobby of ladies. First Norma de Grey and now another one," the inspector commented.

It was the following morning, when reports came in from the seats of the various fires, that Doctor Manson first gained an inkling of where the investigations into the combined cases were leading him. They were full and comprehensive, as had been asked for, and were the result of inquiries made by the local branches of the C.I.D. and the fire services.

Since they play an important part in the mystery, it will be as well to give them in full.

The first of them was signed by the detective-inspector in charge of the C.I.D. at Birmingham.

It ran as follows:

Conflagration, Bric-à-brac shop; request for any unusual circumstances in connection with:

1. The fact that the fire occurred on the one night when the sprinkler extinguishers were out of action is to me an unusual circumstance. Explanation of this, however, was supplied to Chief Detective-Inspector Doctor Manson on his visit here.

2. The purchaser of the business, Mr. James McKay, from the proprietor for 20 years, Mr. Henry Segrand, was a man in very moderate circumstances, whom it was surprising to find in command of the money required to acquire the business. Dam-

ages of £10,500 were paid by the insurance company, but Mr. McKay, who is still in the town, is short of money. Mr. Segrand states that the negotiations for the purchase of the business were conducted by a stranger to him, a tall, well-built man of the name of Close. He did not at any time see McKay, and was astonished when he found that he was the owner of the business. He had known McKay for years. Close, he says, talked with a trace of a foreign accent.

McKay had not been in any kind of business before, and is now a bookmaker's clerk. Have not questioned him without knowledge of the lines and reasons for your inquiries.

Report from the Chief Constable of Liverpool, on Paris Show Rooms, Ltd., fire:

No traces of any unusual circumstances connected with the actual fire. Have not questioned principals who are still resident in the city. Assistant, now employed in woman's outfitter's shop, states that business was not in a thriving condition but that new capital was believed to be forthcoming, as a lady and gentleman had, three days before the fire, spent some time in the shop inspecting contents. The shop had been specially dressed just before their visit, and photographs had been taken, prints of which were sent to a London address. Man cannot now recall the address, as he only saw the envelope by chance on the office desk. The visit of the man and woman followed two days later and the fire occurred three days afterwards.

Report from the Detective-Inspector in charge, C.I.D., Welsborough, on fire at London Fashion Modes:

Unusual features associated with this outbreak are that anyone who had made inquiries in the town should have opened the business at all in goods which were already in supply in old-established and popular houses. Secondly that, for a month before the fire the premises should have been closely shuttered at night. Mr. Montague's explanation of this was given to Chief Detective-Inspector Manson, D.Sc., on his inquiries here. Mr. Montague left the town after the claim had been settled, and his present address is not known.

The constable on beat in the district at the time of the out-break, states that a car with a number-plate not bearing a local registration passed him half an hour before he discovered the fire. It came from a direction which was not a passageway through the town.

Shop assistant, questioned, says that the only strangers to visit the premises were a foreigner a few days after the opening. He was known to Montague, in company with whom he looked over the shop. That was the only time he visited the place so far as she knows.

Report from the superintendent in charge, C.I.D., Sheffield, on fire at Messrs. Fines and Howard:

Fire was always a suspicious circumstance as firm had a bad reputation, and one insurance company had refused to pay out on a claim for alleged theft. Company was in a bad way following the theft, claimed to be an extensive one. Two shop assistants, a Miss Pelham and a Miss Fountain, now employed in Cannells, state that the business was to be closed up, and they had been given notice to leave, when the proprietors obtained fresh cap-ital. This, they think, was provided by a tall, well-dressed lady and a man taken to be her husband, who spent a day with Mr. Fines in the shop, examining the premises and contents. Miss Fountain states that she heard the man say to Fines: "It's a first-class proposition." She assumes from this that the new capital came from the couple. She would, she thinks, be able to identify the couple if she saw them again.

No report had been asked for from Silks, Ltd., and those from the remaining two towns stated that they could not discov-er anything of a peculiar nature in connection with the fires or the businesses.

Doctor Manson, Superintendent Jones, and Inspector Kenway studied them together at a desk in the superintendent's room at Scotland Yard. The fat superintendent grunted.

"Rum do . . . damned suspicious . . . never made inquiries . . . found out . . . time of fire," he said.

"There was no reason to suspect any of these things, Jones," retorted the scientist. "The fire brigade in each case passed the fires as apparently accidental outbreaks. It was not until the insurance societies began to worry over their claims that we, or anybody else, began to look into the fires. No blame that I can see attaches to anybody."

"But it's pretty obvious now, Doctor, that the fires were incendiary," said Inspector Kenway. "The tall man, the foreign gentleman and the man with a foreign accent all seem to me to suggest the same person." The inspector thought for a moment or two. "It looks to me like the stories of the master criminal who plans the coups. That the man should turn up at practically all the places shortly before a fire breaks out seems to suggest that he was the author of the frauds."

"Go further," retorted Jones. "Was he . . . man . . . goin' buy one business . . . and come inspect it. Was he . . . man . . . negotiated purchase . . . business. . . . Bric-à-Brac shop? What say . . . that. Doctor?"

"I think that quite possibly you and Kenway are correct, Jones," the scientist replied. "But that is not the most important point to me in the reports."

"What is . . . important point, Doctor?" demanded the superintendent.

"Two women," was the reply.

"Two women?" The superintendent echoed the words. "What have they to do with it?"

Doctor Manson chuckled, grimly. "Quite a lot, I hope," he replied. "If they haven't, then I've gone badly astray."

"Who are the women, Doctor?" The question came from Kenway.

"That I do not know for certain, Kenway. But I want photographs of Miss de Grey, and of the woman with whom I am quite sure Mr. da Costa is now living. I also want one of da Costa himself. Listen."

He talked to the two officers for a minute or two. They listened in silence. Doctor Manson watched them. No thought of what was in his mind seemed to cross their imagination. The superintendent, however, acceded to the request which the scientist had made.

"I'll put Wendover on the job, Doctor," he announced. "He's a good photographer, and he doesn't look too much like a copper."

CHAPTER XVIII
TELLS OF A PHOTOGRAPHER

ONE OF THE NUISANCES which have followed in the wake of the cinema is the street photographer who as you walk along the street, puts the camera to his eyes and snaps you, immediately presenting you with a card on which is inscribed a number and the intimation that by proceeding next day to the address given and quoting the number you will be able to purchase prints of the snapshot at so much a dozen—or in single copies.

Their haunt is generally the West End of London, or the seaside promenades. Probably only one in twenty people ever ask for prints, but the cost of film is very low, and, since the photographer is paid usually on commission, the syndicate employing the men do not stand to lose much money. Indeed, one in twenty, at the prices asked for the enlarged photographs, should show a wide margin of profit. The sufferer during bad custom is, as usual, the operator.

One such man was having a thin time with his camera in Cumberland Road, Kensington. He had taken a pitch some few yards away from Cumberland Court. The choice would have surprised even the most inexperienced of street photographers, for the class of people who frequented the road, and the residences in the road, particularly those living in the Court, were hardly the class who would journey to the headquarters of the photographic company to obtain a view of themselves. When they desired a reproduction of their faces their venue was mostly one of the more fashionable of the West End Photographic Salons.

The man had snapped some forty or fifty prospective clients without one of them accepting his card of identity up to ten o'clock. The lack of success, or appreciation, did not, however, seem unduly to worry him, for he maintained his operations with a pleasant glance and smile at the customers who passed on.

Most of his snaps were taken as residents emerged from the imposing entrance to the Court. He possibly imagined that the attraction of the background of their luxury home might be an added inducement to purchasing copies of the snaps. At 11.15 a.m. he levelled his camera at a man and a woman leaving the Court, and, as usual, proferred his professional card. His arm was brushed aside by the man, who walked to the pavement edge and hailed a taxi. Putting the lady inside, he gave the Hotel Magnificent as his destination, and followed the lady into the depths of the vehicle.

The blow seemed to be the last straw to the man at the camera for, after a half-hearted attempt to entrap a further couple, he pushed his camera into its case, turned on his heel, and walked down the street, being lost, presently, in the direction of Kensington High Street.

The photographic dark-rooms of Doctor Manson's Laboratory at Scotland Yard contained all that was modern in the apparatus for producing pictures at the shortest possible notice. It vied with the dark-rooms of the most famous of the picture papers of England. The film, once developed, could be quickly cleared of all the unwanted emulsion, it could be washed free of hypo in a matter of a very few moments. The wet film could be dried at remarkable speed by a judicious mixture of methylated spirits and a flow of gently warmed air from a dryer. And once the enlarged print had been taken in the enlarging camera, it, too, could be bone dry within the space of not more than three minutes, after it had passed between the warm blankets of the automatic drying machine.

Thus, within half an hour of the camera man leaving Cumberland Road, Kensington, Detective-Sergeant Wendover emerged from the dark-rooms at Scotland Yard, and placed a print on the desk in front of Doctor Manson. The print was a 10 x 8 inches' enlargement, of Mr. da Costa and a lady. The scientist eyed it critically.

"An excellent production, Wendover," he said, eventually. "Now get me out half a dozen prints of the girl separately, and another half a dozen of the man. You might as well do the same quantity of the pair together. Leave this print of the couple with me, and ask Simmons to come and see me, will you?"

Sergeant Wendover departed on his job. A knock at the door, and an invitation to enter, produced Detective Simmons, the artist of the headquarters of the C.I.D.

"Ah, Simmons," Doctor Manson greeted him. "Have a look at this print of two people." He paused a moment to allow the details of the print to sink into the mind of the detective, and then continued:

"Now, listen. A constable at Shepherd's Bush saw a car and a couple of people walking along a street at eleven o'clock or thereabouts, at night. It was dark. I believe the couple to have been the pair in this picture, and I want to see if the constable can identify them. You will note the difference in height of the pair. I feel it possible that if we could reproduce the effect of the street at that time of night and the couple walking along the street it might wake some echo in the constable's mind. Can you do something like that, do you think?"

Simmons eyed the photograph in contemplation for a minute or so. He held it at arm's length, and studied the figures. He held it nearer at different angles, and studied them again. Finally, he replaced the print on the table and regarded the scientist.

"Could I get a picture of the actual street, Doctor?" he asked.

"Quite easily, I should say, Simmons," was the reply.

"Then I think I could transform the street into the semblance of night, and a bit of montage would put the figures in. I'll have a go at it. Where is the street?"

Doctor Manson provided the address of the street in which Mr. Oppenheimer had lately done business, and the artist departed in search of his quarry.

At 2.30 p.m., he returned with a print. It showed two figures standing in a darkened street. At the corner of the street stood a car. Doctor Manson looked at it with admiration.

"Excellent, Simmons," he said. "How the deuce did you do it?"

"Over-printed a print of the street, Doctor, reduced the figures on Wendover's print to scale, mounted them in the street print, and after retouching it up, re-photographed the print, and printed it from the new negative."

"Well, it's a work of art, and I think it might do the trick." He sent for Inspector Makepeace.

Police-Constable Woodcock stood to attention in front of the inspector, in Shepherd's Bush police-station. Yes, he said, he remembered the fire at the shop of Mr. Oppenheimer, and the inquiries which had been made into it. He remembered a statement which he had made to his own inspector. Inspector Makepeace felt that in asking those questions he had been guilty of what in the view of the Bar would be called putting a leading question, but he felt justified in giving the constable a clue to what he was to be asked to decide.

Without more ado, he confronted the constable with the photograph composed by Simmons. The constable stared at it, startled.

"Why, that's the very couple—and taken in the street, too," he said. "I never saw anybody with a camera."

"What do you mean by that, Woodcock?" asked the inspector. "You can't mean to say that you recognize the people, surely?"

"Not to say recognize their faces, which can't really be seen, sir," was the reply. "But I recognize them by the appearance. One of 'em tall and the other short. It was that which made me notice them in the first place."

"I see. Then you will say that the people in the photograph have every appearance of being the two people you saw walking in that street, a few nights before the fire occurred, and that they are the people to whom you referred in the statement that you made to your inspector following an inquiry from Scotland Yard?"

"I will say that they have every appearance of the couple I saw, sir," was the reply.

"Good enough, Woodcock," said the inspector, and dashed back to the Yard to acquaint Doctor Manson with the result of the test.

The scientist nodded approvingly. "I thought it might come off," he said. "It is not, of course, evidence, and we could not produce it in a court of law, but it strengthens an idea I have at the back of my mind, and it might prove a very strong link in a chain of real evidence."

The inspector looked at the scientist inquiringly, but Doctor Manson made no response. Instead he lifted the receiver of his house telephone, and asked for Inspector Kenway at the moment that that officer opened the door of the Laboratory, and walked in.

"Hallo, I have just asked for you, Kenway," said Manson, smilingly.

"And I want you, too, Doctor," was the retort. "Burlington have just telephoned to say that Enora, the Cat, is now fit to be discharged, and they want to know what they are to do about him."

"Tell them that they must invent some excuse to keep him in the hospital. He must not be released whatever happens. Tell the local inspector to impress upon the hospital that this is the urgent request of Scotland Yard. It will be for only a day or two, and then I hope to have solved the mystery, and we can deal with him accordingly."

"Right you are, Doctor. And why did you want me?" asked Kenway.

Doctor Manson produced the prints of da Costa and the woman. "Have these pictures sent to Birmingham, Sheffield, and Liverpool," he said. "I want them shown to those people who were interviewed, and who told of certain incidents. Include one of our portraits of Miss de Grey with them. What I want particularly to know is whether any of the people can identify either or all the photographs. And send copies, by a sergeant, to Mr. Anstruther, former manager of Silks, Ltd., and see if he can recognize anybody.

"Then, Kenway, you yourself take the picture of the lady known, apparently, as Mrs. da Costa round to all the theatrical agents you can think of, and see if they can give her a name. This is most important—that is the reason I am asking you to attend to it, personally."

Alone in his Laboratory Doctor Manson took a sheet of foolscap paper from a drawer and began to fill it with lines of his small, neat writing. He wrote steadily for a quarter of an hour, read through his notes, nodding his head now and then at points which he regarded as of special interest, and finally locked the M.S. in his private drawer.

Deciding that he could make no further progress until he received the reports for which he had asked, he took a parting look round his domain and left for his flat—and dinner.

CHAPTER XIX
COMINGS AND GOINGS

WHATEVER DOCTOR MANSON expected from the inquiries which he had set on foot he did not convey to his officers. Nor could these officers see much point in them. Kenway had been at much pains to find some association between the fires and Mr. da Costa and the death of Miss Norma de Grey on the stage at the Burlington pavilion. He knew perfectly well that there must be some association, for Doctor Manson had insisted that the hospital should keep the Cat inside that institution for a few further days, and the doctor, he ruminated, had not spent any time investigating the death of the star, but had, on the contrary, seemingly been engaged exclusively on the problem of the fires. Therefore, said Kenway, there must be some association, and a very close one, between the two happenings. What it was, however, he knew not and could not conjecture.

It was his job that morning to get busy on the task of tracing the lady who was masquerading as Mrs. da Costa. The scientist had suggested that he should make a round of the theatrical agents of the Metropolis to ascertain whether they had any knowledge of the lady. Here, again, the inspector saw no reason for the particular choice. Why pick on the theatrical profession? Why not a shop assistant of some kind. There must be some very sound reason for the choice—Kenway knew Doctor Manson too well to suppose that the scientist was guessing or making inquiries at hazard.

However, it was no use surmising. He settled down to the routine task in front of him in the form of correspondence and police reports which had come in during the night. That concluded, he wandered out into the Embankment, and on to Hippodrome Corner, the home of theatreland. The search, unless he was lucky, would, he knew, take him the greater part of the day, for there were nearly a hundred theatrical agents listed in the police register as being congregated round Leicester Square, Soho, and the other haunts of the Profession. He began with the imposing firm of Frasers, probably the oldest and biggest firm of agents, in Leicester Square. His card gave him access to Mr. Harry Fraser himself.

"Identify a certain person in the theatrical profession, Inspector?" queried Mr. Fraser from behind a cigar. He waved a diamond-adorned hand. "I should think it possible. I know most of the members of the Profession and most of 'em have come up these stairs at some time or another."

Kenway produced the photograph, and handed it over. Mr. Fraser eyed it in silence for a few moments. He laid back in his chair and searched his mind and recollection. But without tangible result.

"No, I can't say who she is, Inspector," he announced. "I've a feeling I've seen her sometime, but where it was I can't say. She isn't well-known; I can assure you of that. Is she still in the Profession?"

"That is one of the things I want to know," the inspector replied. "As a matter of fact, we don't even know that she is in the profession at all; it is a suspicion on our part."

"Well, have a go at some of the little agents," suggested Mr. Fraser. "I'd know her if she was an artiste of any reputation. She's probably one of the smaller people and they are usually handled by the little 'uns."

Thanking him, Inspector Kenway left, and proceeded towards his next port of call.

While Kenway was plying his inquiries round the West End, Doctor Manson was waiting in his Laboratory for what might be washed into his net of inquiry, now being trawled by the police of four cities. So important did the scientist think the result of the inquiries, that he had asked that the C.I.D. of the various towns should telephone to Scotland Yard any information they might chance to gather.

First result to arrive, however, was from the detective deputed to visit the manager of the late firm of Silks, Ltd., a Mr. Anstruther. The officer announced that the manager had been unable to recall seeing either of the two ladies, either as friends of the proprietors, or as customers to the shop. The detective added that he had particularly impressed upon Mr. Anstruther the picture of Miss Norma de Grey, because of the scientist's discovery, told to him, that she had possessed two dust sheets bearing the name of Silks, Ltd., which sheets were not sold by the company but were used solely for covering over their own goods at night time. He had insisted that he had never, to the best of his belief, seen the lady.

He had, however, something more tangible to relate when he was shown the photograph of Mr. da Costa. He identified it as that of a Mr. Onslow, who had on several occasions visited Silks, Ltd., and had been shown round the premises by Mr. Bessing, one of the partners. Mr. Onslow had, he said, taken so much interest in the place that he, Anstruther, gained the impression that he was considering purchasing the business. The same impression was gained by other members of the staff of the firm, and it had caused some consternation at the time.

The detective added that, supplied with the names and present places of business of two of the assistants, he had visited them, and they, too, had recognized the portrait of Mr. Onslow.

The detective had hardly left the room when the first of the telephone reports arrived. It came from Liverpool, and dealt with the Paris Show Rooms, Ltd. An assistant who had been previously interviewed on behalf of Doctor Manson, on being shown the photograph of Miss de Grey identified it as that of a lady who accompanied a gentleman to the shop on two occasions, and inspected the premises and stock. Confronted with the picture of Mr. da Costa, she said without hesitation that he was the man who had been with the lady, and whom they (the assistants) thought was a possible subscriber to the depleted funds of the business, since they knew that the proprietors were seeking new capital in return for a partnership. Asked for the approximate time of the visit, the assistant put it as some time in early September. It was within a week or so of her return from her annual holiday, which she had taken in the last two weeks of August.

The next report came from Welsborough. There, the only two assistants formerly employed by London Fashion Modes who could be traced, expressed the emphatic view that they had on one occasion seen the foreign-looking gentleman of the photograph. He was a man who had visited Fashion Modes a few days after the opening of the business. He stayed with Mr. Montague for some time, and inspected the premises. They thought at the time that he was a man from the insurance company. They could not recognize either of the two women. The Welsborough inspector added that the date of the visit was approximately the middle of December, and Mr. Montague and the gentleman had been seen in the town during the late evening. Accordingly, he had thought of inquiring in the hotels for any traces of the stranger. He had been unexpectedly fortunate. At the Bull Hotel the photograph of Mr. da Costa had been recognized by the reception clerk and a chambermaid as Mr. Sylvester, who had stayed at the hotel for one night on December 19th. They were unable to identity Miss de Grey's photograph, but at once recognized the second photograph as that of Mrs. Sylvester, who had occupied the room with her husband.

From Sheffield the police reported that the photographs of Mr. da Costa and Miss de Grey had been identified as those of the man and woman who had visited Fines and Howards about August. They were taken to be husband and wife, and had spent some time looking over the place. Miss Fountains, who had been previously interviewed, expressed the opinion that the man had invested capital in the business, as the notice given to employees of dismissal, because the premises were to be closed down, was rescinded within a few days of the visit of the man and woman. A considerable amount of new stock was ordered following the withdrawal of the notices.

The only other area from which any satisfactory report was forthcoming was from the Fur Warehouse at Nottingham, where a former member of the staff, who had occupied a position in the office, said that she thought she recognized the man as a representative of the insurance company who came to inspect the premises. She could not remember the date, but thought that it was some time in the autumn. She could not identify either of the two women. A member of the staff of the Poultry Hotel, however, thought that the taller of the ladies was one who accompanied a gentleman at lunch one day in the hotel some months back.

That represented the sum total of the urgent inquiries asked for by Doctor Manson, and the scientist proceeded to sum them up. A certain suspicion had been running through his mind when he considered all the facts that had transpired from the many inquiries which had been instituted into the riddle of the fires. He had decided that the information which had now been forthcoming from the various areas would either confirm those suspicions, or dispose of them altogether. If the former, then there were certain other lines which might be undertaken in the way of further inquiries If the latter, then he would have been working on entirely erroneous lines, and a complete new line of investigation would have to be started. He did not think, however, that he had gone wrong. A detailed examination of the reports would, he hoped, prove that to be the case. To begin his examination he wrote down on a piece of paper a précis of the various reports. This, when finished, read as follows:

Mr. Onslow (da Costa) visited Silks, Ltd., on several occasions. No mention of the ladies.

Mr. da Costa and Miss de Grey were visitors to the Paris Show Rooms, Liverpool, in the summer.

Mr. Sylvester (da Costa) visited the shop at Welsborough with his wife on December 19th. Wife identified as the present Mrs. da Costa.

Mr. da Costa and Miss de Grey visited Fines and Howards, Sheffield, during the month of August.

Mr. da Costa visited the fur warehouse at Nottingham some time in the autumn. Miss de Grey stayed for lunch in an hotel.

Mr. da Costa and the present Mrs. da Costa believed to be the two people who were outside the Shepherd's Bush shop, one night, at a late hour.

After studying the tabulation for a minute or two, the scientist took a fresh piece of paper and drew a line across the centre of it, horizontally. At the top of the upper half, and on the left-hand side, he wrote the name *Miss de Grey*. In the same position on the bottom half he wrote the words, *other woman, alias Mrs. da Costa*. He then added in the respective positions the points of the précis he had just concluded. The finished product presented the following appearance:

MISS DE GREY:
> *At Liverpool during the summer.*
> *At Sheffield in August.*
> *At Nottingham in Autumn.*

OTHER WOMAN:
> *At Welsborough, on December 19th.*
> *At Sheffield in January.*

What, if anything, could be gained from the date-line between the appearances of the two women? Doctor Manson asked himself the question. And were they in any way connected? Looking them over, he realized the fact that throughout the summer and the autumn, the companion of the man who was, undoubtedly, da Costa, was Miss de Grey. After the autumn she appeared to fade out of the picture; and from December 19th, the other woman seemed to have been the gadabout companion of da Costa.

Was there anything to be surmised from this point? It was at this stage that the scientist suddenly remembered the evidence of Miss Prue, the Principal Girl of the pantomime. She had said that during the first week of the pantomime the picture of a tall, handsome gentleman friend stood on the dressing table of Miss de Grey. Then, during the second week, it vanished. Miss Prue had said, in reply to a question, that the photograph had not been stolen, or Miss de Grey would have raised hell about it. Now, the pantomime opened on Boxing Day. It was less than a week previously that the second lady, who was now masquerading as Mrs. da Costa, was at Welsborough with da Costa. Might it not be surmised, Doctor Manson asked himself, that Miss de Grey had learned that she had been supplanted in her gentleman friend's affections, and had removed the photograph of him from her presence? Also Miss de Grey had given up her luxury flat in December.

A fortnight later Miss de Grey died—murdered.

"But the link . . . the link?" Doctor Manson said to himself. "Where is the link?"

It was at this precise moment that Inspector Kenway began his return journey to Scotland Yard after a tiring morning and afternoon of patient search. Twelve agencies had been combed without any trace of the identity of the lady friend of Mr. da Costa coming to light. Then, casually glancing at a doorway while on his way to the thirteenth of his recorded addresses, the inspector noticed a white name standing out from a black background board.

FRED FLECKMAN
Theatre, Variety and Concert Parties

On the spur of the moment he entered and asked for Mr. Fleckman, if he was not too busy.

The pert girl at the desk grinned. "Sure, he'll see you," she said.

Mr. Fleckman, after overcoming his disappointment that the visitor was not a long anticipated client, expressed himself as willing to help the Law if it was at all possible. From his briefcase the inspector produced the picture of his unknown lady and handed it across.

"Can you tell me who this woman is?" he asked.

Mr. Fleckman took the photograph and glanced at it.

"Why, it's little Nina Francetti," he said. "Bless my soul, what do you want with her?"

Inspector Kenway cast a wary glance at him. "So far as I know, we don't want her for anything," he replied. "Only thing we are concerned with is who she is. The photograph cropped up in some matters we are inquiring about, and nobody seemed to know who is the owner of the face. You do. Well, who is Nina Francetti, Mr. Fleckman?"

"Well, Inspector, I don't know very much about her. She came to me about five years ago and I found her a small part in a show. I had a better part for her some months later, but she told me that she had left the stage and had retired. Apparently somebody was looking after her. Then, when I'd almost forgotten all about her, she turned up again. I got her a part in *Alice*, the children's play, you know."

"The gentleman got tired of her, I suppose?" suggested the inspector.

"That would be about the size of it, I reckon," was the reply. "Anyway, she appeared in *Alice* for a couple of years, and then turned down another job, saying that she had gone into business. I heard that she was in the studios of a well-known advertising photographer, where she was posing for advertisement pictures half the time and working in his dark-room the other half. I haven't seen her since she started in that game."

"Do you happen to know the name of the firm?"

"Not sure of it, but I think it was Slesmans."

The inspector's next inquiry was of her nationality, and did she dance?

"Sure. She was a damned fine dancer. Her parents were Italian. Came over here with an opera company and stayed. Madame Scarlatina, her mother was. About the best mime artiste we ever had. Treat to watch her. The goods, she was. Played every part in *Alice*. Lord love us, versatility was her middle name. Taught little Nina herself."

Kenway's inquiries at Slesmans confirmed the agent's story. They had, they said, employed Miss Francetti for some time, but she had left them to enter business as the manageress of a gown shop. They knew nothing more about her.

With that story, Inspector Kenway returned to Doctor Manson. The latter listened attentively to the recital.

"So you see, Doctor, she's just another theatrical. Gets more and more muddled, doesn't it?"

Doctor Manson ignored the question. Instead, he asked one himself.

"You say that Fleckman found her one or two small parts. Did you happen to inquire what sort of parts they were?"

Kenway chuckled. "I did, Doctor," he said. "Always very careful to miss nothing when I'm on a job for you. The most minute detail, you know."

A smile from the scientist acknowledged the 'dig'.

" And what kind of parts did she play, then?"

"Several dancing parts, a small imitations role in a revue, and two Christmasses in the kids' play, *Alice*."

"What!"

The ejaculation made Kenway jump at the suddenness and fierceness of it.

"A part in the kids' Christmas play, *Alice*."

"What part?"

"That I don't know, Doctor."

Doctor Manson pointed to the telephone. "Ring up your Mr. Fleckman and ask him," he said.

Kenway dialled a number, and put the question. He listened to the reply and, asking the agent to hold on for a moment, turned to Manson.

"He says one or two minor parts," he announced.

The Doctor motioned for the mouthpiece to be handed to him. He spoke to the waiting man at the other end. Had Miss Francetti played a certain part. He was specifically interested in that, he said.

"Well, she has done, but it's not her best line," was the answer. "Ma was the one for that. It wants a bit more than Nina has."

The scientist asked another question.

"Oh lord, yes," replied Mr. Fleckman. "She don't do it now. Bit too stiff, you gather. But she's still in the business."

Manson replaced the receiver. A grim smile played about his lips. He turned to the inspector.

"Keep this under your hat, Kenway," he said. "Is the *Dick Whittington* company still at the Old Sussex?"

"It is their last few days, Doctor."

"Pop down there and see the stage-manager. Ask him if any of the girls were off on the night that Miss de Grey died. Tell him to think carefully, as it may mean a lot to us. I want to know if anybody was off, and if so who they were, and why they were away. Go in a Squad car, and hurry back."

The journey, however, seemed to be wasted. Mr. Trimble, the stage-manager, was emphatic that there could have been nobody missing from the stage during the evening.

"I'd have spotted a blank space or an odd number in a trice, old man," he said. "Dammit, that's part of my job. I can assure you that there was nobody short on the stage that night, or any other night. I'd have raised hell had there been."

"Doctor Manson attaches the greatest importance to this, Mr. Trimble," insisted Kenway, in an attempt to upset the memory of the stage-manager. "Is there any way in which anybody *might* have been absent—any conceivable way?"

The stage-manager ruminated over the question in the silence of painful thought. He had deliberated for a couple of minutes and was about to shake his head when an idea occurred to him.

"As a matter of fact. Inspector, there *might* be a chance. A very slight one, but a possible chance. I've heard of it happening once before. Not with the regular company, mind you. The only way an absence could be possible without me or the manager knowing it would be through the local girls. Every pantomime company, you know, engages a few local girls as extras. It could happen there. It would be like this. . . ."

He explained in a few sentences the possibility.

Inspector Kenway hurried back to the Yard. Doctor Manson heard his report with a face over which crept the alertness that was a sign to his Yard colleagues that he was seeing a possible way out of an *impasse*. He looked long and searchingly at the inspector.

"You and I will go down to Burlington in the morning, Kenway," he said.

CHAPTER XX
THE LAST CLUE

THE SCIENTIST'S VISIT to the seaside resort had, however, to be postponed. Barely five minutes before he and Inspector Kenway were on the point of leaving, the telephone bell in the Laboratory rang out a shrill demand. Wilkins, the Laboratory attendant, answered it.

"For you, Doctor," he announced.

Manson took the telephone. The voice of Professor Simpkins, of the College of Metallurgy, greeted him.

"You wanted to know, Doctor, what amounts of indium there are in the country, and for what it is used. Well, the only amount I know of this side is about half a pound and we have it here. It's very little known, you understand. As for the use of it, I can't imagine why you are inquiring, but so far as I know it is not used over here for anything. That is, by any engineering concern in their manufactures.

"There is, however, a possible explanation of a small quantity—a very small quantity—in this country."

"Now, Professor, you are getting interesting," retorted Manson. "I have found traces of it in very peculiar circumstances, and I cannot account for its presence. Anything you can tell me that will put me on the track will be, indeed, exceedingly valuable. What is the possible explanation of which you are speaking?"

"This, Doctor. Our engineering department tells me that the American car makers who turn out the Splendide automobile have been experimenting with indium as a lining for pistons or for sleeves in the cylinders. It was purely an experiment, but had been found satisfactory. I gather that some two hundred cars have now been so fitted. Now, there may be two or three of those cars over here, and the metal you say you have traced might, conceivably, have come from the cylinders. Say a car thus fitted has been rebored over here. The garage obviously could not have acquired any supply of indium, and must have used some other metal, probably aluminium. The old sleeves would, therefore, have been thrown away. That is the only suggestion that I can think of."

The scientist, after a word of thanks, rang off; and immediately dialled the Yard's motor expert.

"Who handles the Splendide car over here, Soames?" he asked.

"Alliday and Alliday, Pont Street, Doctor."

Once more the scientist called the telephone into play. He asked for the general manager of Alliday and Alliday. Mr. Alfred Appleton inquired what service he could do the caller.

"I understand that the Splendide car has recently been fitted with indium-lined cylinders, Mr. Appleton. Is that so?"

Mr. Appleton replied that one type of car had been so fitted. "It is our twelve-cylinder model, Doctor Manson," he explained. "Not many have been lined with the metal you name. Why? Do you want one?"

Doctor Manson chuckled. "I'm afraid not, Mr. Appleton," he rejoined. "I am interested in the metal more than the car. Tell me, have you any of that model over here?"

"Quite a lot of Splendides, Doctor. They are exceedingly popular, you know. But if you mean the indium-lined, then I'll have to look up the records. There aren't many. It's an expensive car, the twelve-cylinder one. Costs about £3,000. And only the 12 has the indium. Hang on for a moment, and I'll have a hunt in the books."

The manager was back within two or three minutes. "Are you there?" he called.

The scientist assured him that he was listening.

"Well, then, so far as I can see, Doctor, only three of those cars have been sold over here. We have, until recently, been servicing all three. One we have in the garage at the moment undergoing a three-monthly check. One is on the Continent on a tour, and the third is still in London."

"Who has it, Mr. Appleton? Who is the fortunate fellow?"

"A Mr. da Costa, a City gentleman."

"I see." The scientist thought for a moment. Then: "Can you tell me when the second of the cars went over to the Continent?"

"I can, Doctor. We serviced it just before it went. It is about three months ago."

"Thank you very much, Mr. Appleton." Doctor Manson rang off without satisfying the waiting curiosity of the manager.

He turned to the waiting inspector. "We'll have to put off the trip to Burlington for an hour or so, Kenway," he announced. "Do you know whether the block of flats in which da Costa is housed have a garage, or garages?"

"I don't, Doctor. But I'll soon find out."

He telephoned the flats, and was connected to the hall porter.

"Have you garages attached to your flats?" he inquired.

"Private lock-ups, yes, sir," was the reply.

"Ask him if da Costa has one," whispered Manson.

"He hasn't," was the porter's reply. "Cos why? Cos his big car won't go in any we've got. See."

"Where, then, does Mr. da Costa garage his car?" queried Kenway.

"In the Sun garage just round the corner," was the reply.

"Many thanks." Kenway rang off. He looked at the scientist.

"This, Kenway, is going to be a ticklish business," he said. "I think you had better do the job yourself. Go to the Sun people and find out when da Costa's car was last serviced. I want to know when the sump of the car was last drained, and what became of the oil. They'll probably say that they have never drained it. If so ask them when da Costa last bought oil in a drum, or something like that. But, most important of all, I want you to arrange for someone there to drain the car sump, and keep the oil for me. It is strictly under the rose, of course, and we shall have to pay for the engine to be filled up again with new oil. But make sure that they use a perfectly clean container for the sump oil. That is most important. No suspicion must, of course, leak out. I should think that the best time to do the business will be after da Costa has come in after his night's carousal in the West End. Anyway, see what you can do."

Inspector Kenway departed, and the scientist sat down impatiently to await his return. It was not so prolonged as he had anticipated. In a little over half an hour the inspector made his reappearance. He carried a petrol can in his right hand.

"Easy, Doctor," he announced, gleefully. "We had a bit of luck. The lighting and speedometer of da Costa's car went wrong yesterday, and the thing is in for repair. Da Costa went off into the country by train. I got hold of the manager and he had the sump drained at once. Gave me this petrol can to carry the oil away in. Absolutely new can, so to speak." He handed over the prize.

Doctor Manson took off his jacket, and slipped on a white laboratory coat in its place. He stepped to the centre table and arranged an assortment of test tubes, beakers and other impedimenta. Having lighted a Bunsen burner, and arranged in the dark-room a spectroscope, he placed a chair for Inspector Kenway, and told him to sit down and keep quiet.

For an hour and a half the scientist worked with the aid of Merry and Wilkins. At the end, Manson and the deputy scientist, Sergeant Merry, compared notes. Finally, from his dossier the sergeant took out the results of the tests carried out on the ashes taken from the Shepherd's Bush fire, and he and the scientist went carefully over them together. Point by point, they checked the dossier with the results obtained by their chemistry analysis just completed, looking at the two sets of results for the precise contents of the ashes and the oil.

At the end, they looked across at each other and smiled.

The scientist divested himself of the white coat, and donned his jacket once more. He turned to Kenway.

"Now, Ken way, we will proceed on our journey to Burlington," he said. "We'll stop on the way for lunch."

The pair got into the Doctor's big Oldsmobile, and began the new hunt. Of the results in the Laboratory, Doctor Manson said no word. And the inspector knew better than to ask for information which was not given voluntarily. He made the journey in a very curious and puzzled state of mind.

Inspector Bradley, looking up at the opening of his door, greeted the pair with enthusiasm. He had made arrangements, as requested, for Enora to be retained in hospital for the remaining short period which Doctor Manson had said would be sufficient for him to complete the case of the poisoned Panto Star. He had been puzzled at the delay, but since the affair was in the hands of the Yard, he had to obey instructions. Now, he said, the time had come to get some movement and tangible result from their investigations. He would, of course, share in the credit of the affair, and had worked with the great Doctor Manson of the Yard. He moved forward and waited for the news that the scientist was bringing.

Doctor Manson waved him to his chair and he and Merry seated themselves on two others brought in by an anticipatory constable.

"Now, listen, Inspector," he said. "I take it that the stage-door-keeper at the Pavilion now is still the same man who was there during the pantomime?"

Inspector Bradley nodded.

"Well, first of all I want to see him. I've one question to ask."

"Let's go," said Bradley, with alacrity.

They went.

The stage-doorkeeper, told that he was wanted to give extra information, waited for the question. So did Inspector Bradley. Doctor Manson addressed the man.

"You were on the door here, I take it, on the night that Miss de Grey died?" he queried.

The man agreed that he was. He had also been on the door, he said, every night for the past three years.

"Now, do you know, if any of the girls were absent from the company on that particular night?" Doctor Manson asked him.

The man scratched his head. He threw his thoughts back to the night of the tragedy.

"Well, sir," he said at length. "I can't recall having reported any of 'em, so I supposes they must all have been here." He proceeded to explain. "You see, sirs, I has a day book what belongs to the manager of the company. I keeps it here on the ledge of me box, and when the chorus girls comes in they has to sign on, same like as any man working in a factory has to sign on. Now, if there was one what hadn't signed, I has to report her, see."

"Does that go for the local girls—the girls engaged for the pantomime?" asked Manson.

"Yes, sir, goes for all the girls what ain't principals in the company."

"And you can't recall any of them missing?"

"Not to my remembering, sir. But the day book would show if there was. The manager of the company could tell you from seeing the day book."

"We've already seen the day book in London," Doctor Manson replied. "It shows that all the girls signed on. I suppose you knew most of the local girls by sight. Did you notice if they were all the same that night as on other nights?"

"Bless you, sir, I shouldn't know. I don't see half of the girls come to the theatre. Mebbe I'm busy with something in me box here. So long as they signs, that's all that worries me. If I found there was somebody short, I has to tell the stage-manager. But I don't inspect 'em all as they comes in."

"Right. Then I'm afraid you can't help us much more than you have already done."

Outside the stage door, the scientist turned to Inspector Bradley. "Now, Inspector, I want all those girls who took part in the pantomime gathered together. It's too late, I dare say, to get them tonight, but I'd like to see them first thing in the morning. I'll arrange a private room in the hotel to see them. Shall we say ten o'clock. I'll leave it to you to arrange. But there must not be any absentees. If work is the trouble send round and tell their employers that they have to see me, and that they must be given time off."

Inspector Bradley nodded, glumly. The enthusiasm with which he had begun the expedition had faded gradually away, and it was with a disappointed air that he left the Scotland Yard couple to return to his police-station.

Sergeant Merry chuckled. "You've hit him hard, Harry," he said. "I think he'd a blank warrant in his pocket."

Manson answered with another chuckle. "I know, Jim, but he doesn't know what we know, and I don't want him to until our man is safely in the bag. Any chance talk now might spoil the whole bag of tricks. Come along, and let us have a wash and a brush-up before dinner. That is, if we can get a couple of rooms in the hotel here, or one of them."

They dined, and spent an evening's relaxation in the local music hall. At the time that they were chuckling over the knock-about comedy duo that had the premier place on the bill, Inspector Bradley was bemoaning the fact to his chief constable that they had ever called in the Yard at all. He had gone to his chief with his tale of woe, immediately after he had sent out a couple of constables to round up the girls and summon them to appear at the Royal Hotel by ten o'clock the following morning, no excuses to be accepted.

"I can't see the point of it, sir," he grumbled at the end of his recital of the afternoon's peregrinations. "He said himself that only the cat could have done the murder—he admits it was murder—and there's only two cats. It's got to be one of them. So what has one of the girls being away to do with it? Why waste any more time? The stage-doorkeeper says he can't remember anybody being away. The day book kept by him has been seen by them in London, where the company is now, and that shows everybody signed in, so what's the use? These Scotland Yard men spend too much time following minor details when the course is obvious."

The chief constable regarded his inspector with doubting mien. "Well, Inspector, I don't say you are wrong," he said at last. "But this Doctor Manson is a pretty big man in the Yard, and he's had very few failures. In fact, I don't believe he's had even one failure. If he wants to see the girls, then I feel that there must be something behind it. However, if nothing transpires after he's interviewed the girls tomorrow, I'll see him and suggest that the case is not so complicated as he seems to think. I don't suppose I'll be thanked for it, though."

With that the inspector had to be content. He returned to the station, to wait what the morrow might bring forth.

It produced eight girls in a room in the Bull Hotel, all in varied stages of emotion, fright or expectation. They chatted nervously together, and mostly in undertones, until the Doctor and Inspectors Kenway and Bradley entered. At the unexpected appearance of three arms of the law, the eight were frozen into silence. Inspector Bradley, being a local man, they, of course, knew, it was the two strangers that produced in them a sense of foreboding, however much they searched their consciences and found them without blemish.

Doctor Manson, who was no mean student of psychology, let them wonder in silence for a few moments, then addressed them.

"I understand that you are the ladies who were engaged locally to dance in the pantomime during its stay last Christmas in Burlington," he said. "Is that correct? You *are* the same girls— all of you?"

The eight nodded in their turn, as he eyed them individually.

"Now, you all know the dreadful thing that happened during the pantomime. Miss de Grey, the Principal Boy, died on the stage. It is about that that I want you to help me if you can. It is very important, the thing that I want you to tell me."

He paused, and then put the question:

"On the night that Miss de Grey died, were any of you girls missing from the theatre?"

There was a momentary silence before a chorus of 'noes' came from the combined eight.

Doctor Manson eyed them. "Even missing for no more than an hour or so," he added.

"If they were missing at all, Doctor, it wouldn't be for an hour. They would either be missing or not missing. They could not walk in late, and get away with it," put in Inspector Bradley.

The scientist regarded him with a frown. "Will you let me put the question in my own way, Inspector," he said, tartly. "Anyone could have been in at the start, missing for a time, and then re-appear. Was there anything like that on this night?" he asked again.

There was again a chorus of 'noes'. But Manson, watching the eight closely, thought that he detected a slight hesitation in the rejoinder. He said nothing, but continued to look at the company, as though pondering his next question.

He noticed that the eyes of one or two of the girls strayed embarrassedly from his gaze, and generally towards one other of their number. Inspector Kenway noticed it, too, for he bent forward and spoke to the scientist.

"I think there's something doing with that girl second from the end on the right, Doctor," he suggested.

Doctor Manson nodded. After a pause of a minute or two he turned to the girl.

"What is your name?" he asked.

"Mary Sinclair," she replied.

"Well, Mary, I rather think you are hiding something, are you not, and the others are trying to cover you up?"

The girl blushed uncomfortably.

"There is no need to be frightened. There is no question of any punishment being meted out to you, and there is no reason why the theatre people should know anything about it, if you are afraid that you will not be given another job on the stage next pantomime. All I want to know, or to be sure about, is that you were or were not absent that night. Now were you here, or were you, indeed, away?"

"I was away, sir," came a whisper.

"There, now, that is exactly what I thought." He looked at Inspector Bradley. "These other girls can go into another room,

Inspector," he said. "I will talk to Miss Sinclair without them."
As the girls left the room he drew up an armchair and installed
the guilty party in it. Then, taking a chair himself, and motion-
ing Ken way and Bradley to others, he set himself to probe the
girl's absence from the cast.

"First of all, Mary, the day book shows that you were present
as usual in the theatre. How do you account for that?"

"I don't know, sir. I was surprised when I found out that my
name was there. I knew that someone was taking my place, but
I expected they would sign their own name, and I thought it
would be one of the girls who had trained at rehearsals to take
the place of anybody taken ill."

"You mean that it is not unusual for a deputy to come into
the theatre in certain circumstances, eh?"

"Yes, sir."

"Well, now, how did it all happen? Were you taken ill?"

"No, sir. But I was about fifty miles from the theatre, and
couldn't get back in time."

"I see. And how did that happen?"

The girl's story was soon told. She had, she said, a day or two
before met a gentleman who had been waiting outside the stage
door. He had taken her to supper and a dance in the Pavilion
dance hall, and had been, in fact, very nice. Not at all like some
of the gentlemen who took the chorus girls out after the show.
Then he asked her if she would have lunch with him the following day. The girl said she liked him and agreed.

He drove up to the meeting-place in a car, and during lunch
asked if she would like to have a run into the country.

"I said I should love it, but I had to be back early to go to the
theatre," the girl explained. "He said that would be all right, and
he went off."

"And I suppose the car broke down?" suggested Doctor
Manson.

"I don't quite know what happened to it, sir. I think he said
that the steering had gone wrong, and it would be dangerous to
drive it. He told me to stay and see nobody stole the car while he
went to find a mechanic from a garage to come and fetch it in."

"Where were you then?"

"In the country, miles and miles away. I told him I'd lose my job over it, that there would be a girl short, and he said he would telephone to the pantomime manager, who he knew, and tell him what had happened."

"Which, of course, he never did?"

"No, sir. But I didn't know that for a long time. When he came back, he said it was all right, and I need not worry. Another girl would take my place for the night and I was to go back next night as though nothing had happened and say nothing about it. Which I did."

"How long was he away?"

"Oh, hours and hours. He said he couldn't find a garage who would send, but one had lent him a special tool, and he thought he could get the steering right with it."

"And, of course, he did?"

"Yes, it didn't take very long, sir."

"I see. Well, Inspector, I think we can have the other girls in now, and see what more we can learn about this business."

The seven entered. They were in a more comfortable frame of mind, and they replied with wide smiles to the scientist's look of pained regret at their earlier conduct.

"I have heard Mary's story now," he said, reproachfully. "It was very naughty of you to deny that she had been away, but, I suppose, very understandable. I should probably have done the same thing myself in your places. But now we must discuss the thing very seriously. Who was the girl who took Mary's place?"

"We don't know, sir." The reply came in an emphatic chorus.

"You don't know? Do you mean that she was a stranger?"

"She was to us," one of the girls answered. "We thought that she knew Mary, because when she turned up she said that she had come to take the place of Mary Sinclair, who had gone into the country with a boy friend and didn't want to come back until late. She said that we were not to say anything about it, or Mary would lose her job. She'd signed Mary's name, but of course the dresser knew that she wasn't Mary."

"But, of course, you do have deputies, and you assumed that there was no need to do anything about it, and I suppose the dresser thought the same, eh?"

"Yes, sir."

"Well now, what happened to her during the Highgate Hill scene?"

The girls looked at one another, and then at the scientist. "Nothing happened to her," was the reply.

"She was on the stage, then?"

"Of course, sir. We'd soon have heard about it if she hadn't been. The stage-manager would have rowed us if one hadn't been there, I can tell you."

"And what happened to her after the show?"

The girls looked at the doctor with puzzled faces.

"We didn't know, sir. We never saw her again."

"Did she remain for the entire performance?"

"Oh, yes."

Inspector Bradley started in surprise. "Was she among those I questioned on the stage that night after the show?" he asked.

"Why, yes, sir. She went out with us."

Doctor Manson listened with a frown on his face. His fingers were beating a tattoo on the arms of his chair.

Kenway, hearing it, looked up. "The Doctor's in trouble," he said to himself. "What's gone wrong?" He, like his colleagues at the Yard, knew the signs of perturbation in the scientist.

"Now listen carefully to this, girls," Manson said at length. "Was the lady with you all the time? You keep together, don't you, in your dressing-room?"

"Yes, sir."

"And she was with you all the time?"

"Do you mean on the stage, sir?"

"Both there and in the dressing-room. Take your time and think carefully back. Was there any time when she was not with you or in the company of some of you?"

The girls looked at one another, and talked quietly among themselves. There followed excited noddings, and then one of them elected herself spokeswoman.

"She was with us all the time, sir, except for a few minutes after the shop scene," she announced. "She ran into the dressing-room a bit late, and the dresser had a job to get her changed in time. But it was only about four minutes. We haven't a lot of time for a change."

"Did she say where she had been?"

"She said she had been talking to someone, and had forgotten the time."

"And I don't suppose you, Mary, have seen the nice gentleman friend since?" he asked.

"No"—regretfully.

Doctor Manson produced a copy of the photograph of Mr. da Costa. He held it out to the girl.

"Would this be the gentleman?" he asked.

Mary Sinclair shook an emphatic head.

"Oh no, sir," she replied. "It isn't a bit like him."

Doctor Manson rose. "All right, girls, that's all, thank you. Off you go, and don't talk about this at all. You've been a great help, and you can all have tea in the Pavilion cafe at our expense this afternoon. We'll tell the manageress."

The eight vanished with alacrity, and Manson turned to Bradley.

"Well, Inspector, you see there was a girl missing, after all," he said.

The inspector agreed rather shamefacedly that it was so.

"But what does it matter, Doctor?" he asked. "What has any girl dancer to do with the death of Miss de Grey? She wasn't anywhere near her, except for just dancing past the milestone. . . ."

"Well, don't worry, Inspector. I have no doubt it will all come right in the end. By the way, I'd like to make another inquiry—at the Pavilion."

The three men walked along to the theatre and into the manager's office.

"Mrs. Brough, sir?" repeated that executive. "No, she wasn't on our staff. She was employed by the company and was engaged in London."

Back in the Metropolis the scientist telephoned Mr. Trimble on the stage of the Old Sussex.

"Hello, Doctor," answered Mr. Trimble. . . . "Oh no, she left after Burlington. Said her nerves were upset by the murder and she couldn't go on with another woman. What? Oh yes, genuine enough. She was a nice old soul. No, I don't know where she is now."

Doctor Manson asked one further question.

"I'll ask Miss Prue," was the reply. "She'd be more likely to know than anybody else. Hang on."

A couple of minutes passed. Then his voice came again over the line.

"You there, Doctor? Sure, Pruey says Norma always had a glass of stout and sandwiches in the interval. Standing order. She had one that night. Dresser fetched it from the pub during the Hill scene."

INTERLUDE III
To the Reader

It was at this stage that Doctor Manson regarded his investigations into the two mysteries as completed.

He knew in his own mind the answer to the riddle of the fire frauds, and also the answer to the murder of Dick Whittington.

What remained to be done in producing the evidence necessary to convict was, to his mind, routine work. His case was concluded.

Perhaps the inveterate reader of detective fiction can also name the murderer and the fraudulent fire-raiser. All the clues are in the foregoing pages.

CHAPTER XXI
ARREST NO. 1

THE PRELUDE to the final stage of the dual riddle was played to its crescendo by Inspector Kenway and two sergeants. Their task, entrusted to them by Doctor Manson, was to learn something of the story of the past twelve months of the woman who was now enjoying life under the name of Mrs. Raoul da Costa.

The search by Kenway and his assistants lasted the better part of a day; and the results were presented in precis to the Assistant Commissioner (Crime) at an emergency conference held at the request of Doctor Manson to review for the last time the aspects of the case.

The scientist had made it plain that he was not concerned with the earlier life of Miss Nina Francetti. All he desired to know of her was her story during the last year.

Inspector Kenway gathered it from West End night-clubs, and social rounds; from members of the theatrical profession and from friends and acquaintances of Mr da Costa—and also from those who were antagonistic to the financier.

"As far as we have been able to gather," he told the Assistant Commissioner, "Miss Francetti some twelve months ago had thrown up her stage work and had gone to da Costa as his mistress. They lived together in a flat in Mayfair. I do not think that she passed then as Mrs. da Costa, although, from the flats, I gathered that she was accepted as such, but was held to have retained her stage name. I understand that most ladies of the stage retain the name by which they are well known, even after they marry," the inspector added.

"Anyway, the pair were living together; I have the statements of chambermaids and of the porters who have seen the photographs we took along."

The Assistant Commissioner interposed: "You say, Kenway, that they co-habited. Do you know whether they were, in fact, married?"

"They were not, sir. Da Costa, according to Somerset House, is a single man. At least, there is no record there of his ménage."

"But he may have married abroad, may he not?" asked Manson.

Kenway started in surprise. "Yes, I suppose so, Doctor," he agreed after a pause for reflection. "There would be no record in Somerset House of that."

"And he might have married Miss Francetti, or any other woman?"

"Quite so, Doctor."

Doctor Manson smiled. "It is as well not to jump to conclusions which may put us on a wrong track," he said. He waved to the inspector to continue.

Kenway hesitated. "Where was I?" he asked.

"You had da Costa and Miss Francetti co-habiting in a Mayfair flat, Inspector," prompted the Assistant Commissioner.

"Oh yes. Well, sir, there were, I gather, several rows which disturbed the inhabitants of the other flats and the manager was about to ask the couple to find another love nest when, one night, there was an unusually noisy scene, and da Costa left the flat banging the door behind him. He looked, the porter said, very angry.

"A minute later Miss Francetti came out. She was in a state of hysterics, and said that he (meaning da Costa) had been going round with other women, and she had told him that she would not stand for it. The porter says that he and his wife soothed her, and suggested that Mr. da Costa was only doing what most gentlemen in his station in life did, and that he would be all right in the end.

"Mr. da Costa, he said, did not come back that night. He returned the following morning after Miss Francetti had gone out, and gave up the tenancy of the flat—it was a furnished flat, by the way—paying all dues to the end of the week, which was a couple of days ahead. When Miss Francetti arrived back after lunch she was told what had happened and warned that she would have to vacate the flat at the end of the week. She did leave—and that was the end of the episode."

Inspector Kenway sat back and looked at the Assistant Commissioner. Sir Edward, in his turn, glanced at Doctor Manson.

"That convey anything to you, Doctor?" he asked.

The scientist nodded. "It fits in with what I had conjectured, Sir Edward," he agreed. He turned to the inspector.

"And what happened to Miss Francetti after that?" he asked.

"She returned to the stage for a time," replied Kenway. "It was at this stage that Mr. Fleckman—the agent, you remember—got her one or two small parts. When those came to an end, she went into the advertising office, and she left there to become manageress of a gown shop. . . ."

"Would there have been a fire at the gown shop, Kenway?" Manson interrupted.

Kenway looked across at him. "You know everything, Doctor," he commented. "There *was* a fire, and the shop and all the stock were completely destroyed."

"And twelve months after, or thereabouts, the wheel turns its full circle and Miss Francetti is once more living with Mr. da Costa, who has renounced the other ladies, eh?"

"That's about the ticket," the inspector agreed.

Doctor Manson smiled. "Now let us forget the point for a moment, A.C., and concentrate on the fires," he suggested. "Now . . ."

For a quarter of an hour he spoke rapidly, outlining his evidence. The Assistant Commissioner, at the end, nodded his agreement.

"Then we pull in the two?" he asked.

"I think so—after a little chat," was the scientist's reply. "I suggest that the insurance companies' legal representative's office would be a suitable rendezvous, in the circumstances."

The conference broke up.

* * * * *

Mr. Izzy Oppenheimer, summoned to the office of Mr. Redwood, attended with anticipatory satisfaction at the prospect of a cheque in the neighbourhood of £1,300, or thereabouts. He greeted the lawyer with a cheerful 'good morning'. Mr. Redwood grunted, and motioned him to a chair.

A moment or two later Doctor Manson and Inspector Kenway entered. They nodded to Mr. Oppenheimer, and each took a chair placed conveniently near the lawyer.

With them comfortably seated, Mr. Redwood put aside the pen which he had been using on a document on his desk, and addressed himself to Mr. Oppenheimer.

"Now we will talk business, sir," he announced. "Let me see, what was the total amount of your claim?"

"It vos £1,630," replied Mr. Oppenheimer, and rubbed his hands together. He was already feeling the money. Mr Redwood eyed him menacingly.

"Well, Mr. Oppenheimer, we do not propose to pay one penny of that sum," he announced.

The gown shop proprietor jumped an inch off his chair. He stared, speechlessly, for a moment or two. But only for a moment or two. Then he found his voice.

"Vot? I don't understand," he said. "Vot is it you are trying to do to me, ain't it? My shop has an accident. It vos insured. You take the money for the insurance. I pay you good money, don't I. You don't pay, ain't it?"

He shook a finger at the lawyer.

"All right, I don't say nothings. I get my solicitor. You don't do the monkey business with me."

He rose and picked up his hat. "I'm ratepayer, ain't it? I vill have justice."

Manson spoke quietly to the excited man.

"Justice you shall have, Mr. Oppenheimer. I am an officer of the Law, and so is this gentleman"—he pointed to Inspector Kenway. "We are here to see that justice is done."

Mr. Oppenheimer put down his hat and beamed on the couple. "You vill be a vitness, yes?" he asked. "You are English Law gentlemen."

"Sit down again, Mr. Oppenheimer, and hear what we have to say," responded Manson.

The man glanced anxiously at the two men, and then at Mr. Redwood, who sat, with a slight smile playing over his face. His alarm grew.

"Thank you, thank you," he said, "but I does nothings without my solicitor. Good-bye to you." He again took up his hat.

"Sit down, Mr. Oppenheimer," said Doctor Manson; and his voice had a note of command. "Sit down and listen to me."

Mr. Oppenheimer sat.

"The fire on your premises started at the spot where you say that an alterations and pressing department was situated. Is that so?" asked Manson.

"Yes. That damned woman. She left the iron burning."

"Well now, we say that she did nothing of the kind, Mr. Oppenheimer. On the contrary, we found traces of petrol and oil at the spot—and at other spots. And from that we suggest to you that the place was deliberately set on fire in such a way that it was certain that the entire premises would become involved and a claim for total loss made against the insurance company—in fact, the ancient and remunerative custom of fire-raising. What do you say to that, Mr. Oppenheimer?"

Beads of perspiration were standing on the forehead of the man. His gaze darted furtively from one to the other of the three men.

"But who would do it?" he moaned. "I get no insurance. I am ruined. . . ." he wailed.

"Tell us what you know of a Mr. da Costa?" suggested Doctor Manson.

"Da Costa?" echoed Oppenheimer. "Who vos the man. I know nothings about him. How would he get in my shop, eh?"

"You do not know Mr. da Costa?" Doctor Manson bent an ironic gaze upon Oppenheimer. "But did you not telephone him on the morning after the fire?"

"I telephoned him? Me. I know nothings of any da Costa man."

"Come now, Mr. Oppenheimer," rejoined Manson. "We know when you called da Costa. We know what you said, and we know what was the reply. You walked round the corner to a telephone-box after you left us and the burned-out shop at

Shepherd's Bush. You asked for a number, which was a mistaken number. You then asked for Royalty 07765. A man's voice answered, and you then said, 'There has been an accident.' Now, Royalty 07765 is the number of da Costa's flat. Do you still say that you do not know Mr. da Costa?"

Doctor Manson eyed the man with a quizzical gaze. Oppenheimer swallowed painfully once or twice, and then repeated his denials. "Show me a picture of him," he demanded. "Maybe I know his face."

"I do not think a picture is needed, Oppenheimer," the scientist retorted. "I am alleging that you and da Costa plotted to burn down that shop in order to gain the insurance money. I am suggesting that a night or two previously you had rehearsed the fire by lighting a couple of candles, or maybe more, and letting them burn while da Costa and a woman walked past the shop in the street several times to see whether any light showed from the candles. . . ."

"I'll have the law on you. It's a libel . . ."

"Slander," corrected Doctor Manson. "Libel has to be written. You see, Oppenheimer, although you say that you do not know da Costa, *he* says that he knows you very well. He says that he financed you and whatever may have happened to the shop he was only a sleeping partner and had no part or parcel in it."

Doctor Manson realized that in wording his remarks in the way that he had done, he was twisting da Costa's statement; that he was not strictly within Judges' Rules. It was true that da Costa had stated that he was only a sleeping partner, inasmuch as he had found the capital. Obviously, argued Manson, if he was only a sleeping partner he could not be accounted to have part and parcel with whatever happened. A little sharp thinking, but, Manson decided, permissible in the circumstances.

The effect of the sentence on Mr. Oppenheimer, however, was electrical. He jumped to his feet and flung his hands to the Heavens.

"Vot!" he screamed. "The damned Dago said that? He shopped me. Listen, gentlemens. I'll tell you somethings. That da Costa, he made the fire. He suggest to me that we start a shop and have a big fire. He showed me vot to do. I go away and leave the shop." He wrung his hands.

"I am the mug," he moaned. "I the baby hold."

"And who took away the greater part of the dresses and the rolls of silk before the fire, Oppenheimer?" asked the scientist.

"The da Costa man sends a car for them, mister."

Doctor Manson eyed him sharply. "And so it was all da Costa, was it?" he asked. "Was it da Costa who told us that the dresses had all been lost in the fire and claimed damages for them? Or was it you, Oppenheimer?"

The man made no answer.

"How much of the insurance money were you, the innocent man, going to get?" asked Mr. Redwood.

"Three hundred pounds," moaned Mr. Oppenheimer. "I am a poor man. It was a temptation."

"Well, we are arresting you, Oppenheimer, on charges of arson and attempted fraud," announced Kenway. He charged the man and handed him over to a sergeant waiting hopefully outside.

"And try to think up a story of how you met da Costa and how many other fires you have helped him in," was Kenway's final thrust. "It may help you with the judge."

"He'll want a solicitor when he has had time to think, Sergeant," said Kenway, drawing the officer aside. "You'll have to telephone for one."

The sergeant nodded.

"But make sure you do not get the one he wants for a couple of hours. We've another gentleman to question before this arrest leaks out."

The sergeant nodded again.

From the offices of Mr. Redwood, Manson and Kenway sauntered the easy distance to the two-roomed suite of Mr Raoul da Costa. The financier answered their request for information with an enthusiastically expressed willingness to render Scotland Yard any assistance that lay in his power. About what was information required? he inquired. "I know probably as much about finance as anyone in the City."

"Say rather, about *whom*," Doctor Manson suggested.

"Very well, gentlemen, about whom do you want my information?"

"About Mr. Izzy Oppenheimer."

"What! Him again?"

Mr. da Costa simulated a startled surprise.

"What has he been doing now?"

Inspector Kenway chuckled at the *bonhomie* of the question. But he said nothing. It was Doctor Manson who replied.

"You will recall, Mr. da Costa, that when we asked you on the last occasion about Mr. Oppenheimer, you informed us that you were a kind of sleeping partner to him; that you had, in fact, lent him money on the security of a half-share in the business. Mr. Oppenheimer had, I think you said, done you a good turn once, and you felt that you would be repaying him by lending him the £500 he needed?"

The financier nodded. "That is the exact case," he agreed.

"Now the shop is burned out, Mr. da Costa."

"True. But the stock was insured. I insisted on that, of course. That was my security."

"Quite so. I can well believe it."

Doctor Manson sat back in a leather armchair into which da Costa had pressed him. He pursed his lips, and pressed the tips of his fingers together. He paused a moment before continuing. Then:

"Mr. da Costa, you have lost your £500," he said.

Da Costa stared at him.

"Lost it? Do you mean to say that Oppenheimer was not insured? Damn it, he told me that he had paid the premium."

"Oh yes. Oppenheimer was properly insured. I can assure you of that," the scientist announced.

"Well, then, how have I lost it? Possibly, the insurance people will knock a bit off the claim. The fraudulent devils generally do. But I'll get it out of Oppenheimer. I haven't lost the 500."

"The fact of the matter is, that Oppenheimer was arrested half an hour ago on a charge of maliciously setting fire to the premises with intent to defraud the insurance company, and on a charge of conspiracy to defraud. The insurance company are not, of course, paying the claim. We felt that you, as a sleeping partner, should know where you stand in regard to your money."

Mr. da Costa looked incredulous. Watching him closely, Inspector Kenway noted the play of the eyebrows, the eyes and the hands. He commented silently that the man would have made an excellent actor. He must have realized the peril in which he in all probability stood; but was fighting gamely on an outside chance.

"Maliciously setting fire . . . not an electric iron left burning?"

"Mr. Oppenheimer claims that the fire was accidental, and was caused by an iron left switched on," agreed Manson. "But he made one mistake, Mr. da Costa."

The financier looked inquiry.

"He forgot to leave us an iron to find." Doctor Manson smiled grimly. "Now, fire cannot destroy an electric iron without trace. It doesn't burn away, and it doesn't melt. We did not find traces of an iron, but we *did* extract lead and paraffin from the soot of the fire, and a curious metal from the ash and debris left behind by the flames. It is wonderful what science and chemical analysis can do. You should study the subject, Mr. da Costa. It is really fascinating. Now, those discoveries suggested to us that the flames had been fed with petrol and oil."

Mr. da Costa digested, slowly, the resumé.

"Do I gather that Mr. Oppenheimer has admitted the incendiarism?" he asked.

"Not altogether. But partly. As a matter of fact he states that it was you who suggested the plan to acquire the premises, start a business there and then set fire to it. He states that you financed the entire project, and that you removed a large part of the stock before setting fire to the shop. He says, also, that his share in the divvy out was to have been £300, leaving you with the balance of £1,330."

The two men waited with anticipation the reaction of Mr. da Costa to this bluntly-expressed accusation. It was not likely, of course, that he would make any admissions; he was, they were quite sure, of different calibre from Oppenheimer. Doctor Manson expected a denial, but he was interested, psychologically, in the kind of denial which da Costa would invent on the spur of the moment—and which he would have to maintain in the future.

It was, in fact, two or three moments before the financier recovered his composure. Then he laughed.

"Ha! Ha! A likely story, don't you think, Chief Inspector. A man of my standing engaging in crime for the matter of . . . how much would it be? . . . £1,330, if the claim is settled in full. I can make that much in a day in the ordinary way of business. Do I look the kind of man who would imperil his liberty for a thousand or so pounds?"

He paused as though an idea had occurred to him. He uttered an ejaculation of surprised realization. "Gad, Chief Inspector, it looks to me like a plant, and that was the reason he wanted a sleeping partner, in case anything should go wrong with his plans. He seems to know the ropes of fire-raising, doesn't he? Stock removed, and claimed as destroyed. By the way, how do you know that stock was removed?"

"By the simple process of weighing the ash and debris, and making a quantitative analysis, Mr. da Costa."

"I see. Well, I don't suppose you will pay much attention to his statements. It is, as I have said, a plant. The insurance, I take it, is in his name. Looks to me that he is pretty experienced in the game."

"We have no doubt that he has been concerned in earlier fires," confessed Doctor Manson. "There is, however, one curious feature of this particular fire which may interest you, in view of the fact that you think you have been . . . framed I think is the word, is it not, Kenway?"

"Framed is the word, Doctor."

"And what would that be, Chief Inspector?" asked da Costa.

"You remember I told you that we had abstracted lead and paraffin from the soot at the fire and a curious metal from the ash and debris?"

Da Costa inclined his head in recognition.

"The spectroscope can perform remarkable deeds, Mr. da Costa. It demonstrated to me, for instance, that the metal was indium. It also told me that the metal was contained in the oil which had been used to feed the flames at the spot where the fire broke out to the other parts of the shop. Now, indium is an exceedingly rare metal in this country. There is, to my certain knowledge, only half a pound over here, and that can be accounted for fully. On the other hand there is available a small extra amount. A certain type of American car is being fitted with the metal as an experiment, in the shape of piston linings. The thought occurred to us that the mixture of oil and indium might have come from the sump of a car of this particular make."

Doctor Manson leaned forward.

"While you were away, Mr. da Costa, we drained the sump of your Splendide car and analysed the oil. It contained indium in about the same quantity and proportions as the ash delivered to us from the fire."

"Proves nothing, my friend," retorted da Costa. "Accepting your conjecture as correct"—he emphasized the word conjecture—"I might point out that I am not the only person over here to possess a Splendide car."

"You are the only Splendide owner to have had one with indium linings in this country during the past three months, Mr. da Costa," retorted the scientist. "And, incidentally, I never conjecture; I propound only proved data."

"You will find it difficult to convince a lawyer that such theoretical moonshine can be accepted in legal circles, sir," said da Costa.

"There are other incidents," was the quiet retort. "For instance, last August you visited the Paris Show Rooms, Liverpool, accompanied by a woman. You were thought by the assistants, who have identified your photograph, to be considering finding capital for the business—a sleeping partner. A fortnight later, the top was burnt out, and the insurance was paid.

"Again, you have been identified as a man who had a long interview with London Fashion Modes at Welsborough. This shop, too, suffered a fire calamity shortly afterwards, and again heavy insurance was paid. You had stayed on that occasion at the Bull Hotel in the town. Still further coincidence is the fact that, very shortly after you had inspected the premises of Fines and How-ards, at Sheffield, insurance was paid on another total loss. . . ."

"Was I the only visitor at all these premises before the fire?" Costa waxed sarcastic.

"No, I suppose not, sir," was the tart retort. "But may I refer to the destruction of the fur warehouse in Nottingham, within a week of your paying it a long visit? Among the articles for which a claim for total loss was made was a mink coat. We have found that mink coat, Mr. da Costa. It was left behind at the Burlington Theatre by Miss de Grey who died in that theatre. She accom-panied you to Nottingham on the occasion of your visit to the fur warehouse. We found there, also, dust sheets covering Miss de Grey's clothes. They had been specially made for Silks, Ltd., whose stock, heavily insured, was destroyed, also by fire, after having received a visit of inspection from you. Those dust sheets were never sold; we have the assurance of the manager for that.

"Now, all these coincidences are so disturbing, Mr. da Costa, that I am detaining you on suspicion of being concerned in a conspiracy to defraud."

CHAPTER XXII
ARREST NO. 2

AT 1 P.M. the Elysium night-club in the heart of London's West End, was preparing for another night of profit. At the same time Inspector Bradley was hurrying to the Metropolis in a car, bringing with him a passenger.

And in Scotland Yard, Chief Detective-Inspector Manson, D.Sc., and Inspector Kenway were investing themselves in the sombre black which is civilized man's raiment in which to spend his evenings and nights in social whirl and gaiety.

The final performance of Dick Whittington's death was call-ing overture and beginners.

The Elysium night-club varied but little from the score or so of other clubs which continue to pester and befoul the West

End of London. The difference between it and they lay in the fact that its charges were higher, and the quality of the fare provided lower. In all other directions it resembled its companions. By which you will know that it is housed in a basement (in which nobody would confine a dog), had a collection of eight nondescript musicians who produced a selection of noises alleged to be music, but more correctly designated 'Swing', and had also a crooner, by which is meant a person of either sex with no voice, no ear for music and no knowledge whatever of phrasing or diction. The lady in the Elysium moaned and whined at various intervals, a microphone a couple of inches or so from her mouth, lest her voice should not reach even the front row of tables fining the dance floor.

The Elysium was a bottle party club. That means that it had no licence to sell drink—either in licensed hours, or out of them. However, the ingenuity of bottle party proprietors finds a simple means of getting round that. The customer—the club member—gives an order to a wine and spirit merchant through the club. (The owners of London's night-clubs are, jointly, also the owners of the wine and spirit establishment.) The order is made out for so many bottles of this and that to be delivered on demand.

Thus, when at 2 a.m. the customer wants a bottle of something to raise his jaded spirits he merely writes on a slip of paper an order to the wine and spirit merchant to supply one of the bottles ordered. A waiter repairs to the ever-open door of the wine establishment and returns with the bottle. Thus can you drive a coach and horses through an Act of Parliament.

The Elysium is covered with an expensive red plush and pile carpet, except for a small space reserved in the centre, where a laid pinewood floor space is utilized for dancing. The lights are dimly shaded over intimate tables. The club opens its doors at 11 p.m. It begins to wake up at 11.30 and dies away at about 3.30 a.m.

At 11.45 on the night under review a car drove up to the entrance, at street level, of the club. It paused to allow two evening-kitted officers of the Law to alight. Then, with the constable driver, and a sergeant beside him, it moved on a few paces and parked by the kerbside.

Doctor Manson and Inspector Kenway descended the stairs of the club to the foyer, and after a word with the attendant, entered the office of the manager. Incidentally, the manager was also the proprietor of the club, although he did not know that Scotland Yard was aware of that fact; and had done his best to hide his dual identity.

The lack of cordiality with which he greeted the inspectors was even more marked when he learned the reason for the visit. He raised a shrill voice in protest.

"Listen, Pepi, or Weinberger as you were born," retorted Kenway, "we could do what we are going to do in your dashed club in sight of the customers, but we're showing you consideration which neither you nor your club deserves, so shut up and do as you are told. We want to use this office. Get out somewhere, and stay out."

Mr. Weinberger wasted no more words; he moved out of his office and club.

Inspector Kenway followed. He strolled into the club proper, and sat at a table placed conveniently in a corner of the basement room, and partly hidden by a large palm, the continued life existence of which in the gloomy, stuffy atmosphere would have provided an intensive study for any horticulturist.

At midnight Inspector Bradley and his passenger ended their journey from Burlington-on-Sea, and they, too, wandered through the doorway of the Elysium and into the manager's office, to be greeted by Doctor Manson. They were made comfortable in a couple of armchairs.

"I cannot say how long you will have to wait, Inspector," the scientist apologized. "But I do not think it will be long. Meanwhile I have ordered coffee and sandwiches. They are on the house. If you had wandered inside the club, they would probably have cost you a sovereign."

Time, which according to the proverb, flies, dragged a weary way to twelve forty-five. Then, Kenway, watching the doorway, saw the plush curtain drawn back as by invisible hands and a moment later the entrance framed the figure of a woman.

She was a *petite* slim brunette dressed in a long black evening gown cut low in the corsage. The darkness of her hair and frock emphasized the startling whiteness of her bare arms and shoulders. She stood for a moment like a statue and then moved slowly and gracefully to a table which bore the intimation 'reserved'. A bottle of champagne sat already in the ice bucket. A waiter came forward with a bow; she waved him aside and nestled comfortably in the luxurious depths of her chair. The lady was, it seemed plain, awaiting her escort.

The eight players, having recovered from the exertions of an earlier performance, broke into another cachination of sound. A dozen or so of the couples present rose, and broke into the steps of a Rumba on the pine floor.

Inspector Kenway rose in his place and passed unobtrusively through the curtained entrance to the office. His eyes took in the gathering; he nodded to Bradley and then sent an inquiring glance at Doctor Manson.

An answering nod; and he straightened his tie, pulled the points of his waistcoat into place and, turning, brushed aside the curtain and stood looking into the club.

His eyes passed to the waiting woman—and stayed. Slowly he walked across the floor and stood in front of her. He bowed.

"Mr. da Costa has been detained, madam," he said. The phrase brought a slight smile to his lips. It was, he soliloquized, about the first time it had been used in the circumstances with absolute truth.

"He may be some time before he can join you. I offer my services until he can do so. Shall we dance?"

"Detained—at this hour. How extraordinary." Her lips formed into a *moue*. She looked at the tall figure of the well-groomed man in front of her, noted his air of breeding, his good looks. She rose and, placing her bag on the table, moved towards the floor.

"Might I suggest, madam, that you carry your bag. It is a tempting bait."

"Oh, perhaps you are right. I heard that one was stolen from the club the other night." She slipped it over an arm.

Together the inspector and the woman moved into the dance. Twice they completed the circuit of the floor and then Kenway steered his partner towards the entrance.

Feeling the carpet beneath her feet the woman looked up in surprise. Her mouth opened, but before she could frame the obvious question the inspector proferred his explanation.

"There are three friends of mine who I particularly want you to meet," he said.

"It's a little unusual, surely. I do not even know you," the woman insisted.

"Nevertheless. . . ." He took an elbow and ushered her, protestingly, through the curtain, across the tiny foyer, and into the office of Signor Pepi (born Weinberger).

Doctor Manson and Inspector Bradley rose. The woman eyed them in mute inquiry. Doctor Manson turned to the passenger whom Inspector Bradley had brought up from Burlington.

"Do you know this lady?" he asked her.

He waited for her reply, a marked anxiety in his face. He was satisfied in his own mind that his deduction was correct. But it was, after all, deduction. None knew that better than he; and none knew better that he had no evidence which would satisfy a jury as to the accuracy of that deduction. One word from Bradley's passenger could produce that evidence—or destroy it.

The word came.

"Yes. She is the lady who took the place of Mary Sinclair in the pantomime on that night."

"Thank you." Doctor Manson nodded towards the door and Inspector Bradley took the Burlington girl by the arm and shepherded her into the foyer.

"Sit there for a few minutes, will you?" he asked, and returned to the office.

The three figures stood silent, awaiting him. The smooth whiteness of the woman's face had changed to a haggard grey. Her eyes were opened in dilation, and her hands were clenched so that the whites of the knuckles showed plainly through the skin.

At a nod from Doctor Manson Inspector Bradley stepped forward. He raised his voice.

"I am Inspector Bradley, of the Burlington-on-Sea Police Force," he said. "These gentlemen are detective-officers from Scotland Yard. *I am arresting you, Nina Francetti, on a charge of being concerned in the murder of Norma de Grey on the stage of the Pavilion Theatre at Burlington, on the night of . . .*"

"Catch her, Kenway," said Manson sharply.

The inspector supported the fainting woman, and laid her on the settee.

"You will have to warn her when she comes round, Bradley. Fetch her cloak."

Five minutes later Nina Francetti left for the last time the club where her nights had been spent in song and dance. The strain of 'You'll Miss me Sometimes' from the swing band ushered her departure. The shuffling of feet on the dance floor sounded to her ears like the rustling of a shroud.

* * * * *

At 1 a.m. Raoul da Costa was roused from his bed in his cell. Inspector Kenway accosted him.

"We have just arrested Nina Francetti on a charge of being concerned in the murder of Norma de Grey," he said. "I am now adding to the charges already made against you a further charge of being an accessory before and after the fact of the murder of Norma de Grey."

The man rose in terror.

"It's a lie," he shouted. "I knew nothing whatever about the death of Norma until afterwards. I'll make a statement. I'm not going to swing for a damned woman."

"You are not bound to make a statement, but—" began Kenway.

"I know all that jumble," was the retort. "I'm telling you what happened."

He began to speak in a high-pitched, frightened voice. . . .

* * * * *

In Doctor Manson's room in Scotland Yard, the scientist, Kenway, Bradley, and Merry sat drinking coffee. Inspector Bradley's passenger had been made comfortable for what remained of the night in the women police quarters of the Yard. The inspector himself now congratulated the scientist on the completion of the case.

"Though, how you came to suspect that damned girl, I'm hanged if I know," he announced to the company at large. "It's genius."

"The completion of the case?" Doctor Manson repeated the words after him. "We haven't completed the case, Bradley. Far from it."

"B—b—but—" began Bradley.

Doctor Manson interrupted.

"You arrested both Nina Francetti and da Costa on charges of 'being concerned in the murder' and with being an accessory before and after the fact, Bradley. We have not charged either of them with being the actual perpetrator of the deed. Neither were they. That is why I suggested the wording of the warrants. We have still to arrest the actual murderer."

"N—n—not the Cat?" asked Bradley.

Doctor Manson smiled.

"Neither of the cats, Bradley, I promise you," he said.

"The Francetti girl was on the stage, Doctor. And at the time. She had Mary Sinclair kept away on purpose—"

"Agreed, Bradley. That is part of the conspiracy. She went there, I think, with the intention of murdering Miss de Grey. But she was stopped by someone or something, and somebody else did it. She did not commit the murder because the murder was committed by the Cat. Now, Miss Francetti was not the cat. She couldn't have been the cat, because she was dancing in the ballet scene when the Cat was lying with Whittington on the Hill. Wasn't she?"

Inspector Bradley reluctantly agreed that it appeared that way.

"Then who the hell did do the murder, Doctor," burst out Kenway. "I was banking on Nina Francetti from the inquiries we've been making. Where do we look for the murderer now?"

"I think, perhaps, the murderer will come to us, Kenway," was the reply. "Which reminds me. I want the arrest of Nina Francetti put in the papers. See the Press Bureau and ask them to request the Press as a favour to the Yard to give it prominence. Get it to the Press Association and the Central News, too. Here, I'll draft the paragraph."

He wrote for a few moments and then read out the result:

Miss Nina Francetti, dancer and actress, was arrested early today, charged with the murder of Miss Norma de Grey on the stage in the 'Dick Whittington' pantomime at Burlington-on-Sea. She will appear in court today. A sensational story is likely to be told by detectives engaged in the case.

"But, Doctor, she wasn't charged with the murder," said Bradley. "Only with being concerned in."

"I know, Bradley. But this paragraph is designed for a purpose. Just let it go this way."

It was at nine o'clock the same morning that the case was completely solved to the satisfaction of Inspector Bradley. At that hour the telephone bell rang in Doctor Manson's flat. He answered it.

"Kenway here at the Yard, Doctor. There is a woman here to see you. Says she must do so at once. It's a matter of life and death, according to her. She won't give a name. . . ."

"She doesn't need to, Kenway. I know her. I'll be round at once. Put her into my private room, will you, and get Bradley to join you."

A quarter of an hour later the three men entered the room. A woman sat hunched in an armchair; and the face that stared at the three men was ashen and dead. She glanced from one to another and whispered a query. "Doctor Manson?" she asked.

The scientist stepped forward.

"I am Doctor Manson," he said, "and you, of course, are Helen Brough, who dressed Miss de Grey at Burlington."

She nodded, and held out a newspaper, folded at a column. "Is this true, sir?" she asked.

The scientist nodded.

"It is true that Miss Francetti has been arrested, yes," he replied.

"She didn't do it, sir. I killed Miss de Grey. I played the Cat—for the last time." A thin smile showed for a moment on her face. "I doped Enora, and used his skin."

"So I supposed."

The scientist spoke gently.

"I expected you here this morning. I knew that you would have to come; that you would not be able to help it."

Gently, he charged her.

* * * * *

At eleven o'clock Nina Francetti and Raoul da Costa were placed in the dock on the charges made against them.

Inspector Kenway stepped forward and addressed the magistrate.

"A third person has been arrested this morning and charged in this case," he explained. "I ask that all three shall appear together. I shall ask for a remand."

The magistrate nodded.

Helen Brough was brought up from below into the dock. Nina Francetti looked at the bowed figure.

"Mother!" she screamed. "Oh. . . . Oh. . . .*MOTHER!"* She collapsed.

CHAPTER XXIII
DÉNOUEMENT

THE PAVILION THEATRE at Burlington-on-Sea was ablaze with twinkling lights which flickered with pleasing warmth from the revolving ball at the top of the theatre to the colours which ran round the illuminated sign telling from the front of the building the programme that was within.

Beneath the lights, the dark streets were thronged with advancing columns of people jostling one another in a jolly and friendly way as they converged from various directions on the square of pavement that gave way to the vestibule of the theatre. It was the opening night in Burlington of Mr. Henri de Benyat's new musical comedy, *Dolores*, which had been produced in Wimbledon the week before. The visit was of especial interest to Burlington, for it contained leading members of the cast, as the posters put it, "after their phenomenal success in the pantomime *Dick Whittington*".

Miss Prue, who had been Alice Fitzwarren, was now in the leading role of Dolores. The Glee Brothers provided the comedy motif; and King Rat, in other words Mr. Frederick Barnson, was the villain of the piece. Enora, the Cat, now happily recovered from his pantomime experience, had a new animal role, specially created; and the secondary lady was Miss Heather Low who, in the pantomime, had played the Fairy Queen. Mr. Trimble was once again Mr. Henri de Benyat's stage-manager. The dancers and chorus were substantially the same as in the pantomime.

A slight air of restraint made itself felt among the crowd. Rather unusually the ladies and gentlemen of the company were gathered in the Green Room some eighteen or twenty minutes before the curtain was due to ring up. Mr. Frederick Barnson had slipped, in make-up, through the stage door to the Green Man. He now reappeared, a newspaper, folded, under one arm.

The chatter died into silence as he entered.

"Any news, old man?" asked the Captain of the Glee Brothers.

Mr. Barnson nodded. "All found guilty," he announced.

"Never thought they would be, from what we knew," opined Miss Low.

"That fellow Manson got 'em clicked," explained Mr. Barnson. "Remember him coming to us?"

Supporting nods from a dozen heads acknowledged the recognition.

"Marvellous stories the papers have of him."

"What's he say, Freddie?"

Freddie opened his paper. "We've got a bit of time," he said. "I'll read his bit out." He cleared his throat and began.

Chief Detective-Inspector H. Manson, D.Sc., the eminent scientist, told a remarkable story of the investigations which led to the arrest and conviction of the accused. He described the conditions in which Miss de Grey was found dead on the stage of the theatre at Burlington, and the Cat, Enora, was found poisoned in his dressing-room. "There was evidence of bad feeling between the Cat and the dead woman," he said, "and the Cat was the only person at the side of the dead woman during the fatal few minutes on the stage.

"It was obvious to me from the start," he continued, "that the murder could only have been carried out by the Cat; it was obvious also that it had been carefully planned. The Cat was seen to leave the stage immediately after the curtain had been rung down.

"It seemed a reasonable supposition from the appearances that the Cat had injected the poison from which Miss de Grey died and then, knowing that there was no prospect of his escaping the penalty, had taken the same poison in his dressing-room, immediately afterwards. It was when I inspected the dressing-room that I became convinced that this supposition could not be upheld."

The Attorney-General (prosecuting): "Why not?"

Doctor Manson: "Because of three rather curious circumstances. In the first place there were no make-up materials in the room, although Enora not only had to make up the lower part of his face for his part, but was, in fact, actually made up at the time of his poisoning. Secondly, he had drunk a liquid in which the poison had been contained. Now, the action of this particular poison is so rapid that the man would be unconscious within a few seconds of taking it. He would not, therefore, have had time to dispose of the vehicle from which he had drunk. The third circumstance was the complete inability to find the hypodermic syringe which had been used by the murderer."

The Attorney-General: "I take it that that led you to discard the theory of murder and suicide on the part of the Cat?"

Doctor Manson: "On the part of *Enora*, the Cat, sir, yes. I had, accordingly, to start again. The Cat had, of course, an understudy. The question arose as to whether the original Cat had been poisoned by the understudy, who had then carried out a revenge for wrongs on Miss de Grey. There was, however, no evidence of any ill-feeling between Miss de Grey and the understudy either during the run of the pantomime, or in any period before. In addition, the understudy had an alibi that was cast iron, to quote a popular description."

Doctor Manson then described what he said was another curious circumstance. The stage-manager in the scene in which the Principal Boy died, stated that Miss de Grey's cue to the Cat was not at once taken up, and that he leaned forward to see what had happened. "Where's the blasted cat?" he asked, and then, after a short interval, saw the animal enter the stage but rather further back on the stage than usual.

"Now this, to me," said the Doctor, *"was very interesting, for entrances once made by an artiste are seldom changed except at the request of the management for matters of policy or convenience. There were no such reasons in this case. In fact, the place of entrance was actually in the script."*

The scientist described how he returned to London with the skin of the Cat and examined it under a microscope. "I found a number of hairs," he explained. "I had obtained through Inspector Bradley, of the local police, hairs from the head of Enora. Most of the hairs from the interior of the Cat's head mask corresponded with, and were identical with, those of Enora. The shape of the ends of the hairs corresponded with the natural growth after a hair-cut which it was proved that Enora had had a day or so previously.

"There were, however, a few other hairs which were foreign to Enora. These I plucked from the canvas lining, evidence that they had been caught there and pulled from the head of a wearer. That was further evidenced by the fact that each of these hairs had a living root. The code measurements of Enora's identified hairs were 1/350 and the sedullary index 0.132. The hairs for which I had no known owner measured 1.450 with a sedullary index of 0.148.

"*These are the measurements of the hairs from the head of the average woman.* They were not, however, the long strands of hair which are usually associated with a woman's hair. I was forced to the conclusion by careful examination, that these hairs had come from the head of a woman who affected what is known as an Eton crop. From the evidence then before me I arrived at the decision that, since Enora could not have been the poisoner, and the deputy Cat had an alibi that held up against all investigation, some person other than these two had played in the Cat's skin during that fatal scene, and that the person who had done so was a woman."

The Attorney-General: "In fact, one of the two women prisoners at the bar?"

Doctor Manson: "At that time I had no knowledge of the existence of Nina Francetti or Madame Scarlatina. I knew only that some woman had been in the skin."

The Attorney-General: "Will you tell the jury, Doctor, how you came to associate the women prisoners with the skin."

Doctor Manson: "When I began to investigate the past life of Miss de Grey I found out that she was, or had been, the mistress of the male prisoner, Raoul da Costa. I was already inquiring into the activities of da Costa in connection with another case. . . ."

The Judge interposed at this point. "You must not introduce any matter relative to a prosecution, or investigation, not before this court, Doctor Manson," he said.

Doctor Manson: "I will take great care of that, my Lord."

The Doctor then proceeded to describe how he found that a woman had been associated with da Costa in certain activities up to the production of the pantomime, and how, in the course of investigations, he had identified the woman as Miss de Grey. After December, he added, he discovered that another woman was associated with da Costa in the same activities. The change corresponded with a date on which a photograph of da Costa had disappeared from Miss de Grey's dressing-room. He told how a photograph had been taken surreptitiously of da Costa and the second woman.

"Inspector Kenway identified the woman as Nina Francetti," said Doctor Manson. "He identified her, also, as an actress who had played various parts, including those in the children's play *Alice*.

"This opened up a very important line of investigation, because many parts in that play are animal rôles. *Miss Francetti had, in fact, not only played animal rôles, but had actually played the Cheshire Cat.* I was convinced that she had played the Cat on this occasion of Miss de Grey's death, particularly as she had been at pains to get into the cast on this night. I was working on that assumption."

The Attorney-General: "What led you to change your mind, Doctor?"

Doctor Manson: "The discovery that Miss Francetti had danced all through the ballet. That was vouched for by the seven other local girls. She could not, therefore, have been in the Cat's skin. She was away from the other girls only for about four minutes and that was before, and not during, the fatal scene."

The Attorney-General: "So you transferred your attentions to Madame Scarlatina?"

Doctor Manson: "I transferred them so far as the actual murder was concerned to another woman. It had to be a woman because of the woman's hairs from the Cat's skin. And it had, of course, to be someone inside the theatre."

The Attorney-General: "And your suspicions then became directed against the older woman prisoner?"

Doctor Manson: "There were one or two incidents for which I could see only one explanation after Miss Francetti was eliminated from the actual deed. Someone had taken the make-up box and the glass and bottle from Enora's room. Someone had to assist the pseudo Cat into the skin of Enora.

"*Now, the one person who could carry a make-up box and a bottle and glass without attracting attention is a dresser*, part of whose job it is to fetch and carry drinks for the artistes, and, on occasions, carry make-up materials to the stage for a quick change. When I came to consider whether a dresser might have removed the articles on this occasion, I discovered that on the night of the murder Miss de Grey's dresser had not accompanied the Principal Boy to the stage for the Highgate Hill scene, *which had been her invariable custom*, to put the finishing touches to the costume. Her explanation, made to the inspector on the night of the murder, when everyone was questioned, was that Miss de Grey had asked her to get some stout and sandwiches in her dressing-room ready for when she came off, and had said that she would manage for herself at the side of the stage. Now, this was not true, because Miss de Grey always had a glass of stout and sandwiches during the interval, and the dresser had procured them without fail *after she had attended to Miss de Grey, and while the Highgate Hill scene was in progress.* I asked myself why the woman had lied, and what was the real reason for her absence from the stage that night.

"Taken in conjunction with the time of her alleged going for the sandwiches and drinks while Miss de Grey was 'managing for herself', the absence for some four minutes of Miss Francetti at the same time, seemed to me to be a matter of high suspicion."

The Attorney-General: "You did not know that the dresser was Madame Scarlatina?"

Doctor Manson: "No, sir. But I recalled the statement of the variety agent, in the course of inquiries into Miss Francetti that, although she had played animal rôles she was 'not good at it' but that the mother was 'the one for that'. She had played all the parts in *Alice*. Now, a considerable number of those parts are animal rôles, and I elicited that Madame had been a great performer as the Cheshire Cat.

"I came to the conclusion that the dresser had been the actual murderer because she was the only one in the theatre with the opportunity, and because she could leave the theatre without question, and because by so doing she could carry away without suspicion the bottle and glass and the make-up box and the hypodermic syringe.

"I came to the conclusion that the poison had been supplied by Miss Francetti, who had gone to so much trouble to get into the theatre, and who could have obtained it during her employment in a photographic studio, where such stuff is used.

"Finally, I came to the conclusion that the dresser must be someone whom Miss Francetti knew would never betray her, and who could play the part of a cat—a difficult part—perfectly and without arousing suspicion, and would not have to leave the theatre afterwards, thus arousing suspicion, but could mix freely with the other people. I therefore came to the belief that Helen Brough, the dresser, was Miss Nina Francetti's mother. I was quite sure that if that was so she would come forward when her daughter was charged with the murder. She did so."

"Then there's a bit about the fellow da Costa," went on Mr. Barnson. He continued reading the report:

Mr. da Costa denied any knowledge of the murder. He said that Miss Francetti had previously been his mistress and that he had discarded her for Miss de Grey. "Then I got tired of Miss de Grey's extravagance, and wanted to break with her," said da Costa, "but she was blackmailing me because she knew too much about the fires business. I met Miss Francetti in the street, and she asked to come back to me. I told her I couldn't break with Norma because she knew too much about me. I didn't really want either of them.

"I said jokingly to Miss Francetti that if she rid me of Norma de Grey I'd even marry her. I knew nothing until I read of the death of Norma and Miss Francetti came to me and told me that she had carried out her part of the bargain. I didn't mean when I said get rid of her that she was to murder the girl. I meant get rid of the blackmail part."

The Attorney-General: "And knowing that she had, according to her confession, or your version of it, killed that unfortunate girl, you took her to live with you?"

Da Costa: "Yes."

"Overture and Beginners, please," came the voice of the call-boy.

"Buck up, Freddie," begged Miss Prue. "Is there any more?"

"Only a bit about the dresser. I'll read it quickly, Pruey."

Madame Scarlatina, in evidence, said: "I had not seen my daughter for some time, because she had been living with da Costa, who was a man I did not like or think well of. She did not know that I had taken a job as a dresser. You see, the theatre is in my blood, and when I could no longer act, I still wanted to be in it. When I saw her in the passage dressed for the part of the chorus, I got her in the laundry-room and asked her what it was all about. She told me that she was going to have a baby by da Costa and the only way to get him to marry her was to get rid of Norma de Grey who was blackmailing da Costa into marrying her. She said she had come to kill Norma and she told me she meant to play the Cat and do it that way, because she had watched from the front of the house and knew it could be done once she got into the theatre. I tried to dissuade her, but she said it was either that or she would commit suicide.

"I knew she couldn't play the Cat without being found out, and anyway, the absence of the real chorus girl would be found out. When she still said that she would commit suicide and kill the unborn baby at the same time, I said I would do it for her, if she would help me to dress in the skin. I wanted to save her name; we have always been a respectable family, and I wanted to give her baby a future, for I knew I could make da Costa marry her if Miss de Grey was out of the way. So I did it. I carried the glass and bottle back to the Green Man after the Hill scene, and broke up the syringe at the same time and dropped the remainder down one of the street sewers."

Mr. Barnson put down the paper.

"That's all," he said.

"Poor old soul," said Miss Prue. "That's a mother all over. Sacrificed herself for her daughter."

"Everybody on the stage, please. Come along, ladies and gentleman," called the stage-manager.

From in front of the curtain the strain of the opening bars came liltingly to the company.

"Stand by, everybody."

The eyes of stage-manager Mr. Trimble looked round his domain at the wailing players. Everybody was present.

He pressed a button.

The curtain rose.

THE END

Lightning Source UK Ltd.
Milton Keynes UK
UKHW022351060319
338640UK00005B/96/P